To Live Again

L.A. WITT

ISBN-13: 978-1543223392
ISBN-10: 1543223397

Copyright Information

This is a work of fiction. Names, characters, places, and incidents are either the product of the author's imagination or are used fictitiously. Any resemblance to actual persons living or dead, business establishments, events, or locales is entirely coincidental.

Second edition

First edition published by Samhain Publishing

Cover Art by Lori Witt
Editor: Linda Ingmanson

ISBN-13: 978-1543223392
ISBN-10: 1543223397

THE WILDE'S SERIES

The Best Man
The Distance Between Us
A.J.'s Angel
The Closer You Get
Meet Me in the Middle
To Live Again
Before There Were Three: Ethan & Rhett

Written with Aleksandr Voinov
No Distance Left to Run
No Place That Far
Missionary

Chapter One

"Well, that part's done." I dropped onto a barstool at the island in Rhett and Ethan's kitchen. "Thanks again for all your help."

"Don't mention it," Ethan said.

Rhett nodded. "Just let us know if you need help moving it all from the storage unit to your new place."

"Will do," I said. We'd just killed an entire Saturday lugging a million pounds or so of my stuff into my storage unit, and a handful of boxes into their downstairs bedroom, where I was living for the moment. When they'd found out that I was living in a hotel while I made arrangements to move into an apartment, they'd insisted I stay with them, and they'd been a godsend when it came to the grunt work. "Question is, what now?"

Ethan grinned. "Clearly, you need a beer."

"That goes without saying," Rhett said. "I think we all could." While Ethan pulled three bottles from the fridge, Rhett watched me across the island. "So, you doing all right?"

I shrugged. "I'm not really sure what counts as 'all right' in this situation."

Sighing, he nodded. "Yeah, I get that." As Ethan uncapped each of the bottles, Rhett rested a hand on the small of his back. "When we were separated, I just felt completely lost for a while."

"Me too." Ethan looked at him, and their eyes locked for a second. I could almost feel the brief spike in tension, as if they'd both been hit by a sudden wave of *shit, what if we'd never fixed that?* at the same time. Then they shook it off, and Ethan kissed Rhett's cheek before turning to me again. "It's not easy." He slid the bottle across the counter. "And we're serious—you're welcome to stay here as long as you need to. We both know damn well how long it can take to find your bearings."

"Thanks."

He sipped his beer and rested his other hand on top of Rhett's. My chest tightened, and I pulled my gaze away from their hands.

"Well." I took a deep swallow of beer. "I'm afraid I don't see me and Becky putting things back together like you two did. I think… I think I'm just still in shock." Pressing the bottle against my forehead, I muttered, "Maybe I should've seen it coming." I lowered the bottle. "Be honest. Am I an idiot for being surprised?"

"No, but…" Ethan shifted his weight. He turned to Rhett, eyebrows up as if to say *help me out here.*

"Well…" Rhett hesitated. "No, I don't think you're an idiot. It's a lot easier to see things from the outside than the inside."

"Speaking from experience," Ethan said quietly.

I drank a little more beer. "So, did you guys see something I didn't?"

Rhett fidgeted beside his husband. "To tell you the truth, neither of you have ever seemed particularly happy. Not as long as I've known you."

"He's right." Ethan's voice was unusually gentle. "I don't think I ever saw you argue with her, but you both seemed…well, pretty miserable whenever I saw you together."

Staring into my beer bottle, I sighed. They were right, and I'd known for a long, long time that something was wrong. I'd just imagined us working it out, maybe seeing a counselor or whatever. Once the kids were grown and the chaos of raising them was over, we could focus on us. That was how it had played out in my head, anyway.

But then, our youngest went off to college, and suddenly we had an empty nest, and my wife decided it wasn't empty enough.

Ex-wife. It wasn't final yet, but…ex-wife.

Tomorrow was twenty-five years since we said, "I do." Today was three weeks since she said, "I'm done."

Happy anniversary, honey.

"Well…" I exhaled, thumbing the label on my beer. "I really appreciate you guys letting me crash here. Hopefully I'll be out of your hair before too long."

"No rush," Rhett said.

"Thanks." I swallowed and then looked up at them. "If you don't mind my asking, what did you guys do when you were first separated?"

They exchanged uneasy glances.

"Fought a lot," Ethan said.

"We were stuck under the same roof." Rhett wrapped his arm around Ethan's shoulders. "That was, uh, not a fun period."

"I can imagine," I said. It had been awkward enough, coming by the house while I got my shit together and moved out. Having no choice but to live together through all of this? "That must have been hell."

"Yep," Rhett said quietly.

Ethan gave a dry laugh. "That's probably why we both spent a fair amount of time getting laid."

"Ethan!" Rhett laughed, his cheeks turning bright red. "Really?"

"What?" Ethan shrugged. "Don't act like it isn't true." Gesturing at me with his beer bottle, he added, "Greg might find it…I don't know, useful."

I chuckled. "I have to admit, I've thought about it. Becky and I weren't, uh…for a long…" I exhaled hard, my shoulders sagging. "Guess that should've been a sign, shouldn't it?"

"Sometimes it is," Ethan said. "Sometimes it isn't. But all joking aside, it can be good to put yourself back out there, or it can make things worse. I needed to blow off steam. You might need more time."

"Blowing off steam does sound pretty tempting. Maybe I—" I hesitated, my stomach twisting with panic, but really, if I was going to finally say the words out loud, these two were hardly going to give me hell for it. Could be a good opportunity to get the hang of admitting things about myself that even my wife—ex-wife—didn't know. I tamped down the panicky feeling and quietly said, "Maybe I need to find a guy this time."

Rhett choked on his beer, clapping a hand over his mouth as he nearly spat it across the counter.

"I told you!" Ethan laughed. "I fucking *told you*!"

I blinked. "You told him, what exactly?"

Ethan watched Rhett, grinning smugly.

Rhett finally recovered, clearing his throat a couple of times, and I couldn't tell if his cheeks were red from coughing or from something else. "We, uh…" He glanced—more like glared—at Ethan before turning to me. "Ethan said a while back he thought you might not be completely straight."

I lifted my eyebrows. "So what gave me away?"

Rhett turned to Ethan again, silently putting the ball back in his court.

This time it was Ethan who blushed a little. "Uh, one of our house parties last year. I don't know, something about the way you were looking at Sebastian."

"Sebastian?" I cocked my head. "Which one was he?"

"The tattoo artist," Rhett said.

"Oh. Right. Him." Yeah. *Him.* I took another deep swallow, hoping they didn't notice the shiver that ran through me. I'd seriously considered getting my first tattoo just as an excuse to have that guy's hands on me. "He was, uh, pretty hot."

"Mmhmm." Ethan grinned. "That's what I thought."

I chuckled into my beer bottle. "That wasn't the reaction I expected the first time I told someone I'm into men."

Rhett elbowed Ethan. "Always expect the unexpected with this one."

"So I've learned."

Ethan just laughed.

Rhett sobered a bit as he met my gaze. "So, are you…gay? Bi?"

"Not gay." I shifted in my seat. "I definitely still find women attractive. And I've, well…I guess you'd say I'm bi-curious since I've never actually been with a man."

They both blinked, and in unison asked, "Never?"

"Never." I played with the label on my beer again, self-conscious under the weight of their stares. "I've been married since I was twenty-two. Didn't figure out I was even attracted to men until after that, and didn't admit it to myself until my mid-thirties. So…never had the opportunity. Maybe now's as good a time as any."

"Well," Ethan said. "If you decide you want to hook up with a guy, we can certainly point you in the direction of places to find them."

I worked at the label some more. The offer *was* tempting. Whether I liked it or not, I was single. I'd continuously felt like shit for the last couple of weeks. Indulging in some decade-old curiosity was quite possibly what I needed. A night out—particularly if I wound up in someone else's bed—might be exactly what the doctor ordered to get my mind off the fact that I was no longer welcome in my own house.

"You know what?" I sat straighter. "I think I'm gonna take you up on that."

Ethan grinned, but Rhett stared at me incredulously.

"Really?" he asked. "Are you sure you—"

"To be honest, I need it. I need…well, something other than sitting on my ass, feeling sorry for myself, and pining after someone who doesn't want me anymore."

"That's the spirit." Ethan glanced at Rhett, and they had one of those telepathic exchanges they always seemed to share. Kind of like Becky and I used to—

Stop it, Greg. Stop it.

Facing me, Ethan said, "I'd be happy to take you to one of the clubs on Capitol Hill. Maybe let you feel out the gay scene before you start diving into any of the apps and hookup sites." He glanced at his watch. "It's still early for a Saturday, so if you're not too tired, we could go tonight."

This time it was Rhett who produced the wicked grin, and he nudged Ethan with his elbow. "You could take him to Wilde's."

"I could."

I raised my eyebrows. "Wilde's? Isn't that place… I mean, I've heard it's…"

"A meat market," Ethan said matter-of-factly. "It's a meat market."

I swallowed. "Right. That's what I've heard."

Rhett nodded. "It's true. Which means if you want to meet someone just to fool around and get your mind off everything…"

"It's perfect," I said. "Sounds like exactly what I need."

Rhett glanced back and forth between us, and then shrugged. "Hell, if you guys are going, I'll go. They do have pretty damned good Kamikazes."

Ethan laughed. "That's just because you like the guy who mixes them."

"Yep. Guilty." Rhett looked at me. "Kieran's a bartender there. His Kamikazes are second to none."

His ass isn't losing any competitions either.

"He's married, though, isn't he?" I asked.

"Yep," Ethan said. "Half the bartenders there are now, which is a damned shame. But there are plenty of guys there who aren't."

"And most of them?" Rhett whistled, tugging at his collar. *"Hot."*

"Well." I drained my beer. "What are we waiting for?"

Chapter Two

Maybe this wasn't such a good idea.

After grabbing a shower and a shave, putting on something presentable, and getting into a cab with Ethan and Rhett, we were here. At Wilde's. At a gay bar.

I looked around, my heart pounding so hard it almost drowned out the thumping bass. So this was the infamous Wilde's. The guys—especially Kieran and his husband—always had colorful stories from this place, which they'd tell at house parties after a few drinks, but I'd never actually been here until now. In fact, it had been ages since I'd set foot in anything that qualified as a club, and this was nothing like the places I'd been back in that era.

There were fewer women, for one thing, though I saw a few here and there. At least one bachelorette party, judging by the cluster of women—one of whom wore a fake bridal veil—laughing hysterically over margaritas at a booth near the back.

But for the most part, this crowd was male. Gorgeous. Dressed to flaunt every asset they had. Dancing. Drinking. Kissing. Male. All of them male.

My heart beat faster.

Even the employees were a sight to behold. The bouncers were as hot as they were intimidating. Ethan had said something about a couple of them being ex-Legionnaires, and I didn't doubt that—they stood like they were used to standing in ranks, and studied every man who came through the door like they were ready for anything. Pity all three of them had wedding rings on, or I could've tried my luck there without moving into the rest of the club.

At the edge of the room, the bartenders all wore tux shirts and cummerbunds, and against a colorful backdrop of top-shelf liquor, every last one of them could've graced an ad for something strong and expensive. A stunning blond deejay kept the dancefloor lively, though I was pretty sure the men moving together on that crowded floor would've done just fine without him. Or maybe they would've given up on dancing and started fucking right there in the middle of the club—some of them looked like they were close to it already.

I swallowed. Ethan and Rhett had insisted this was the best club in Capitol Hill, Seattle's gay neighborhood. Ethan said the men were hotter. Rhett said there were fewer illegal activities going on here. I took their word for it.

As I looked around, I couldn't say one way or the other about Rhett's comment, but I definitely believed Ethan. The men here were stunning. Absolutely stunning.

And intimidating as fuck.

It wasn't just that most of them looked like they were half my age and had recently leaped off the pages of a menswear catalog or a porno. That part didn't help, but it wasn't what had me standing at the sidelines, wondering what the fuck I was thinking by coming in here.

They were all so…comfortable with each other. Physically. Those who weren't dancing or making out stood close—some touching, some nearly so. Without flinching, they made the kind of eye contact I'd been terrified to make with a man ever since the first time a stubbled jaw and a wicked smile had given me a hard-on.

Jesus. I didn't think I'd be comfortable enough to get that publicly intimate with a woman. A man? Forget it. I was definitely attracted to men, but I'd never gone further than fantasizing about them or staring at them on a screen or a page. How the fuck was I supposed to put myself on someone's radar? And what was I supposed to do if I did?

There was no way in hell I could be that bold, or not freak out if someone was that bold with me. Not even if I would've sold my soul to be that guy pressed up against the wall with another man's lips exploring every inch of his throat. Or the one at the bar who'd clearly made a connection with the guy next to him. That kind of eye contact was unmistakable even without a hand on a knee.

Those guys were all getting laid tonight. No doubt about that.

Me? I didn't belong here.

Some of the guys here were my *kids'* ages, for God's sake. I was ninety-nine percent certain all three of my kids were straight, but I prayed like hell that if either of the boys weren't and they hadn't yet worked up the nerve to tell me, they didn't walk in here while I was making a feeble attempt to get over their mother with some young leather-clad guy.

Yeah. This was a mistake.

"Greg?" Ethan touched my arm. "Why don't we grab a booth, and Rhett can get us some drinks."

"What are you drinking?" Rhett asked.

How about a huge glass of Get Me The Fuck Out of Here?

I swallowed. "Um. Uh…you said…"

"Kieran's working tonight." Ethan gestured toward the bar. "You want to try one of his Kamikazes?"

I looked at the bar, and my God, there must've been some trick lighting in this place. Kieran had always been attractive—going to house parties always meant struggling not to ogle him or Alex—but something about the tux shirt, the light, the bottles behind him, the flirty grin…wow.

"Greg." Ethan elbowed me. "Kamikaze? Or…?"

"Yeah. Yeah. A, uh, Kamikaze sounds great."

Rhett took off toward the bar, and Ethan led me to a booth that was far enough from the stage for us to hear each other. A little closer to the cackling bachelorette party than I would have liked, but I'd live with it.

"This really is your first time in place like this, isn't it?" Ethan shouted over the music.

I laughed dryly. "You noticed?"

"Relax." He smiled. "If it helps, most of the guys here are after the exact same thing you are."

I looked out at the crowd of undiscovered supermodels and porn stars. "Something tells me most of them aren't looking for a guy like me. If they're into someone my age, I doubt they're after someone with my level of experience."

"Don't sell yourself short. I mean, yeah, there are guys here half our age. But…" He hesitated. Leaning toward me, he lowered his voice, and sounded uncharacteristically shy as he said, "You're not a bad-looking guy at all."

My cheeks burned.

He gestured out at the crowd. "And I've already seen a couple of them checking you out."

I couldn't make myself turn. "You're shitting me."

"Not at all."

"How much you want to bet I could turn them off the instant I open my mouth?"

"Depends on what you're thinking of doing with your mouth."

My teeth snapped shut. Ethan chuckled. I was used to this side of him—he'd always been the brazen, uncensored half of that pair—but he was also one of two people on the planet who knew I wasn't straight. And he'd only known since earlier this evening. I wished I could believe everyone in my life would be so relaxed about me coming out. Hell, Ethan hadn't even been surprised, and he was already to the point he could joke about it as if it were no big thing. God, I wished I was at that point.

"Look, I'm serious." He folded his arms on the table and locked eyes with me. "Greg, you're a single man. You're in a club full of horny, single men. All you have to do is get out there and break the ice with one or two, and you're golden."

"Yeah. Easy for you to say." I fidgeted on the bench. Maybe I just needed a moment to collect my thoughts. Something to get me away from all these lights and all that skin. "I'm, uh, gonna hit the head. I'll be right back."

"Sure." He gestured past the dance floor. "See that exit sign? Go past that, and there's a hallway. Restrooms are back there."

"Great. Thanks." I got up and headed in the direction he'd indicated.

Halfway to the dancefloor, I met the gaze of a beautiful twenty-something with a smile that almost made me stumble. He lifted his eyebrows and beckoned to me.

Go for it. Go for it!

But I just returned the smile and kept walking. Maybe I'd find him when I came back. I had to escape for a second, though, or I was going to lose it.

I kept my eye on that exit sign like it was a lighthouse in a storm, and finally managed to shoulder my way through the throngs of people and slip past it. As soon as I was around the corner, the noise of the club diminished enough that I could hear myself think.

I stopped and leaned against the wall. Eyes closed, I took a few breaths.

What was I so afraid of? I'd been out of the game with women for so long, it wasn't like I'd be *that* much less awkward with them, but men may as well have been an entirely new species for all the confidence I had in approaching them.

And the divorce was still a fresh wound. Three weeks ago, the thought of approaching anyone for sex had been an alien concept, because Becky and I—

The wall I was leaning on suddenly gave.

I stumbled back. "What the—"

"Shit!"

I almost caught the doorknob, but missed, and crashed into someone and the boxes he was carrying. He lost his balance. I lost what was left of mine.

Someone tried to grab us both, but we tumbled into a heap.

I quickly got off him—well, managed to get on top of a guy tonight after all—and scrambled onto my knees. "I'm so sorry. Are you all right?"

"You fucking idiot," the kid who'd tried to catch us snapped. "Why the hell were you leaning on—"

"Hey." The other guy sat up, dusting off his black Wilde's shirt. "Take it easy, Evan. Just go unlock the van, okay?"

With a huff, the kid—Evan, apparently—stomped past us, keys jingling in his hand.

I watched him go, then turned back to the guy I'd knocked over. "I'm really sorry about that. You okay?"

"I'm good."

Our eyes met.

And my heart stopped.

I couldn't put my finger on his nationality—Hawaiian, maybe?—but holy shit. His black hair was cut neat and short, his tan much too deep for someone living in Seattle, and those eyes…

I gulped. They were dark. Almost black.

He cocked his head. "Hey. You all right?"

"I'm fine. I'm…" I started to stand. "Sorry. I…guess I didn't realize I was leaning on a door."

Chuckling, he moved onto his knees and reached for one of the boxes he'd dropped. "It's okay."

"Here, can I give you a hand?" I reached for the second box, which had landed on its side. "None of this is breakable, is it?" *Oh God, please tell me it's not.*

"No, it's not breakable." He rose. "Just a bunch of T-shirts."

"Oh good. Do you, um, want some help taking them out?"

He seemed to ponder it for a moment, then shrugged. "Sure, if you really don't mind."

"It's fine." I chuckled. "I think I kind of owe you."

The guy laughed, which did funny things to my blood pressure. "It's okay. I'm surprised it doesn't happen more often, actually."

"Well, that's encouraging." I picked up one of the boxes. "So, where do these go?"

"This way." He picked up the other and led me out into the hallway.

As he walked ahead of me, I couldn't help staring. He was roughly my height and looked like he spent a good chunk of his time at the gym. Maybe he was one of the bouncers. They were well-dressed just like the bartenders, though, not clad in skintight T-shirts and jeans that held on to that ass like…

I shook myself and tore my gaze away before I wound up on my own ass. *Again.*

At the end of the hall, the guy pushed open the door with his hip, and held it with his foot so I could step out. Around the corner, Evan stood beside a van with its back doors wide open.

"Just put them in here," the other guy said, and we tucked the boxes in amongst some crates and electronic equipment.

Evan bristled at my presence but kept his mouth shut. He handed the keys back and then went inside, leaving me alone with…

This guy.

He didn't even have the lights and ambiance of Wilde's to bolster his looks. Out here in the blanched glow of the streetlights, even with harsh shadows on his face, he was jaw-dropping.

After he'd shut the van and pocketed his keys, he extended his hand. "I didn't catch your name."

Probably because I didn't make the greatest first impression.

"Greg." I cleared my throat as I shook his hand. "Greg Douglas."

He smiled. "Sailo Isaia."

"Interesting name."

"In a good way, or a bad way?" He narrowed his eyes slightly, but the effect was playful, not irritated.

"Good, of course. Just…not a name I've heard before." And I realized my hand was still clasped in his. We both glanced down and quickly let go.

"It's, um…" He muffled a cough, shifting his weight. "Samoan. Not very common around here, I guess."

"I suppose not." I paused. This was the point where we were supposed to go back inside and disappear into the crowd, wasn't it? Now or never, sink or swim, nothing to lose but a little bit of dignity…

I swallowed. "Listen, I feel terrible for what happened in there. I don't suppose I could buy you a drink to make up for it?"

"Much as I'd love to take you up on it"—he grimaced apologetically—"I'm on the clock."

"Oh. Right." My face was on fire now. "You're…" I gestured at his shirt. "Right. Anyway…"

The grimace softened to a smile, which did nothing to help my disappointment over his understandable rejection. "I'm off at midnight, though. If the offer's still open…" His eyebrows rose.

"Yeah, sure!" *Way to sound cool and not the least bit eager, idiot.* I schooled my expression and my tone. "I mean, I'm just here with some friends. I'd be happy to wait for you."

"Sweet." He motioned toward the doorway. "I'll see you around midnight, then."

"Great. See you then."

Chapter Three

"There you are!" Rhett chuckled as I slid back into the booth. "Thought you might've gotten lost back there."

I laughed. "No, I didn't get lost. I was, um, giving somebody a hand with…"

They both smirked.

"Goddammit, you guys. That is *not* what I meant." Rolling my eyes, I added, "I bumped into someone—literally—and helped him carry some boxes out to his van."

Rhett's eyebrow climbed. "Is that…all you did?"

"Yes."

"Mmhmm."

"I call bullshit." Ethan gestured at the bar. "I'm going to get another round." He pointed at the glass in front of me. "Should I grab you another since the ice is almost melted in that one?"

"No, this will do me." I picked up the sweaty glass. "Watered down is probably just as well right now."

"Suit yourself." He kissed Rhett's cheek. "Refill?"

"Please."

Ethan kissed him once more—a quick peck on the lips this time—and left the booth.

Rhett faced me. "So, you just carried a box."

"Yes. Why the third degree?"

"Because I've known you for a long time, and I have *never* seen you grin like that."

As soon as he pointed it out, I realized he'd busted me. I sipped the Kamikaze. Wow, even watered down it was good. Wrapping my hands around it to cool myself off, I shrugged. "Well, he was… I mean—"

"All right, gentlemen," the deejay's voice boomed over the speakers, making both of us jump. "That's it for me tonight, but keep on dancing, and give it up for *Sailooooo*!"

My head snapped toward the stage and my jaw dropped.

The blond deejay stepped away from the console, and yes, it was him. Sailo. Under the magic Wilde's lighting that made everyone look good was the beautiful Samoan man who was meeting me for a drink at midnight.

And whoa, that lighting was kind to him as well. He'd changed out of the T-shirt and wore a black tank top now, which revealed more of his tanned, toned body, and also the intricate tribal tattoo covering his left arm all the way to the shoulder and disappearing under the front of his shirt.

The music switched to something way more upbeat than before, as if to keep time with my racing pulse, and I just…stared. He was on his feet, smiling broadly and encouraging the guys in front of him to dance.

And he was dancing too. Mostly from his hips. Jesus *Christ.*

"Earth to Greg?" Rhett shouted over the music, snapping me out of it.

I shook myself and turned back to him. "Sorry, what?"

His eyes flicked toward the stage, and he chuckled, raising his mostly empty glass. "Enjoying the scenery, are we?"

"What's not to enjoy?" I took a drink, wondering if I should get a stronger one, or maybe hold off until Sailo joined me. No point in being drunk when he did. I'd probably say plenty of stupid shit without the alcohol's help.

As I poked at the remaining ice cubes with my straw, I said, "I'm surprised you and Ethan come here. Doesn't really seem like your scene."

Rhett shrugged. "We usually come during the week to harass Kieran. When it's not quite so"—he gestured at the crowd—"busy."

I couldn't imagine this place when it wasn't packed, but it made sense that the weekdays wouldn't be so crazy. Presumably most of these guys had jobs besides looking hot and groping on a dance floor. Unless, of course, they *were* models and porn stars.

I let my gaze slide back toward the stage. I wondered if he was only here on the weekends. It probably wasn't in the best interest of the club's budget to have a deejay here all the time, and the stage looked it could readily accommodate a live band. So was this his full-time job? Maybe he was one of those deejays who worked weddings and parties too. Or maybe he did something else. I couldn't picture him putting on a shirt and tie and sitting behind a desk in a cubicle, but stranger things had happened. One of my coworkers was the drummer in a heavy metal band during his off time. A thin enough dress shirt would hint at the tattoos he kept hidden—not that I'd ever quietly ogled him—but otherwise, no one would ever guess.

Did Sailo have coworkers who'd be stunned to learn he was a deejay in a gay bar?

And why was I so interested?

I took another drink right as Ethan rejoined us and put a couple of glasses in front of him and Rhett.

"I think someone's rather taken with the deejay," Rhett said.

"Oh yeah?" Ethan glanced toward Sailo, and grinned. "Can't imagine why. Wow."

"He's…" I hesitated. Oh hell, why not? "He's the guy I was talking about. With the…"

"The one you gave a hand?" Ethan asked, chuckling.

I laughed as heat rushed into my cheeks. "Yes, that one."

"Nice," Rhett said. "Too bad he's working."

"Well, I offered to buy him a drink, and he said he'd take me up on it when he's off the clock." Checking my watch, I added, "Which is about two hours from now. Hopefully he'll remember."

"I'm sure he will," Ethan said. "And you've got two hours to stare at him."

"So do we." Rhett's voice barely carried over the music Sailo was playing.

My arms prickled with goose bumps. Oh, I'd definitely be staring at him for the next two hours…

~*~

At midnight, the blond deejay returned, and Sailo disappeared backstage.

Rhett and Ethan had left twenty minutes ago, wishing me luck on their way out. I was grateful they'd stayed this long. That they'd come with me in the first place. I couldn't imagine walking into this place without at least some backup.

But now I was on my own. I'd moved to the bar to keep from occupying a booth that would better serve a group, and I drummed my fingers on my knee, keeping my hand safely beneath the bar so no one—least of all the man I was waiting for—could see my nerves. As the minutes crawled by and Sailo didn't emerge from the crowd, those nerves were tougher and tougher to ignore. Twelve oh-five. Twelve ten. Twelve twenty.

When my phone said it was twenty-five minutes after twelve, my heart sank. Maybe he'd hoped I wouldn't stick around this long. Or when he realized I had, he'd ducked out the back and sped off in that packed van. It wasn't like I could make mental excuses—he was stuck in traffic, he was finding a place to park, he was looking for the club—because he was right here in the same building.

Maybe the promise to meet for a drink had just been a way to placate me so I'd get out of his hair. Or to see if I'd really be gullible enough to stick around. And anyway, I couldn't imagine I'd made the greatest first impression, so—

There he was.

I gulped as he emerged from the crowd like a mirage taking solid form. He'd changed clothes, losing the black shirt in favor of a plain blue one, untucked with the top two buttons undone. His black hair was neatly arranged and damp, and he smiled when he saw me.

He made his way across the lounge and joined me at the bar.

"Sorry to keep you waiting," he shouted over the music. "I wanted to grab a shower after…" He nodded toward the stage, where the current deejay was working up a hell of a sweat.

"I can't blame you," I replied. "So, I think I owe you a drink?"

He leaned in a bit. "What?"

"A drink." I pointed at the bar. "What'll you have?"

He scanned the colorful bottles against the wall and pursed his lips. "How about a rum and Coke?"

I nodded and flagged down the bartender. After he'd made our drinks, I paid him, and then faced Sailo again. Raising my glass, I said, "Sorry for crashing into you earlier."

He laughed and clinked his drink against mine. "Oh, I don't know. I got a free drink out of it." He winked, which sent an electric charge straight down my spine.

I took a drink too, needing the cold more than the alcohol.

He said something, but the music smothered it.

Tilting my head toward him, I said, "What?"

He leaned closer, and I swore I felt the warmth of his breath on my ear—*oh God*—as he repeated, "Is this your first time at Wilde's?"

I nodded, drawing back to meet his gaze. "You?"

"Uh, no." He chuckled, tilting his glass toward the stage. "I work here."

I cringed. "Right. Sorry. I…" Well, there was no coming back from that one, so I just laughed and shrugged. "Sorry."

He smiled, which crinkled the corners of his eyes and made my heart flutter. Good God. If I'd had any lingering doubts about my attraction to men—any reason to call myself bi-curious instead of bisexual—they evaporated right then and there.

Or maybe I'd just had a little too much to drink tonight.

He leaned in. "So what do you do?"

"I'm an engineer," I shouted.

"Computers?"

"Planes."

"Oh. Cool."

I wasn't sure what I could add that would be interesting and wouldn't require a longwinded explanation that he'd barely hear anyway. On the bright side, the booze and nerves didn't make me quite stupid enough to ask what *he* did for a living.

I sipped my drink, searching for something to say. Something to ask about him that he'd hear. That he could answer without wearing out his voice. This was going to get exhausting fast. Carrying on a conversation in here with my friends had been challenging enough—trying to communicate with someone who barely knew me would be…difficult. We didn't know each other's speech patterns well enough to fill in when the music drowned out the actual words.

Sailo shook his head and turned to me. "It's way too fucking loud down here."

Scowling, I nodded. "I know."

In the space of a few seconds, I convinced myself he was about to shrug and bow out, but instead, he asked, "You want to go someplace quieter?"

My heart skipped. Going someplace quieter… Wasn't that a come-on of some sort? Oh hell. Maybe it was. And maybe I really was getting too old for this shit, because the club *was* a bit too loud for my tastes. Someplace quieter—come-on or not—definitely sounded appealing.

So, I nodded.

He raised a finger as if to say *just a minute*, and turned toward the bar, beckoning someone over. One of the bartenders—a good-looking and somewhat scruffy guy with his sleeves rolled to his elbows—came over. They both leaned across the bar, speaking directly into each other's ears. Sailo gestured toward the back. The guy glanced in that direction.

With a decisive nod from each, they separated.

Before I realized what was happening, Sailo took my hand. It took me a second to make sense of that casual contact, the warmth of his gently callused fingers between mine, and by the time I got my head around that, I realized I was following him through the crowd. That he was leading me between throngs of dancing, drinking men, and my feet were keeping me hot on his heels despite my brain going *wait, what?*

So I didn't argue.

I just followed him.

Chapter Four

Sailo led me into the back hallway where we'd crashed into each other in the first place, but when the glowing Exit sign indicated we should go left, he went right. The hallway turned again, as if we were doubling back and going around the club we'd just exited. Halfway down that hall, he stopped at a door marked VIP LOUNGE—PASS REQUIRED.

He went in ahead of me. We took a staircase up to another door where we paused. Keys jingled. The lock clicked. He pushed the door open and gestured for me to go inside.

Behind me, he shut the door, and he wasn't kidding about this being someplace quieter. The stairway had already diminished some of the noise from the club, and the door cut off most of what was left.

Sunken lights came on above our heads. The room was sleek and posh—red leather booths. A chrome-edged bar. An enormous flat-screen TV. I could just imagine this place full of gorgeous men, clinking martini glasses together and using those plush booths the way they used the ones in the main club.

My spine tingled as the bass from downstairs thumped beneath my feet. What kinds of things happened in here?

After all, I knew what kinds of things happened down there. I doubted people had private VIP parties to talk about current events.

A row of tinted windows overlooked the rest of the club. For a moment, we watched in silence, shoulder to shoulder while men below us were bumping, grinding, kissing, groping. Somehow that had all been easier to ignore when we were in the heart of it. Here, at a distance and still watching, I was about as comfortable as if a porno had just started playing on the giant TV.

"Ugh." Beside me, Sailo wrinkled his nose. "Max *always* overdoes it on the bass." Then he rolled his eyes and chuckled. "Don't know why I worry about it—the guys here would dance to anything. They just need a beat to break the ice so they can dance a bit before they go fuck."

I blinked. "Really?"

"Well, yeah. Look at them."

Oh, I am…

He turned to me. "That *is* why guys come here, isn't it? To get laid?"

"I…guess they do."

Sailo studied me for a moment. "Is that why you came here?"

Our eyes locked. My heart was giving the bass a run for its money right then, and my mouth went dry. "To be honest, I'm not really sure what I'm doing here."

"Do you mean you don't know why you're here?" He stepped just close enough to make my stomach flutter. "Or you don't know what to do now that you are?"

I swallowed. "A little of both, I guess?"

He came even closer, moving well into my comfort zone. "Well, let's narrow it down. I assume you didn't come here with the express purpose of *not* hooking up with someone, right?" The upward curl of his lips told me that, yes, it was meant as a lighthearted joke. But laughing meant breathing, and I wasn't doing much of that at the moment.

Sailo's smile turned less playful and more friendly, as if he sensed my nerves and wanted me to relax. "I'm right, aren't I?"

He'd asked a question. He'd…right. Question. I cleared my throat. "Yeah, you are. I don't think I'd have come here if I didn't want to get laid."

As soon as the words were out, my teeth snapped shut, and panic shot through me. Was I really doing this? Did I sound as desperate and scared as I felt? Fuck, I felt like a teenager just then—nervous as hell, certain I was going to screw this up at any moment, and simultaneously almost giddy with arousal as a whole lot of blood rushed south. Gazing into Sailo's dark eyes made my pulse go haywire. Before tonight, I'd never had a chance to entertain the idea of going beyond looking at someone—at a *man*—and suddenly there he was, and there I was, and—

And had he really just inched even closer to me?

"Why are you so nervous?" He spoke so softly that, without thinking about it, I leaned in closer to hear him over the bass from downstairs.

"I'm…" I moistened my lips. "This is…" *New? Terrifying? Hot?* "I'm…"

Sailo reached for me, but his hand didn't come to rest on my hip or my side. He didn't touch my arm, didn't snake his hand around and draw me across that remaining sliver of space between us.

No, he went straight for the front of my pants, and as he slid his fingers and palm over my cock, he grinned.

"That's what I thought."

"What you—"

He kissed me.

And the rest of the world just…vanished.

It wasn't like I'd never been kissed before, but it had been years since a kiss had been anything more than "see you tonight" or "how was your day?" I'd forgotten what it was like for the soft contact of lips on lips to send shudders down my spine, or how my knees could turn to liquid when the tip of a tongue slipped underneath mine.

I curved my hand around the back of his head, my fingers sliding through short, damp hair. His lightly stubbled chin grazed mine. His hand drifted down my back, and when he pulled my hips to his, there was no way he didn't feel my hard-on just like there was no pretending I didn't feel his.

Oh. My. God.

There was no mistaking that I was kissing a man this time. For the first time in my life, after years of wondering and fantasizing and thinking this would never happen, it was. I was overwhelmed. Turned on. Disbelieving. I was…I was kissing a man.

Trembling all the way down to my curling toes, I opened to his gently probing tongue and let him explore my mouth. I explored his too, the faint taste of his rum and Coke reminding me of those awkward moments at the bar, of the beautiful man who'd been sitting beside me, fucking with my senses and turning me inside out. The man who was up against me now, touching and kissing me until I couldn't tell the bass from my heartbeat anymore.

He drew back. Eyes locked on mine, he sucked his lower lip into his mouth, and before I knew what I was doing, I mirrored him, searching for one last taste of his kiss.

He swallowed. "Have I narrowed down why you let me drag you up here?"

You don't have to drag me anywhere. "Y-yeah. I think you have."

"Thought so." He grinned, screwing up my blood pressure all over again.

My heart sped up, and it wasn't all arousal this time. Sailo didn't waste any time. He probably knew exactly what he wanted, how to get it, what he expected from me, and I…

I knew nothing.

He started to draw me back in, but I put a hand on his chest and gently stopped him.

"W-wait."

"What?" His eyebrows shot up, and he backed off a little. "Something wrong?"

"No. I mean…well…" I tried and failed to hold his gaze. "Look, before we go too much further, I should…" Finally, I managed to look him in the eye. "I should probably be, um, honest about something."

He cocked his head. "What? Are you pos or something?"

"Pos?"

"Yeah. You know, HIV?" He shrugged. "I mean, it's cool if you are, so—"

"No, no." I shook my head. "It's not that. But I, uh…" I steeled myself, not sure what reaction I expected. "I've never done this before."

Sailo's eyebrow rose. "Which part?"

"All of it." I swallowed. "With a man, I mean. I'm not a virgin, but I haven't been with anyone but my wife in twenty-five years, and—"

"Your *wife*?" He drew back. "You're married?" He put up his hands. "Because that's something I won't—"

"Oh God, no. I'm sorry." I shook my head, grimacing at how stupid I must've sounded. "I'm still getting used to calling her my ex-wife. It hasn't been that long."

He lowered his hands, and something softened in his expression. "Recently divorced?"

I nodded. "Very."

"Oh." He gulped. "Um. Sorry to hear it."

I raked a hand through my hair. "I'm sorry. I completely killed the mood, didn't I?"

"Nah." He came closer again and put his hands on my waist. "Better to tell me now than give me a chance to push you too far. *That* would be a mood killer."

"Fair enough. You are right, though. I did come here to get laid." Renewed heat rushed into my cheeks, not to mention below my belt. "I think I'm just more nervous about it than I thought I was."

His eyebrows pulled together. "Nervous enough you want to stop?"

I swept my tongue across my lips. "No. Definitely not."

The creases in his forehead vanished, and his smile came back. "Good." He wrapped his arms around me and kissed me again.

As I held on and returned his kiss, I couldn't help but relax. There was nothing even remotely threatening about Sailo. He'd already backed off once when my nerves had gotten the best of me. If I was going to put myself out there and try to find a man to satisfy my curiosity, I couldn't ask for a better one to stumble across. Literally.

Sailo broke this kiss again, and his wicked grin tied my tongue even more than his kiss had. "I know your type, by the way."

"My type?"

He nodded. "Newly single, curious about men, and horny all at once."

"That's…that's me."

He grinned. "Well, as it happens"—he cupped my hard-on again—"I'm single." He kneaded me gently, reducing my knees to a wobbling mess. "I know my way around a man." He pressed a little harder. "And I am *seriously* horny tonight."

"Good." This time, I kissed him, and God, that was liberating. Maybe I didn't know what the fuck we were doing, but Sailo obviously did, and as he slipped his tongue past my lips, his confidence erased what was left of my nerves. Whatever he had in mind for tonight, I wanted it. As long as we found our way to a flat surface, and these clothes found their way to the floor, I was game for just about anything.

He was out of breath when he spoke again. "We…we should definitely go someplace else."

"Yeah, we should."

"We should. But I'm too impatient for that right now." He pushed me back a step, and a split second after the *oh shit, I'm gonna fall!*, the wall caught me. And then Sailo was kissing me again, and unzipping my pants, and those lightly callused fingers brushed my very hard cock, and thank God for that wall keeping me upright.

Please don't be a door this time.

His lips left mine and inched their way to my neck. Without really thinking about it, I tilted my head, and he took full advantage.

Holy. Shit.

Just like that, I understood why women liked this so much. No one had ever kissed my neck before, and the softness of his lips, the warmth of this breath, the ticklish brush of his goatee—*fuck*. For a few seconds, I even forgot about his hand on my dick, and then he squeezed just right, and suddenly my senses were divided between him stroking my cock and awakening erogenous zones from my throat to my ear.

My back arched off the wall. My fingers dug into his shoulder and the back of his neck. I didn't have a say in any of it anymore—my body responded to his touch and to my need for balance, and thank God, because my brain was checking out.

"Jesus," I breathed. "You're…gonna make me come if you keep doing this."

"I haven't even started yet," he murmured against my throat.

"I think…I think you're underestimating how long I've—" I gasped as he nipped just above my collar, and he had to have felt my cock get even harder in his hand. "How long I've wanted…"

His lips curved into a grin, and he kissed the spot he'd bitten. Then he lifted his head and met my gaze. "Well, if you come fast, that just means I can take my time getting you off the second time."

A *second* time? Was he—

He dropped to his knees, and my mind went blank.

I'm dead, right? Or hallucinating?

That had to be it. There was no way in hell this gorgeous man was kneeling at my feet, and absolutely no way his perfect, slim lips were around my dick.

"Holy fuck," I murmured, stroking his hair as I stared down in disbelief. "Holy…"

His eyes flicked up to meet mine right as he ran his tongue around the head.

I gulped. Fuck. Yeah, I was definitely going to come fast. Really fast.

I'd had blowjobs before, and getting one from a man didn't feel much different from getting one from a woman, but I couldn't remember the last time I'd been this turned on. Just knowing those lips and fingers belonged to a man aroused me beyond words. When I looked down at his short hair and broad shoulders, watching my dick sliding between that perfect pair of lips, I could barely breathe.

And we were in public. Something I hadn't done in years. No one could see us, but when I turned my head and forced my eyes to focus, I could see them, all the men at Wilde's who were grinding against each other and dancing to the beat of my pounding heart.

"D-don't stop," I pleaded. "You're so…so…good."

He groaned around my dick, and that was it.

My knees buckled. I flattened my hands against the wall, feebly trying to keep myself upright as my hips thrust into his mouth like they had a mind of their own. He didn't stop, either—he stroked me with both hands and teased the head of my cock relentlessly with his lips and tongue until I managed a pitiful, "S-stop…"

Sailo kept a hand on my hip, as if he knew how much trouble I was having with the whole "not collapsing on my ass" thing. He looked up at me and grinned as he wiped his lips with the back of his other hand.

"So," he said, "any chance I can talk you into coming back to my apartment?"

Well, that was a fucking no-brainer.

"You don't have to talk me into anything."

He just grinned.

That devilish, narrow-eyed grin that said I had no idea what I'd gotten myself into.

Chapter Five

In the passenger seat of Sailo's van, I was still shaking. Not visibly, I hoped, but my knees were still wobbly, my hands still jittery. Anticipation, nerves, that orgasm—God knew how I'd made it down the stairs and out to the parking lot without breaking my neck.

I didn't know if I was more excited or nervous. If what he'd done in the VIP lounge was a sample of what was to come, I was going to be dead before sunrise, but damn, what a way to go.

"So you've really never done this before?" he asked as he pulled out of the Wilde's parking lot.

Thank God it was dark so he couldn't see the beet red that was undoubtedly appearing in my cheeks. "Isn't it obvious?"

"Not really." He glanced at me, and the streetlights offered just enough light to illuminate his mouthwatering smile. "You don't kiss like a virgin."

"I'm not a virgin. I've just never been with a man."

"Fair enough." His expression turned a little more serious. "You're still just nervous, though, right? Not having second thoughts?"

"Not enough to make me back out, no." I *was* nervous as hell, though. Sailo didn't make me feel unsafe, not by any means, but I didn't know what was going to happen once we were alone behind closed doors. I suspected I'd find out before too much longer.

He drove a few blocks down Broadway and down a side street, then into a secure parking garage beneath a modest apartment building. After he'd parked in a reserved spot, he killed the engine, and we both unbuckled our seat belts. Before we got out, he glanced at me. We both grinned, but didn't say anything. I wasn't sure what to say. What was the protocol for conversation in this situation? How exactly *did* someone say, *So, I'm horny as hell, and I want you so bad I can't see straight, but this really is my first time with a guy and I'm scared out of my damned mind.*

I did the only thing I could think to do right now—I followed his lead. He hadn't led me wrong so far.

Neither of us spoke as we walked up the stairs to the second floor. At the landing, he took out his keys, and three doors down from the stairwell, he stopped.

Thank God. I didn't mind going up stairs, but if I had to wait much longer—

He pushed open the door and gestured for me to go inside. Heart thumping, I stepped into his dark apartment. Sailo turned on the light. I had about two seconds to curiously glance around, but the click of the dead bolt brought my attention right back to him.

Eyes locked on mine, he reached for my belt. He pulled me to him and kissed me, and we both stumbled this way, that way, until my back hit a wall and he pushed me up against it. "Usually I'd be polite and offer a drink," he murmured between kisses, "but that's gonna have to wait. Because I can't."

"Neither can I. Don't need a drink. Just you."

He kissed me even harder. Then he broke away, took my hand, and led me down a short hallway to his bedroom. There we managed to toe off our shoes and, in what I could only describe as a slow motion controlled fall, we landed on his bed together.

Jesus. Making out with him up against a wall was hot, but lying down in a tangle of limbs was mind-blowing. Without the need to stay upright, to accommodate for balance and gravity, we were free to kiss and touch. I was on my back, and I couldn't keep my hands off him, and he didn't seem to mind at all, so I let my fingers and palms explore his powerful, masculine shape. Never in my life had I felt a clothed, hard dick pressed against mine, and it turned me on so much, I could barely breathe. Every time one of us moved, that thick ridge rubbed just right to send my pulse soaring. It was a constant, delicious reminder that I was with a man this time. Not just a man—an aroused man who was probably about to blow all of my gay fantasies out of the water.

We rolled over. Then again. I fucking loved having him on top of me. My ex-wife was quite a bit smaller than me, but Sailo matched me inch for inch, pound for pound. Everything about him screamed strength and power, as if he could throw me around if he wanted to. And that thought aroused me a lot more than I'd expected it to. It also made his gentleness so much more erotic.

I could get rough with you, said the soft touch of his fingertips, *and maybe I will eventually. But not now.*

His kiss was deep and slow, as if he wanted to savor every taste. Or let me savor every taste. Or both. He kissed and touched with a verve I hadn't felt with my ex in ages. Not because she was a woman and he was a man, but because he wanted me, even if it was only for a one night stand. I may have been the nearest warm body for him, a way to wind down after putting on a show, but there would be no cold shoulder tonight. That, more than a man, was what I needed.

"I hope you're not in a hurry." I swept my tongue across my lips. "This is all pretty new to me." Thinking I sounded like an inexperienced idiot, I grinned and added, "I want to enjoy it."

Sailo returned the grin, teasing my nipple through my shirt. "Do I look like I'm in a hurry?"

He had a point. Hell, we weren't even undressed yet. Nothing about this—and especially not his kiss—said "get on with it so I can go to sleep."

We shifted position again, and now I was on top, straddling him and kissing him and oh God, my cock still rubbed against his. If it was this hot with our clothes on, I could only imagine how it would be once we were naked. I wanted to get us there, but damn it, that meant stopping this, so…fuck it.

Sailo combed his fingers through my hair, then closed his hand and tugged my head back. As if that didn't give me goose bumps, then he lifted his head to kiss my neck.

"Jesus," I groaned, pressing my hips against his as every soft kiss threatened to turn me inside out. "That is so…"

"Like it?"

"Uh-huh."

"Good." He planted a lingering kiss beneath my jaw. "You don't have to be anywhere tomorrow, do you?"

"N-no. Pretty sure I'd be canceling my plans if I did."

"Good." He released my hair, and when I kissed his mouth again, we sank back down to the pillow.

"You really don't mind taking this slow?" I asked.

"Do I mind?" He ran his fingers down my arm. "Why would I be in any rush? I've already got what I want."

"Do you?"

"Yeah. You in my bed." He tugged at my shirt, then slid his hands up my back, grinning when the touch of his rough, warm palms made me shiver.

He pushed me onto my back and sat up over me. "I'm not in any hurry, but I do think we're both a bit…overdressed."

And right then, he peeled off his shirt. Oh, sweet Jesus. His intricate tattoo sleeve continued up his arm, shoulder, and pec, but I didn't have a chance to really drink it in because he came back down to me. Tattoo could wait. Kissing couldn't.

And now that his shirt was off, the rest of our clothes followed. Every time an article of clothing came off, Sailo zeroed in on the newly bared skin. He'd been with other men before, but he caressed, kissed, explored like this was his first time too. As if being his first time with *me* warranted the same kind of curiosity and fascination as my first time with any man.

It was strange to feel attractive again. Earlier tonight, I'd wondered who in his right mind would be interested in a newly-divorced semi-virgin on this side of forty-five. I kept myself fit, but I wasn't twenty anymore.

And Sailo didn't seem to give a damn. Maybe he was fantasizing about someone else, but I didn't care as long as he kept pulling off clothes and touching my skin.

He dropped my boxers off the side of the bed, and when he pulled me close again, his bare skin warmed mine. No clothes left. Nothing between us. Before tonight, I'd never touched another naked man, and now I was wrapped up with this one, both of us stripped down and rock hard and making out like we weren't kidding about taking our time. And I was right—feeling his cock against mine without the layer of fabric in between was *mind-blowing*.

"Let me…" I licked my lips. "Let me see you."

"See me?" He grinned and sat up over me.

"Yeah." I ran my hands over his chest. "First time, remember?"

"Look all you want." He winked. "And feel free to touch."

"Oh, I will. Believe me."

No surprise—Sailo had a gorgeous body. Nothing like the men I'd fantasized about, but only because I hadn't thought to imagine a man like him. My mental harem was all a bunch of generic porn stars. The stereotypical image of what was hot. Six-foot-something dudes with six packs and modeling contracts.

Sailo wasn't one of them, but he was fucking stunning. The tattoo on his arm and chest had nothing on the one covering his lower abdomen and upper legs. The design was even more intricate than the other, with thin black lines and tiny geometric patterns forming bands that dipped into a deep V just below his navel and continued, one after the other, to his knees, covering every inch of skin except his cock and balls. It must have taken ages to complete.

I wanted to run my fingers over it, look at every single line and angle, but the only thing fascinating me more than all that ink was the man who wore it.

His abs were smooth, his chest and shoulders broad. Not much hair—a few dark sprinkles here and there—aside from the thin trail that started below his navel, and led my gaze downward to where it disappeared into his elaborate tattoo, and below that toward his thick, untattooed cock.

"Like what you see?" he asked with a playful grin.

"Very much so." I reached up and curved my hand around the back of his neck, and he came down into my arms for another long, toe-curling kiss. Now that I had his lips against mine again, I explored his tattoos with my fingers. They were ever so slightly raised, especially the one on his lower body, and I traced the lines, marveling at the unusual texture. Every little bump and groove reminded me that this was someone completely new, that my hands were no longer on the familiar soft skin of my wife. Everything about Sailo was different, from the shape of his body to the lines etched onto his skin, and every touch drove home that I was with someone completely new for the first time in a quarter century.

I wasn't just overwhelmed by him, but by how much I wanted this. Touching another man's body, feeling his cock against mine, turning him on—and I'd doubted if I was really attracted to men? Oh, I was. I couldn't even remember being this drawn to a woman, or this turned on by one. Maybe it was just because this was shiny and new. Whatever the case, I was loving every second.

"Question." Sailo lifted himself up and met my gaze, his eyes absolutely *smoldering* with lust. "You said you've never been with a man, right?"

"Right."

"You ever had anal before?"

I gulped. "With my wife, yes."

He tilted his head. "She ever peg you?"

"Peg—no."

"So you were always the top?"

I nodded. "Always."

He pursed his lips. "Well, you've been a top before, but I don't bottom."

My heart sped up again. I realized I hadn't even thought that far ahead. Whenever I'd fantasized about sex with men, I was on top. I'd only ever *been* on top when I'd had sex with anyone, and I hadn't seen myself in any other position. It simply hadn't occurred to me.

But now that Sailo put it out there, the idea of bottoming was…hot. Unnerving, yes, but hot. Some of the pornos I'd watched over the years flashed through my mind, and God, yes, I wanted to know what that was like, being on my knees or flat on my back with a man *pounding* me. "I've definitely never done that."

"Relax." He leaned down and kissed me. "We won't go that far tonight. If you're game to hook up a second time, though…"

I nodded without hesitation. I couldn't imagine not being game to hook up with him again. Especially if we weren't going to fuck tonight. I was kind of disappointed about that, but relieved too. I wasn't sure if I was ready for that yet. Only that I *wanted* to be ready for it. My curiosity had been piqued, and now it wouldn't shut up.

"Now that I think about it, though," he went on, "I'm actually quite tempted to let you top me one night."

That mental image made my dick even harder. "Are you serious?"

"Mmhmm. You know why?"

"Tell me."

"So I can see your face the first time you're balls-deep in a man."

Oh. God. *Yes.*

I swept my tongue across my lips as I drew him back down to me. "Now you're just teasing."

He laughed. "And you like it."

"I do." I kissed him lightly. Then I nudged him to roll over again, and once I was back on top, I started working my way down to his neck. He tilted his head back, baring his throat as he dug his fingers into my arms. The skin was vaguely rough where he'd shaved, and I liked the way it felt beneath my lips. I liked his body heat, the salt of his skin, the gentle abrasion of his stubble—I could explore him with my mouth all damned night.

I trailed kisses over his collarbone and started on his chest.

Sailo squirmed, lifting just enough to brush my hip with his cock. "Now who's teasing?"

I glanced up at him as I kissed the middle of his chest. "Only a tease if I don't follow through, right?"

His eyebrows rose. "You…gonna follow through?"

Nerves tightened my chest, but I refused to let them show. "Maybe."

He bit his lip.

I kissed lower.

"Fuck…" He squeezed my shoulder and lifted his hips to press against me once more. "You do, I'm not gonna last long. Too fucking turned on not to come."

Oh shit. Was I ready for that?

Guess I was about to find out.

"Just give me some warning, okay?"

"Yeah. Yeah. Definitely."

I trailed kisses lower, his chest rising and falling faster as I continued downward. "You, um, know I've never done this before, right?"

"S'okay." He pushed himself up on his elbows and gazed down at me. "You're a perfect kisser, so you know how to use your mouth."

No pressure. Awesome.

I kept inching downward. Every time I kissed his skin, I moved a little lower, working up more and more courage with every inch I gained. As I reached his lower abdomen, I moved from smooth skin to the intricate tattoos. The lines were odd beneath my lips. Odd, and fascinating. I kissed along the grooves and contours, flicking my tongue here and there and grinning whenever he shivered or moaned.

The tattoos abruptly curved downward below his navel, and like runway lights, led me right toward his fully erect cock. So I followed them. All the way. And the lower I went, the more he cursed under his breath as his abs quivered beneath my lips. By the time I'd reached his cock, I was too turned on by his moans to be self-conscious about my lack of experience.

Here goes…

I steadied him with my thumb and forefinger around the base, and ran my tongue around the head. He pulled in a sharp hiss, so I did it again. Slowly, I worked up the nerve and took him between my lips. First just the head, then more, until I was dangerously close to testing my gag reflex.

"D-don't have to go so deep," he panted. "Use…use your hand."

Right. I always loved that. In fact…why was I so worried about how to do this? I knew what *I* liked.

Quit overthinking this and do that.

So I stroked him exactly the way I liked it—my grip just loose enough to create the perfect friction—and teased the head of his cock with my lips and tongue.

"Oh yeah." He groaned, his hips squirming beneath me. "Fuck, that's good."

Relief and arousal both rushed through my veins. He liked it? God, yes. He liked it. So I tried other things I'd enjoyed. I fluttered the tip of my tongue against the soft skin of his balls, and his throaty groan nearly made me come unglued. Then I teased his balls with my fingertips while I licked and sucked the head of his cock, and he arched off the bed. His fingers gripped my hair, twitched in my hair, pulled my hair enough to make my scalp burn and my dick unbearably hard.

"God, this feels good," he murmured. "You don't know how bad…how bad I wanna fuck you."

Oh Jesus.

"When you're ready for it…" He tensed, sucking in a sharp breath as his cock got even harder between my lips. "When you're ready for it, I will pound you into the goddamned mattress."

Please do. Please, please, please—

"Gonna make me come," he moaned. "You can…stop if you…*fuck*…"

Stop? Not a chance. The thought of him coming in my mouth didn't worry me now. It turned me on. Turned me on like crazy.

I didn't stop. Sailo's cock got even harder, even thicker, and the faint taste of salt met my tongue, so I tightened my grip and quickened my strokes, and his whole body seemed to tense as a low, throaty groan faded into a helpless whimper.

"C-coming," he breathed. "I'm…oh, God…"

And just like that, hot liquid rushed across my tongue and the roof of my mouth. I immediately swallowed it before it could hit the back of my throat, and had to swallow again before he moaned and relaxed. If he was anything like me, he was about to go from coming to extremely—and uncomfortably—hypersensitive, so I let him go.

I pushed myself up on my arms, and Sailo grabbed, dragged me down on top of him, and—despite the fact that he'd just come in my mouth—kissed me. Before we'd even landed back on the pillow, his fingers were around my dick. And they were slippery. Coated in lube. Where had it come from? Oh who cared, because his slick strokes felt amazing. My body once again had a mind of its own, and my hips were suddenly thrusting against him, fucking into his hand. Breaking the kiss, I exhaled, my lips grazing his, and then he grabbed the back of my head and kissed me again.

He pumped my cock as we kissed breathlessly, and apparently my body forgot that I'd already come once tonight because I was heading there again, faster and faster with every stroke. I thrust harder, and he gripped me tighter.

"You gonna come again?" he murmured against my lips. "You gonna—"

"If you keep doing that." I squeezed my eyes shut, breaking the kiss and tilting my head back as I fucked against him for all I was worth.

"Oh yeah," he groaned as if he were the one falling to pieces. "*Come*, Greg."

I looked down at him and met his gaze. There was a wild gleam in his eyes, an intense, focused hunger, and—

"*Shit!*" I thrust once more, and shuddered violently, and Sailo kept stroking me as I came on his hand and his stomach and his chest.

The world spun. I might've even blacked out for a second. One instant, I was crying out and coming, the next, I was slumped over him.

He wrapped his arm around me and kissed my cheek but didn't say anything. I didn't say anything. I just held myself up on shaking arms, squeezed my eyes shut, and breathed.

Well. That answered that question.

I am definitely not *just bi-curious.*

Chapter Six

After we'd cleaned ourselves off, Sailo pulled the sheet up to our waists. For the longest time, we lay there, loosely wrapped in each other's arms, kissing lazily. I had actually forgotten what it felt like to make out like this after sex—it had been way too long since an orgasm had been a precursor to anything besides rolling over and going to sleep.

Eventually, we pulled apart enough to see each other. We were on our sides, fingers laced together between us. This was so perfect and blissful, I could *almost* pretend we weren't a couple of complete strangers who'd picked each other up in a bar.

"So," he said with a sleepy grin. "Your first time with a man wasn't disappointing, I hope?"

"Not at all. I mean, I can't remember the last time I came twice in one night." I laughed, and swore I sounded drunk. "Thought I was too old for that."

He arched an eyebrow. "How old is too old?"

"Is that a tactful way of asking how old I am?"

He shrugged. "Not sure how tactful it was, but okay."

I chuckled. "I'm forty-seven."

Sailo blinked. "No shit?"

"Yep."

"Wow. I figured you just had a few years on me."

I gestured at my hair. "With this much gray?"

He laughed. "Could've grayed young."

"Well, I did raise three kids."

"That explains it." He pointed at his own hair, which now that I looked more closely, had a few flecks of white here and there. "My boy is already turning me gray."

"I didn't realize you were a dad."

He smiled. "Yeah. My son is six."

Six. Holy shit.

"What?" He cocked his head. "You're not weirded out by sleeping with another dad, are you?"

"No, no. It's not that." I laughed. "It's the fact that my granddaughter is the same age as your son."

"No way." His jaw dropped. "You've got *grandkids*?"

"One grandkid," I corrected. "And to be fair, I started young, and my daughter started even younger."

"You don't say. How old are your kids?"

"Eighteen, twenty-one, and twenty-three."

"Wow."

I studied him, trying to add up the faint lines in his skin and the little bit of gray in his hair. "At the risk of being impolite, how old are you?"

"Thirty-seven." He chuckled. "I, um, started a bit later than you with the whole kid thing."

"Smart."

"Eh, maybe." He shrugged, rolling onto his back. "I had my shit together when he came along, but sometimes I think it would've been easier when I was younger and had more energy."

"And sometimes I think it would've been easier when I was a little older and had a bit more experience." I propped myself up on my elbow, resting my other hand on his tattooed chest. "Not to mention money." I laughed, shaking my head. "Jesus. We're already talking about our kids. Isn't this kind of a breach of one-night-stand protocol?"

Sailo burst out laughing. "Yeah, probably." He slid his fingers between mine on his chest. "But we were already talking about meeting up again." He winked. "You know, so I could fuck you."

I gulped. "You were serious about that?"

He sobered slightly. "Were you?"

"I'm sure as hell not going to say no." I moistened my lips. "This is all new to me, but now that I have the chance, I want to try everything."

"Well." He brought my hand up to his lips and kissed my palm. "With the way you kiss and the way you suck dick, you're not going to have to twist my arm to hook up again."

"In that case"—I grinned—"don't let me leave without your number."

"Oh, I won't." He let go of my hand and reached for my neck. Drawing me down to him, he added, "And I want yours too."

He definitely wouldn't have to twist my arm…

~*~

My alarm went off way, way too early. At least I didn't have to be at work at five in the morning like the machinists, but still… Fuck this shit.

Bleary-eyed and cursing, I picked up my phone to turn off the alarm, and my heart skipped.

It wasn't my usual alarm. Today was Sunday, after all. No, I'd set myself a reminder. One I'd programmed in on the day I'd bought the phone.

Anniversary.

I swallowed. Twenty-five years ago today, I'd said, "I do" to the future mother of my children. And less than twelve hours ago, I'd said, "Yes, please" to the man who'd spend half the night turning me inside out.

A few weeks ago, I wouldn't have believed anyone who'd said this was where I'd be now, and now that I was here, I felt…

Nothing.

Which was weird. It was my wedding anniversary, after all. Our silver anniversary. Something I'd had every intention of commemorating with an expensive dinner, that bracelet she'd been eyeing for the last couple of years, maybe a trip somewhere. We'd exchange gifts and cards. The kids would call. Becky and I might've even had sex for once.

But now, on the morning of that milestone anniversary, I was lying in the guest room of a friend's house, counting twinges and hoping I had a shot at another night with the man I'd just met. He'd driven me back here last night, kissed me in the car and given me his number, but did that mean anything would actually happen if I got in touch with him again? No idea. But I sure hoped so.

Eyes closed, I smiled. My brain kept rewinding last night, and over and over I saw myself leaning against that wall in the VIP lounge with my cock down Sailo's throat. Or stripping each other down as we made out in his bed. Or the way he'd grinned up at me as he'd made me come for the second time.

Against my will, my mind wandered to a more sobering set of thoughts—the sex life I'd had until recently. Before last night, I hadn't realized what sex had become in my marriage. It wasn't a chore, or something we didn't enjoy, but we approached it with the same enthusiasm as watching TV in the evenings. It had become a way to unwind after a long day. An orgasm apiece so we could sleep, but no real enthusiasm anymore.

"We haven't done anything in a while. You want to?"

"Ah, hell. There's nothing on TV. Why not?"

Okay, so the conversations weren't really that dull, but the sentiment was. And if I was honest with myself, so was the sex. Not because she was a woman. Not because I was more interested in a man. No, it was because we'd both stopped caring enough to put in the effort.

That thought made me sad, but it also settled something in me. Maybe Becky was right. Maybe our marriage *had* run its course, and it *was* time to move on.

And with that uplifting thought, I wasn't going back to sleep.

I sat up. Aching from head to toe, I felt like a much older man than I was, but couldn't help grinning as those twinges swung my thoughts back to last night instead of my past life. Well, if it was time to move on, I could definitely think of worse ways to do it.

I rolled to my feet. Stretched. Creaked. Gingerly rubbing my lower back, I shuffled into the bathroom for a shower.

By the time I'd dried off, I felt somewhat closer to human. Coffee would help. And either I was hallucinating, or I could smell some coffee coming from the kitchen. So, I followed the scent down the hall.

When I stepped into the kitchen, Ethan was at the island, the same place where they'd decided last night to take me to Wilde's. He was in shorts and a T-shirt, his face unshaven and his dark hair slightly ruffled as he nursed a cup of coffee.

"Morning," I said.

"Morning." Ethan watched me for a moment, then lifted his eyebrows. "Good night?"

"Hmm?"

"Come on." He chuckled. "You're walking kind of stiff, and we did leave you at Wilde's to meet up with that deejay. Plus I heard you come in this morning."

"Oh. Sorry. Didn't mean to wake you guys up."

"It's fine." He gestured dismissively. "I normally sleep through anything, but I happened to be awake right then anyway."

"Really? At that hour?"

With sheepish grin, he said, "Well, we hadn't actually gone to sleep yet, so…"

I laughed. "And here I was trying to be all quiet and sneaky on my way in."

"It's the thought that counts."

"Right. So where's Rhett?"

He pointed at the floor above us. "Still sleeping." Clicking his tongue, he shook his head. "Those late nights are rough on a man his age."

"Um, aren't you older than—"

"Shh, shh." He waved his hand. "That's irrelevant."

"Sure it is."

Ethan flipped me the bird, then gestured at the coffeepot. "There's plenty left if you want some."

"God, yes." I took a mug down from the cabinet. It felt weird to be this familiar in their house, but they'd insisted, *mi casa, su casa.* After I'd poured myself some, I took a seat at the island.

"I'm gonna give Rhett another hour or so," Ethan said. "Then I'll make some bacon and eggs. You want any?"

"Sure, that sounds great." I carefully sipped my piping-hot coffee. "This is what I need right now, though."

"You and me both."

"Why aren't you sleeping in?"

"I would," he muttered into his cup, "but then I'll fuck up my sleep pattern and won't be able to get up for work tomorrow."

"Ugh, yeah. I get that. After last night, I could've slept till this afternoon, but I'd pay for it all week."

"Mmhmm." He paused. "You had a good night, right?" His tone was playful, but the lift of his eyebrows suggested he really was concerned.

"Yeah, it was…well…" I coughed into my fist. "I definitely don't have any doubts left about being attracted to men."

"Oh really?" He grinned. "That deejay, eh?"

"Yep." I sighed, rolling my stiff shoulders. "And Jesus…it was amazing. Best I've felt in the last three weeks, that's for sure."

"If that grin's anything to go by, I'd wager it's the best you've felt in longer than that."

I wanted to argue, to insist that I'd been perfectly happy up until three weeks ago, but he was right. "Well, I'll take what I can get these days." I thumbed the handle on my coffee cup, replaying last night and adding it on to the timeline of the past three weeks. When had my life become this surreal roller coaster of *wow, did not see that one coming*?

Ethan tilted his head. "You okay? You seem like you had a good time, but…not."

"No, I did. It was great. But it, um, definitely drove home how inexperienced I am with men."

"Eh." He shrugged. "We've all been there. The learning curve isn't as bad as you think."

"That's encouraging." I rested my elbow on the counter and idly ran my finger back and forth along my lower lip. "It is, um, pretty new territory, though."

"Yeah, but it seems more intimidating than it actually is."

"For you, maybe. I guess, um…" I cleared my throat. "There are some things I'm less sure about than others. Like…well… Okay, at the risk of sounding like a total idiot…"

Ethan watched me for a moment. Then he chuckled. "No, bottoming doesn't have to hurt."

I blinked. "Huh? What? How did you—"

He patted my arm. "I've seen that look before."

"What look?"

"The one that says 'I was with a guy last night, I'm curious about doing more with him, but I'm scared out of my mind.'" He inclined his head. "Am I close?"

"Uh. Yeah. Actually." I shook myself. "How the hell did you know?"

He laughed. "Trust me—you're not the first who's wanted to have that conversation. And I had it myself a long time ago. Seems like any guy I've ever talked to who's just starting out with men, that's the first thing they're worried about."

"Was it something you were worried about?"

"Of course." He shrugged. "That and what it would be like when a guy blew his load in my mouth, but at least I was pretty sure that wouldn't hurt."

No, no, it would not. It did not. God, that was hot…

I shifted, suppressing a pleasant shudder just so he wouldn't notice. "I think I'd have felt a bit less insecure having this conversation as a clueless twenty-something than…well…now."

Ethan waved his hand. "No reason to be insecure. A lot of guys go all the way through life without ever having the chance or the self-awareness to even have this discussion. Or they go through any of the motions we're talking about. You're further ahead of the curve than you realize."

"Sad, isn't it? That so many people never figure it out?"

"Well. Here's to today's generation. They're light years ahead of ours."

"Isn't that the truth?" I leaned back in my chair. "So, when you say bottoming doesn't *have* to hurt, what exactly does that mean? I mean, I've done it with Becky before, and she loved it. So obviously it isn't always painful. Or is it and she just liked that?"

"No, it's not painful. If the top knows what the hell he's doing, it won't hurt at all." He quirked his lips. "Unless you *want* it to, I mean."

"Beg pardon?"

He chuckled and gestured dismissively. "It's really easy to make it completely painless. There are things you can do beforehand to make it easier. Things you should do anyway, but…" He waved a hand again. "Anyway, make friends with toys and lube, and by the time you're ready for him to top you, you'll be good to go."

"Make friends with them?" I laughed. "Interesting way to put it."

"Trust me. They are your friends if you want to have anal and enjoy it." He pointed in the general direction of the rest of Capitol Hill. "Check out The Oh Zone on Broadway. There are a couple of places on Pike too."

"Do you recommend any in particular?"

He seemed to mull it over for a moment. "You can't go wrong with The Oh Zone. There's Heat over on Pike, and I think Devil of Lace is still open." He wrinkled his nose. "Just don't bother with The Black Curtain."

"Why's that?"

"They're…" He picked up his coffee. "Let's just say the quality of their merchandise doesn't match the prices. And besides, places like The Oh Zone and Heat, they know what they're talking about. You have a question, I guarantee they can answer it."

My cheeks burned just thinking about it. "My God. I can't even imagine going in and asking some of the questions on my mind."

"Nah. There's no reason to be embarrassed in those places." He brought the coffee cup to his lips. "Trust me—they've seen and heard everything."

I smirked. "So what you're saying is, you and Rhett are regulars?"

"Hey!" He lowered the cup and glared at me. "What's that supposed to mean?"

"Are you denying it?"

He pursed his lips. "Well…"

"That's what I thought."

"Hmph." He sipped his coffee again and set it back down.

I chuckled, but my humor didn't last. I leaned back, rubbing the stiff muscles in my neck. "I feel like such an idiot, even needing to go ask people questions like this."

"Greg." Ethan's voice was unusually gentle, his expression completely serious. "You're not as rare a breed as you think. The kids now, yeah, they're coming out when they're fourteen and nobody's batting an eye. We're from a different generation. When Rhett and I used to have the odd three-way, I can't tell you how many times we hooked up with someone who was our age and had never touched a naked man in his life."

I nodded, chewing my lip. "So, you guys don't do that anymore? Threesomes?"

He shrugged. "Oh, we occasionally hook up with one other couple, but it's not something we do as often anymore with people we don't know. Logistics and all—it's kind of a headache."

"Logistics?" I laughed. "Guess that's another world I'm not familiar with."

"What? You and the wife weren't swingers or anything like that?"

"Uh, no." I tapped my fingers on my coffee cup. "Is that weird too?"

"Nah, I'm just busting your chops." He flattened his hands on the counter and leaned over them. "So, this guy from last night—any chance you'll see him again?"

I nodded, a grin trying to form on my lips. "Yeah. That's actually why I was wondering about bottoming. He said he'd like to top me, and I'm…" I groaned. "I have no idea what to expect."

"You'll be fine. As long as he takes his time and uses plenty of lube, and as long as you *relax*, you'll probably love it." Ethan paused. "And if you don't love it the first time, don't give up on it. It can be a bit of…an acquired taste."

"Speaking from experience?"

He nodded. "I was a dedicated top for a long time because my first few experiences weren't so great. Then Rhett came along, and…" He whistled. With a grin, he added, "Let's just say I saw the light. So, give it a chance, but if it's really not for you, then it's not for you. Some people don't ever warm up to it. It's not their thing."

I drummed my nails on my coffee cup again. "That's…encouraging."

"It's actually quite fun. I'm just putting it out there so you don't feel like you *have* to do it, or that it's the be-all end-all of sex with a man." His smile was gentle, and not the least bit patronizing. "Do whatever you enjoy, and don't do the rest."

"And if the guy I'm with enjoys something I don't?"

"Compromise?" He shrugged. "It's no different than with a woman, I would assume. If it's an absolute deal-breaker—something you absolutely won't do and your partner can't live without—you wish them the best and move on. If it's not your favorite thing, but you're willing to do it to make your partner happy and they understand you don't want it all the time? Great."

He had a point. Becky and I both had our limits, and we'd made concessions for each other over the years. She wasn't a huge fan of going down on me, but she knew I liked it, so she did it sometimes. I thought sex in the shower was a pain in the ass, but she enjoyed it, so I did it sometimes.

So why would it be different with a man?

I picked up my coffee and cradled it between my hands. "Well, I'll give it a try, and I guess…I guess we'll see how it goes."

Ethan smiled. "Good luck. I think you're in for a pleasant surprise."

I just sipped my coffee and hoped he was right.

Chapter Seven

As promised, Ethan made breakfast after Rhett finally stumbled out of bed. Then they had some errands to run, so after we'd eaten, they left for the afternoon.

On my own, I wasn't quite sure what to do with myself, but I also couldn't get this morning's conversation out of my head. Maybe Ethan was right, and I just needed to go to one of those shops and ask some questions.

In the room that was temporarily mine, I sat back on the queen-size bed and propped my iPad on my knee. I did a quick search for shops in the area that carried sex toys. No surprise—there were a lot of them. Seattle was a pretty liberated place, after all.

Ethan had recommended The Oh Zone, so I clicked on their site. Might as well see what kinds of things were available before I actually walked into the shop. Did that make me a coward? Probably. I had no doubt I was overthinking everything, but I was an engineer. That was what people like me did. And besides, this was new and somewhat terrifying territory. So, what the hell.

Holy shit. The options were daunting to say the least. Dildos and vibrators of every imaginable shape and size. Butt plugs that seemed anatomically unrealistic. And there were *how* many different types of lube?

I rested my head against the headboard and stared at my screen with wide eyes. It wasn't like this was my first foray into sex shops. Becky and I had gone into places like this early in our marriage, or when we were on one of those rare vacations without the kids and wanted to spice things up. And I'd gone in alone a couple of times to find something for an anniversary or Valentine's Day.

But somehow, this was more intimidating. It wasn't a pair of fuzzy handcuffs or an extra-soft flogger. It wasn't a set of lacy lingerie that would spend most of the night on a hotel floor. It sure as hell wasn't a DVD that we'd watch for five minutes, and then use as background noise while we fucked.

Swallowing hard, I tapped the icon for dildos. Surprise, surprise—half a billion options. I had never even given the toys and vibrators a second look before, especially not with the intent of getting one for myself. I had thought it was as simple as going in, picking one out, paying for it, and leaving. But no—I'd need to find the one that was just the right size, shape, and material. What was I supposed to do? Write down the product name and number, walk in, and ask them to grab that specific one for me?

Then a link caught my eye: Home Delivery.

Wait, what?

I sat up a little as I tapped the link. No shit, for a nominal fee, the company would box up anything I wanted to buy, package it discreetly, and bring it to my—well, Ethan and Rhett's—door. Within three hours.

Which meant I could get anything without having to wander into one of their shops. If it wasn't what I needed, well, I was out fifty bucks.

This was ridiculous. I was a grown man, so I shouldn't have been embarrassed about any of this. On the other hand, if I was honest with myself, the thought of even buying condoms made my skin crawl. Buying a couple of phallic toys, lube, and some books about anal play? Wasn't gonna happen.

But this home-delivery thing was a game changer.

I started perusing the site all over again, this time with the knowledge that it would be discreetly delivered right to my waiting hands. Before long, I'd filled the virtual shopping cart with about two hundred dollars' worth of things I'd never imagined myself buying. My pulse was racing and I was already imagining how things might play out during the few seconds of interaction with the delivery driver, but I tapped the Submit Order button, and it was done.

Now that the order was in, I couldn't help feeling kind of excited about its arrival. I felt a bit…adventurous! The thought of experimenting like this, trying something completely new when I'd previously considered myself to be quite experienced, was a hell of a turn-on.

Come on, driver. Pedal to the floor.

Ethan and Rhett weren't due back for a few hours, and delivery was guaranteed within three. So as long as the driver wasn't late and the guys weren't early, I didn't have to worry about them crossing paths. Hopefully.

I was right—the delivery driver beat Ethan and Rhett, thank the Lord, and the transaction was quick and easy despite me feeling like an idiot. She handed me the unmarked box, had me sign a form saying I'd received it, and she was gone.

I hurried back into my rented room, shut the door behind me, and opened the box. One by one, I removed each item and laid it out on the bed. Then I tossed aside the empty box, and I had to laugh at the items arranged in front of me. Three different size dildos. A butt plug. Two types of lube, in case I didn't like one or the other. Condoms to keep the toys clean. Four books on anal play. Basically, a box full of parts and a goddamned instruction manual—could I have *been* more of an engineer about this?

Chuckling to myself, I sat back on the bed beside everything, and thumbed through one of the books. It amazed me that there was enough to say about anal sex that it could take up this many pages, but there it was. And that was just one of four books, not to mention a dozen more I could order if these didn't fully enlighten me.

There were chapters about positions and rimming. I'd read those later. For now, I concentrated on the ones that talked about stretching, prepping, and penetrating for the first time. Everything that had anything to do with taking it up the ass without pain. I went through the second book. The third. They said basically the same thing Ethan did—start with toys and make friends with lube.

I had toys. I had lube.

Time to make friends.

Heart speeding up, I closed the book and set it aside. I got up and locked the door—not that I expected one of the guys to barge in—and closed the blinds. Then I stripped off my clothes and lay back on the bed beside the array of toys and lube.

Well. Here goes nothing.

As recommended, I put a condom over the toy. Apparently that made it easier to keep them clean. Fine—I just wanted the practice since I hadn't used a condom in *mumble* years. Better to get the hang of it again with a toy than in front of Sailo.

Once the condom was on, I put the toy aside for a moment and opened one of the lube bottles. I poured some on my hand, leaned back against the pillows, and spread my legs.

The books recommended fingers first, so that was what I started with. The position was awkward—it'd probably be a hell of a lot easier with someone else doing the fingering. Or me fingering them. Except then I'd be a nervous wreck, so awkward positions would have to do for now.

Staring up at the ceiling with unfocused eyes, I pressed one finger in. Weird. Very…weird. I gritted my teeth, but that didn't help. And hadn't both Ethan and my reading material said that relaxing was important?

I closed my eyes and took a few slow, deep breaths. I concentrated on relaxing, and kept my fingertip there until the muscle finally obeyed. Pressing in this time, I had more luck—my finger slid in to the first joint. When I withdrew it and tried again, it still took some work, but the third time, it was easier. The burn was bizarre. This turned people on? Different strokes, maybe. Still, I was determined to give it a chance, and pushed my finger in again.

Little by little, I slid it deeper. After a while, I added a second, which didn't take nearly as much work as the first by itself. Before long, they were sliding easily in and out.

Okay. So fingers weren't bad. No pain. Weird, but no pain. In fact, the longer I did it, the better it felt. Still an intense burn, but not unpleasant. Kind of…kind of addictive, actually. Wow.

I blinked my eyes into focus and looked at the condom-covered toy beside me. I swallowed. Time to level up.

I slipped my fingers free, and had to pause for a moment to catch my breath. I wanted them back inside me. Like *now*.

Which meant I really, really wanted to get on with it with this toy, so I quickly put on some lube, not caring that a few drops landed on my stomach or ran down the side of my wrist. I'd probably take a shower after this anyway, so whatever.

Like I had with my fingers, I pressed the toy's blunt end against my ass. I paused to breathe, to relax, and then pushed in. To my surprise, I took it easier than I had my finger, and much more quickly than before, I got used to the thick, smooth presence. Eyes closed, I took more long, deep breaths and slow, deep strokes. It was a strange, invasive feeling. Even more so than with my fingers, since this thing was thicker. It didn't hurt, per se. Felt strange, definitely, and intense, but was it pain? I wasn't even sure I could define it.

And how different would this be when I was with someone else? When instead of a toy, I was taking Sailo's cock? With his body over mine, his lips touching mine…

I shivered. As I took another stroke, I imagined that instead of a toy, this was Sailo's cock. That he was sitting over me, easing himself inside, and…

Oh. Yes. Oh yes. I wanted to try the real thing.

In all those pornos I'd ever watched, the actors had pounded their partners' asses. And my ex-wife had always begged me to do it harder, just like when I'd fucked her pussy. Could I handle it harder?

Only one way to find out.

I sped up my hand, fucking myself harder with the toy, and couldn't help moaning aloud. I didn't even care if the guys had come home and heard me. I did it even harder, until my vision blurred and my arm ached.

Fuck. This was *amazing*. And I needed to come. My neglected cock was rock hard and desperately needed attention.

I wasn't sure I could contort myself enough to move the toy in and out while stroking myself, though, and I wasn't ready to give this part up. My dick could wait a few more minutes. I was enjoying this too much, feeling something moving inside me and imagining I was being fucked by the man who'd rocked my world so hard last night. How much more amazing *would* this be when it was Sailo's dick? Would he moan like he did when I was sucking him off? Cursing and gasping?

A shudder rippled through me. I shifted a little, and—

Whoa.

Whoa.

That was what the book was talking about when they mentioned the male G-spot. Holy fucking…oh God. I couldn't get enough. I tilted the toy a little more, not caring about the vague strain in my wrist and elbow, and moaned as I fucked myself harder. My balls tightened and my eyes rolled back.

Am I going to…whoa, is this really going to make me—

"Fuck!" The word burst out of me, and then I arched off the bed as semen landed on my stomach. I kept pounding myself with the toy as my eyes watered and my toes curled and my whole body seemed to levitate off the mattress, and I didn't stop until it was suddenly too much.

With a long sigh, I sank back to the bed. I withdrew the toy and lay back, staring at the ceiling with tear-blurred eyes. I'd been scared to death that anal would hurt, and then…this? I had never—*never*—come without me or someone else touching my cock.

"*When you're ready for it,*" Sailo's voice echoed in my mind, "*I will pound you into the goddamned mattress.*"

I closed my eyes and shivered.

Yes, please…

Chapter Eight

When the alarm went off on Monday morning, it was not an anniversary reminder.

Time to go to work. This is not a drill.

I showered, shaved, and slipped out as quietly as I could. Rhett and Ethan didn't have to be up as early as I did for work, so I did the best I could not to wake them.

Then it was onto the freeways and my new commute to the job I'd had for most of my adult life. So weird to be driving to the same place from a new place. Just another reminder that everything had changed, apparently.

Everything, that is, except traffic in Seattle. Clinging to my coffee cup, I crawled alongside all the other bleary-eyed commuters. Ten minutes—and about ten feet—down the freeway, I vowed to myself that once I was settled into my new place, I would find an alternate route. I didn't care if it involved back roads through the worst neighborhoods—I was going to find a way to work that didn't involve…this.

Stop and go. Stop and go. Stop and go. Finally, a couple of miles south of Seattle, the worst of it broke up, and I flew down the freeway at a breakneck speed of about thirty-five miles an hour. Better than nothing.

I trudged into the office about ten minutes early, working my way through the familiar maze of cubicles on autopilot before I made it to my own desk and dropped into my chair. The day started. Coworkers came by, sometimes for small talk, sometimes for work-related conversations.

Nobody seemed to notice that I was more bleary-eyed than usual. Then again, everyone at this place was half-dead on Monday mornings since we all had to be here obscenely early, so nothing short of a bullet hole or a missing limb was going to register with anyone. Fine by me. And thank God no one at work knew or remembered or cared that it was my anniversary over the weekend. I wasn't even sure I could cope with a sympathetic "That must be hard" or "How are you holding up?" today.

The kids hadn't called or e-mailed over the weekend either, and for that, I was thankful. They probably knew as well as I did that the best course of action was to let the day slip by as unnoticed as possible.

Easier said than done, though. It had gone without saying, I thought, that my twenty-fifth anniversary would *not* be spent struggling to stay awake or feeling guilty every time I moved and felt a twinge or an ache still lingering from my first ever night with another man. I sure as fuck never saw myself spending that particular afternoon with a dildo and a stack of books in preparation for that man's dick.

Sitting at my desk, gazing at my familiar surroundings while I thumbed the bare spot where my wedding ring used to be, I took stock of the things that had changed and the things that hadn't. The awards and certifications on the wall had been there so long, the fabric behind them was probably a few shades darker than the rest of the cube wall. The framed photos of me and Becky were gone. The ones with the kids remained, but I'd taken down the one of all five of us.

Little by little, the divorce was sinking in. I was moving out while Becky continued living in the home we'd shared for all those years. In theory, we should've sold it as part of the divorce settlement, but she'd inherited it from her parents, so it didn't seem right to take it from her. So, I was on my way out. The lease was signed, my stuff was in boxes, and soon I'd move into a new apartment in a new neighborhood with a mix of old and new furniture, dishes, decorations…

I sighed, overwhelmed just thinking about it all. An earthquake couldn't have rearranged my life like this divorce had. And yet some things hadn't changed. It was funny how it was the things that had stayed the same that felt the weirdest. Missing pictures? Fine. Body twinging and aching from sex with someone I'd just met? Cool. A commute from a different place via totally different roads? Whatever.

But aside from the missing pictures, everything here felt exactly the same, and that left me off balance. Like a lone building still standing in the middle of miles of devastation, they may as well have been signposts reminding me of what used to be.

"Greg?"

I shook myself and looked up as Liz, a coworker, leaned into my cube. "Hey."

She tilted her head. "You okay? You were kind of staring into space." Her brow pinched slightly. She knew what was going on in my life—everyone did, thanks to the office grapevine.

"Yeah, yeah." I laughed. "Just crunching some numbers in my head." Eh, close enough.

"Oh." She straightened, grimacing a little. "I didn't mean to interrupt. Here." She handed me a stack of folders. "Could you have a look at these before this afternoon's meeting?"

"Sure. No problem." I glanced at them, comprehending absolutely nothing on the handwritten sticky note on top, and smiled up at her. "I'll get on them right now."

"Thanks." She smiled hesitantly, holding my gaze as if she were debating continuing the conversation. Fortunately, whatever was on her mind, she let it go, thanked me again, and left my cube.

I set the folders on my desk, took a deep breath, and turned back to my computer screen. Life was going on. This was a good thing. My job was the same as it ever was, and the rest of my world would settle into place soon enough.

And one of the new things in my life was definitely more distracting than the rest.

Sailo.

The hair on my arms stood on end. Sex was nothing new, but that kind of sex? With someone who was as patient and enthusiastic as he'd been? Someone who, at least for that night, wanted me? God, yes.

Especially since yesterday, I'd given myself a solo intro to the kind of sex he'd promised. And I'd liked it. Hell, I could still feel it. Every time I moved, the vague soreness reminded me of the toy that had gone where no man had gone…yet.

I grinned as I started perusing the e-mails that had been stacking up during my daydream. I could not get him out of my head, so I didn't try. Was it just the novelty of a man finding me attractive and introducing me to a world I'd only fantasized about? Or was it *him*?

Either way, the conclusion was the same—I had to see him again.

And *soon*.

~*~

After slogging through my day and crawling "home," I let myself in through Ethan and Rhett's front door. I was ready to collapse and catch up on some sleep, but if I didn't see Sailo again, I was pretty sure I'd go out of my mind.

Before leaving work, I'd sent him a text to see if he was free. Now that I was out of the car, I pulled my phone out of my pocket, and—yes! He'd responded.

At Wilde's tonight. 7-close. Show is over at 11:30. Meet me at the bar at 12?

I grimaced. Midnight? On a work night? Probably not a good idea, or I'd be even worse off tomorrow than I'd been today. Though I could call in sick, I supposed.

Then again, my attorney had said there would be hearings and meetings throughout the divorce process. It would probably behoove me to save my time off until everything was finalized, just in case.

Well. There would be other nights. So, hoping my disappointment didn't come through, I wrote back:

Have to be on the road to work at 5. Later this week?

For reasons I couldn't quite explain, I thought he'd tell me to just forget it and that would be the end of it. Apparently I was really in denial about this guy being interested in me.

Thank you for the self-esteem boost, divorce. Really needed that at this point in my life.

My own thought made me roll my eyes. Without the divorce—dented self-esteem and all—I wouldn't be making arrangements to sleep with Sailo anyway, so whatever.

My phone buzzed.

Free Wed or Thurs?

So much for my stupid ego and its insistence that Sailo was just humoring me. We texted back and forth a few times, and settled on meeting for drinks on Wednesday night. Then he had to get ready for work, and I busied myself making something to eat.

I was restless as hell, though. Tired from a long day, but twitchy. More than once, I reread our texts and wondered if I could survive tomorrow if I did in fact meet

Sailo after his show. It was a stupid thought. I'd be miserable tomorrow, and probably fall asleep halfway through tonight anyway.

Stupid thought or no, it refused to leave me alone. Sailo and I had made arrangements to meet on Wednesday, but damn it, I couldn't wait to see him. Not two more days, anyway.

Oh, to hell with it.

I changed into something more presentable, grabbed my wallet and keys, and headed out before I could talk myself out of it. With my heart thumping against my ribs, I drove through Capitol Hill, down Broadway, right to that familiar neon sign above the swanky club with tinted windows.

Wilde's had its own parking lot, unlike a lot of places in the neighborhood, and apparently they weren't that busy this early in the week. I found a spot near the front and walked inside.

After I'd paid the cover and made it past the bouncers, I continued into the lounge, which was practically empty tonight.

As I approached the bar, Kieran saw me and smiled. "Hey!" He shook my hand over the bar. "Guess the place didn't scare you off?"

"No, not quite. I'm actually meeting somebody." Sort of. He didn't exactly know I was coming. Would he be…okay with it? Oh fuck. I should've texted him.

"Can I get you something to drink?" Kieran asked.

What's the strongest thing you've got?

"Um…" I definitely didn't need any alcohol, but something cold sounded good. "Just a bottle of water. I'm, uh, driving." Probably soon. After Sailo saw me and asked what the hell I was doing here. What the hell *was* I doing here? Was this desperation? Would I look like an idiot, showing up two days before we'd agreed to meet?

Kieran handed me a water, and after I'd paid him, I took a couple of deep swallows. He and I made some small talk since the club wasn't yet loud enough to keep conversations from happening.

Maybe I should've gone for some booze. I was way too wound up to be here without some liquid courage. I hadn't even seen Sailo yet, and nerves were already fucking with my head.

Then movement from the corner of my eye caught my attention, and I turned my head.

Yeah, that cold bottle of water wasn't going to do much. Not with that gorgeous dark-eyed deejay making his way across the dance floor.

I glanced across the bar. Kieran was gone, leaving me here. Alone. With nowhere to go and no one to—

"Hey! You're here!" Sailo put a hand on my waist and kissed me.

It took a second to register that we were kissing in public. Out in the open.

But hell…it was Wilde's. There was almost no one here, and those who were probably didn't notice us, especially since they were doing a lot more than kissing.

"I didn't think you were coming," he said. "What changed your mind?"

I think you know.

I gulped. "Well, I…" I shrugged, probably not coming across as even remotely nonchalant. "You said you had a show tonight, so…"

He held my gaze, and the corner of his mouth lifted. He saw right through me, didn't he?

Then he looked at his watch and back at me. "We've got some time if you want to finish that"—he nodded toward my water bottle—"someplace quieter."

I glanced down at the water, which was mostly empty. "Actually, I think I'm done with it." I screwed on the top and set it on the bar.

Sailo's grin came completely to life. He took my hand and tugged it gently, and as I followed him, he added, "Come on."

We hurried out of the lounge, past the glowing exit sign and into the back. I knew exactly where we were going, and my heart was already at full speed before we'd reached stairs, before I even saw the VIP LOUNGE—PASS REQUIRED sign.

At the top of the steps, his keys jingled. "I'm glad you came," he said as he unlocked the door and waved me in. "Sorry I couldn't get the night off."

"I'm surprised they have you here." I stepped into the lounge. "It's a Monday night."

"Ugh. I know." He rolled his eyes, toeing the door shut behind us. "But there's a private party coming in soon. Normally, if I'm working on a Monday, it's a freelance gig." Then he reached for me, curved his hand around my neck, and kissed me again. "Enough about work," he murmured. "God, I want you…"

I pressed my hand against his lower back so he could feel my hard-on through our pants. "Likewise."

He grinned against my lips. "You're not as nervous as you were last time."

"I don't know about that." I kissed him, then added, "Still nervous. Especially since…" The words died on my tongue. How nervous was I? Nervous as fuck, definitely.

He met my gaze, concern creasing his forehead. "Since, what?"

I swallowed. Those nerves got the best of me, and I shook my head, drawing him back in. "This is just new. All of it."

"New is fun," he breathed, and pressed his lips to mine.

Couldn't argue with that.

I pressed harder against him. He groaned, deepening the kiss. My head was spinning, and damn it, I wasn't close enough to him, so I shoved him back against the door, and we kept right on making out, and I suddenly didn't care that we were here instead of on our way to his apartment. After fantasizing about him for days, imagining all the things we could do once we were together again, I didn't want to wait another minute either. Fuck. I wanted him naked. I wanted skin against tattooed skin. I wanted his dick rubbing against mine or sliding between my lips or moving inside me.

What the hell *were* we waiting for?

Well, besides his show. I supposed we didn't have the time or necessities to actually fuck here, never mind before he had to be onstage. Everything I'd read in those books said the first time couldn't be rushed. And I didn't want it to be rushed. I wanted to enjoy it. Savor it. Really feel what it was like to be fucked by a man.

The thought of him pushing his cock into me sent a shudder right through me, and I broke the kiss with a gasp.

"What?" He blinked. "You okay?"

"Yeah, I…" I licked my lips. "Just really, really turned on."

"Good. That's how I want you."

"Yeah? What if I told you I want more than just a quickie in the VIP lounge?"

"I'm not going to argue." He drew back and squinted slightly, as if trying to read me. "How much more are we talking about?"

"I want you to fuck me," I breathed. "Tonight. Been thinking about it…the last few—"

"Hell yes." He pulled me back in and kissed me hard, his fingers digging into my scalp. "Anything you want. Because I've been thinking about it too." He paused, meeting my gaze again. "You don't have to rush into this for my benefit, though."

"I'm not." I shook my head. "I, um, did a little experimenting on my own, and…" Goose bumps sprang to life along the length of my spine. "I liked it. A lot."

"Did you?" Sailo swept his tongue across his lips.

"When you told me you wanted to," I said, speaking quickly and barely remembering how to enunciate, "I got curious. So I…I tried a few things on my own and—"

He silenced me with a deep kiss. "You liked it? Playing by yourself?"

"Very much so." I rubbed my hard-on against his. "It was…so much better than I expected."

"Yeah?" He brushed his lips across mine. "You're jonesing for the real thing now, aren't you?"

"*Yes.*"

"Oh, this is going to be fun. If you're really serious—"

"I am. Very. I want—"

"Good," he said, panting hard. "After my show, meet me back at my place. And I'm going to fuck you until you beg me to stop."

"Oh God," I breathed, not giving a damn about how much tomorrow was going to suck at work. "Yes, please."

"If I could blow off my show," he whispered, "I so would. Jesus. I want to take you home right now and…" He shivered. So did I.

"You have some time, right?"

"Some." He swallowed. "Not enough for that."

"That can wait." I slid a hand over the front of his pants, my knees trembling when he groaned. "But I think we have enough time for—"

"Please." He grabbed my wrist and pressed my hand even harder against his erection. "Or I'm gonna fucking lose my mind."

I kissed him again, kneading his dick through his clothes as the door held both of us up. Then I gently freed my wrist from his hand and knelt in front of him. I had to hold on to his hip for balance because I was so goddamned dizzy, but between the two of us, we managed to get his pants unzipped.

The instant his cock was bared, I had my lips around it, and a shudder went through me. It was like *this* was what I'd been craving since the other night—his cock between my lips, his hand in my hair. And I realized I had been craving it. I wanted him. Kissing, fucking, blowing each other, doing anything and everything we could think of to drive the other wild.

"Jesus, yes," he groaned, raking his fingers through my hair. He rocked his hips slightly, fucking my mouth, and I teased him with my tongue as he slid in and out of my lips. I was going to get addicted to this, I just knew it—his enthusiastic moans, his fingers in my hair, his cock sliding across my tongue.

I closed my hand around the base and stroked him. With my hand to keep him from getting too far into my throat, I stroked him faster, and he took the hint—he thrust harder.

And then I realized, this was how he'd move later tonight. When he was inside me. Fucking me. My own cock hardened even more, and I groaned around his dick, giving him everything I had as I imagined him slamming himself into me, over and over.

His fingers tightened in my hair. His groans turned to sharp, uneven gasps. Then he shuddered violently, and as he came on my tongue, I was surprised I didn't come too.

He swore under his breath and sagged against the door. I rocked back on my heels. When I was sure I wouldn't black out or something, I rose, and he wrapped his arms around me and kissed me deeply, still panting and trembling between my body and the door.

"Told you I couldn't wait till Wednesday," I murmured.

"Me neither." Another kiss, lighter this time. "I've been looking forward to seeing you again since the other night."

"Glad I'm not the only one."

"Not at all." He looked at his watch, and his shoulders dropped. "Shit. I have to get downstairs." He met my gaze, brow pinched apologetically. "I want to return the favor, but I—"

I kissed him. "You can return it tonight. When we're in bed."

He squirmed between me and the door. “I will. Promise.”

“I can’t wait.” I brushed my lips across his. “And I’m serious about what I said before. I want you to fuck me.”

Hands sliding up my sides, he released a long, ragged breath. “You’re really sure?”

“Oh yeah. Definitely sure.”

He kissed me. “I’m looking forward to it.”

“So am I.”

“I should hope so.” He winked, wrapped his arms around my neck. “I’ve got plenty of lube and condoms at home.”

“Then I’ll see you after midnight.”

“Yes you will.”

“You’d better get to work. I don’t want to get you in trouble.”

“Damn all this adult responsibility.”

Our eyes met, and we both laughed. We kissed once more, and then headed downstairs so he could get onstage. Another kiss—okay, a few more—and we separated. I went to the bar to get something cold.

I still had some nerves, but it was mostly anticipation crackling beneath my skin. If being with a man was anything like what I’d done with those toys, then the only thing I had left to be nervous about was coming too soon.

I was going to regret the hell out of this tomorrow. When I had to be up at a painfully early hour, and function in an office full of people and fluorescent lights while I dealt with technical minutiae and micromanaging e-mails…yeah. Hell.

But it’d be worth it.

After Sailo’s show, I’d meet him at his place.

Because I just couldn’t wait another night.

Chapter Nine

I hung around the club for his show, keeping myself well-caffeinated so I wouldn't nod off at the bar. By the time he was wrapping up, I was starting to second-guess this whole plan. I'd been awake since four, and now it was nearly midnight. I was going to stay up *how* much later?

But then the show was over, and we drove to his place, and suddenly we were in his apartment, kissing and pawing at each other's clothes, and oh yes, I was awake now.

Somewhere between his front door and the bedroom, he broke the kiss and whispered, "I could use a shower before we do this. Want to join me?"

The mere thought of him, naked and soaking wet, made the answer a no-brainer. "Lead the way."

In the bathroom, we stripped off our clothes and stepped into the tub. It was fairly spacious for an apartment shower, which was good, since neither of us was exactly small.

While we soaped and rinsed ourselves, I couldn't stop staring at him. My mental image of him didn't hold a candle to reality. Suds slid over slick skin, pausing here and there on his tattoos, which seemed even blacker now that they were wet. Black hair plastered to his forehead. A few drops clinging to his goatee. And I'd ever questioned being attracted to men?

Our eyes met. As hot water rushed over both of us, we exchanged grins and pulled each other into a long, lazy kiss. Then he broke away, turned me around, and wrapped his arms around me. As he kissed his way up and down my neck, he slid his hands all over my chest and abs. I covered his hands with mine, closed my eyes, and tilted my head to expose more skin.

"Do you know how hard it was to concentrate on my show tonight?" His voice was soft, his breath hot in my ear. "I've been thinking about you since the other night, but after you said you wanted me to fuck you…" He trailed off into a moan, pressing his thick erection against my ass. "And after you gave me that fucking awesome blowjob."

I slipped my fingers between his on my chest and leaned back against him. "And here I thought you'd think I was overstepping some bounds by showing up."

"No, no, no." He kissed beneath my ear. "Showing up at my apartment, maybe. But there's a reason I told you I was at Wilde's." His lips curved into a grin against my hairline. "I was hoping you would."

"Glad I didn't disappoint."

"Not at all." He nipped my earlobe. "What do you say we take this to bed?"

I turned off the water. "Thought you'd never ask."

He laughed as I turned to face him. "Just didn't want to rush."

"But why wait?"

"Good point."

We dried off and moved into his bedroom. Those nerves started coming back to life, but I was too hard, too dizzy with pure arousal, to give them much attention.

Sinking back into his bed was like letting go of tension that had been gripping my shoulders for too many days—we were back, returning to the place where we'd fooled around the first time. Second time, if the VIP lounge counted. The first time I'd ever been literally in bed with a man, though.

Though it was already late as hell, and I was too turned on to think straight, we weren't in any rush. We took our sweet time, kissing and running our hands all over each other as if we'd never touched before. I traced his tattoos as if I could possibly memorize every loop and line, and he kissed his way up and down my neck like it was the most fascinating thing in the world. We lay on our sides, and then he was on top, and then I was. Every minute we spent doing this was one less minute of sleep I'd have before work tomorrow, and around the time he rolled me onto my back and started stroking my very hard cock, I decided for the hundredth time that this would be well worth any lost sleep.

He pushed himself up on his arms and gazed down at me. "If you're still onboard, I can get a condom."

Oh, hello, nerves.

I gulped, then nodded. "Yeah. Definitely."

"You sure?"

Licking my lips, I nodded again. "Nervous, but sure."

He held my gaze as if searching for uncertainty, then leaned down and kissed me again. Lifting himself up, he said, "Get on your hands and knees. You'll be okay holding yourself up for a while, right?"

"I think so? I guess we'll find out."

His lips quirked slightly. Then he shrugged. "Just say so if you start getting uncomfortable. That goes for everything. If it hurts, or you just don't like it…"

I nodded. "Got it."

One last kiss, and we shifted around. My heart skipped as he opened the nightstand drawer. Condoms, lube. Oh fuck.

But I turned onto my hands and knees as he'd requested. He took the condom and lube, and moved them beyond the edges of my peripheral vision. Their presence both excited me and unnerved me—this was it. And he was kneeling behind me, now. A hand on my back. A very erect cock that I couldn't see anymore but was very, very aware of.

Sailo leaned over me, wrapping an arm around my waist. He kissed the back of my neck. "You okay?"

"You haven't done anything yet."

"No." He kissed the same spot. "But nerves are funny things."

"They are. I'm okay, though."

"Good." He trailed soft kisses down my spine. Every light, warm touch made my skin prickle. No one had ever kissed me in those sensitive, strangely erotic places, but he took his time, kissing along my vertebrae as if they were the most erogenous zones imaginable. Beneath his lips and the soft brush of his goatee, they *were* pretty erogenous. My God.

I closed my eyes, letting my head fall forward as another shiver ran through me. I thought I knew all the places I was sensitive. Evidently not.

At the small of my back, he paused. Then his lips lifted away from my skin, and I held my breath, not sure what was coming next.

He gently kneaded my ass cheeks, and as he parted them, I bit my lip. *Now it starts. Fingers first, right?*

No.

Not fingers.

Tongue.

My eyes flew open. The air in my lungs didn't move, and neither did I.

Oh…my God.

His tongue felt…unreal. He made slow circles, probing gently and redefining the word *erogenous*. Whoa.

He shifted a little, and his hand materialized on my balls. He teased them gently, cupping them as he kept making those mind-blowing little circles with his tongue.

"Fuck," I breathed.

"Feel good?" he asked.

"Very." *Now get your tongue back to—*

Yes. Like that. Jesus.

I wasn't even sure exactly what he was doing, only that it took my breath away. It was an alien feeling in an area that, up until very recently, had never been stimulated sexually, and I had to grip the sheets just to remind myself not to collapse flat on my face. Holy hell.

Yeah, those little circles feel…no, don't stop. Don't—okay, fluttering like that is pretty good too.

Wow, that is really *good. Keep…keep doing…*

What the hell are you even doing now? Don't care. Just don't stop.

I was distantly aware of some fatigue in my shoulders from holding myself up like this for so long, but whatever. They could be sore as hell tomorrow for all I cared. This was well worth some muscle pain later.

Sailo stopped, and I opened my eyes.

Wait, why'd you stop?

He shifted around behind me—sitting up, I guessed—and his hand drifted up my side. "You still okay in this position?"

My shoulders were definitely getting tired, but I nodded. "Yeah. I'm good."

"Good." The lube bottle clicked.

Oh fuck. That's right. He was warming me up for more.

Am *I ready for this?*

I closed my eyes again, breathing slowly and reminding myself over and over that I wasn't scared. A toy was different—I was in control, and if it hurt, I could stop—but if I really thought he wouldn't stop, I wouldn't be doing this. Or, more to the point, letting him do this.

I want this, I reminded myself. *Badly.*

He cupped my hip with one hand. "It's just gonna be my finger for now, okay?"

I nodded.

"Might be a little cool." His fingertip met my ass, and I jumped, but it was more nerves and anticipation than the coolness. "Relax," he whispered. His finger didn't move. He just kept it there, as a constant presence while I took a few long, slow breaths.

I'm okay. We can stop any time. And I don't want to stop.

"We'll take this as slow as you need." His voice was low and soothing, and I concentrated on that while he pressed in gently. "No hurry at all. I want to make sure you're completely relaxed first."

His finger slid inside, and my breath caught. This was…a lot more intense than when I'd done it on my own. His fingers weren't any thicker than mine, but they sure felt like it. Or maybe I was just tenser now?

"Relax," he whispered. "We've got plenty of time, and I promise I won't give you more until you're ready for it."

Closing my eyes, I exhaled slowly and willed myself to relax. He withdrew his finger. Slid it back in. Withdrew it. Just as it was when I'd done this myself, it felt strange and invasive. Uncomfortable, but not painful. And that had eventually turned into something amazing, so I didn't tell him to stop. I let him slowly, gently fuck me with his finger.

Sure enough, as I got used to it, the discomfort shifted to intense but very, very good. He kept going for a moment longer, then added a second—fourth?—finger, and my vision blurred. Was that his whole hand?

No. No, just two fingers. Have to get used to it all over again. I concentrated on breathing, on relaxing, and as expected, every slow, slick stroke of his fingers was better than the last.

The burn intensified. He must've been separating his fingers to stretch me. Wasn't that what one of the books recommended? Maybe. Guess so. It felt…it felt fucking awesome, though.

"You ready for more?" He sounded as breathless as I felt.

Am I? I licked my lips, letting him slide his fingers in and out a few more times. "Y-yeah. I'm ready."

"Okay." He withdrew his fingers. "I'm just going to put on a condom. Give me a sec."

I nodded but didn't speak.

Behind me, the wrapper tore. My heart thumped against my ribs as I looked over my shoulder to watch him roll on the condom. Our eyes met, and we both grinned.

Once the condom was in place and he'd poured on some lube, he positioned himself behind me again, and I exhaled, reminding myself to relax, relax, relax.

"There's plenty of lube," he said softly. "But I can always add more. Just say the word." He pressed the head of his cock against me. "Anything to make you comfortable."

I nodded, but couldn't speak. Not with him slowly, *slowly* breaching me with his thick cock. This wasn't that much more than his fingers, but somehow it seemed ten times thicker. Maybe because I was so hyperaware of what it was—that he was…he was fucking me. His cock was inside me. He—

Sailo pushed deeper, and a twinge made my breath catch.

Christ, that was…

He paused. I found my breath again, and the faint pain dulled.

Another stroke, and suddenly it was intense enough to blur my vision.

He stopped again, and ran a hand up my back. "Am I hurting you?"

Kind of.

"*And if you don't love it the first time,*" Ethan's advice echoed in my head, "*don't give up on it. It can be a bit of…an acquired taste.*"

"No." I licked my lips, trying not to wince. "You're…you're good." Sort of. Not really. The toy had nothing on the real thing. With a piece of plastic, there was no warm skin against mine. No soft breath rushing past my neck.

The toy also hadn't been this painful. Maybe I should've picked a thicker one. Or maybe this wasn't such a good idea. Ethan had warned me that it wasn't everyone's thing.

I was about to say something, to suggest we try this again another time, but suddenly the unpleasant burn was gone. Wait, no. It was still there, but it felt…it felt great. Intense. Mind-blowing. I exhaled, and my muscles—especially the ring of muscles around his thick cock—relaxed a bit more, and that intensity was quickly turning into something very different from before. It was still intense, but it was…

Oh my God. This was what I'd experienced on my own. No, better. As he slid in and out of me, every stroke was more amazing than the last, until I was dizzy from forgetting to breath. I rocked back against him, seeking more. How did I make it through forty-seven years without ever knowing how good it felt to be fucked by another man? I didn't care if he ever let me top him as long as he never stopped fucking me just like this.

I wasn't hard, but I was turned on. Not something I'd experienced before. Not something I could really explain. Hadn't the books said something about that? That not all guys…

Fuck, what did I care? God, he felt good. I didn't give a damn if I was hard or if I came. *He* was hard, and *he* was fucking me, and…Jesus…

Sailo leaned down a little, wrapping his arm around my waist and changing the angle of his cock just enough to hit that sensitive spot inside.

"Oh fuck," I moaned.

"You all right?" he asked, panting in my ear.

"Y-yeah. It's good. Real good."

He kissed the side of my neck. "You want it harder?"

I had no idea how that would feel. I'd done it pretty hard on my own, but no way in hell had I been able to fuck myself as hard with the toy as he undoubtedly could now.

"Yeah." I moistened my lips, which had suddenly gone dry. "Harder."

He shifted behind me, sitting up again, and grasped my hips firmly. Then he withdrew almost all the way and—

"Holy fuck!" I dropped down onto my forearms.

"You all—"

"Don't stop." I sounded like I was sobbing. Maybe I was? Didn't care. Just wanted him to keep doing that, keep driving himself into me. Did it hurt? I didn't even know anymore. I couldn't name or define a single one of the sensations rushing through me and electrifying my nerve endings. All I could do was beg him not to stop. Over and over, slurring so badly he probably couldn't understand me anymore, I begged him to keep going.

Gripping the edge of the mattress, I squeezed my eyes shut and buried my face in the pillow. I wasn't going to come this time, and I didn't care. He felt so good. So, so good. Orgasms were…whatever. He was fucking me into a whole different kind of oblivion, and coming just didn't matter.

"You feel so good." He dug his fingers into my hips. "You're gonna…make me come…again…"

I pressed the heels of my hands into the mattress and rocked back and forth as much as I could with his tight grip. It must've been enough, though—he released the most delicious, throaty moan, and his thrusts took on a more earnest cadence, his hips slamming against my ass hard enough to knock the breath out of me.

Then he forced himself as deep as I could take him, and shuddered. My head spun and my heart pounded as if I were the one coming. *How* had I gone my whole life without experiencing this?

With a long sigh, he relaxed his grip on me. He withdrew, and as he stepped away to get rid of the condom, I somehow managed to turn over and flop onto my back.

Holy. Fuck.

Sex had never left me feeling like this. Exhausted. Wrung out. So far beyond bliss, I couldn't put it into words.

Yep. Definitely gay. Or at least bi. Something. Not straight.

A moment later, Sailo returned from the bathroom and lay beside me. "So…you all right?"

"All right?" I laughed, pulling him into an embrace. "I feel amazing."

"Good." He wrapped his arms around me and pressed his lips to mine.

Then his fingers started down the middle of my chest, tracing a very deliberate downward path. My abs contracted beneath his featherlight touch. My cock was already hardening, and as he closed his hand around it—oh God. I deepened the kiss. Rocked my hips in time with his strokes. Fuck, I was already lightheaded from the way he'd fucked me, and now he was going to turn me inside out and…

Yes, please. Whatever you're going to do, please do. Just don't let me stop feeling like this.

He pushed me onto my back. His kisses moved from my lips to my jaw. My neck. My chest.

God, yes…

If his hand hadn't already coaxed my erection to life, the brush of his lips and goatee on my stomach would've done the job. It was just like when he'd kissed along my spine earlier, and that memory made me gasp and shiver. What he'd done with his tongue, how he'd turned me on and relaxed me all at the same time—everything he did was magic.

Eyes closed, I mouthed silent curses as he traced my hipbone with light little kisses. Then his lips were gone.

No longer touching me. And I knew—somehow, without even looking—I knew what was coming next.

Oh Jesus. I would sell my soul to be half as good at sucking cock as you are. How do you even do that with your tongue?

He wasn't done, though. He pushed my legs apart, and as his lips and tongue teased my cock, his hand drifted up my inner thigh.

Is he…No, he isn't really going to…

Yeah. He was. Gently, he slipped his fingers into me.

My eyes flew open. My lips parted, but I didn't make a sound. Had I meant to? No idea. All I knew was…

Oh. *Wow.*

I reached back and gripped the pillow, desperate for something to hold on to, and resisted the urge to thrust into his mouth. His head bobbed over my cock. His fingers slid in and out of my ass. Then they…moved. Bent? Something. Somehow, they were different now, and they pressed against the spot inside, and suddenly my eyes were rolling back and my spine was off the bed and I heard myself curse as I came in his mouth.

Everything went white for a moment. I dropped back onto the bed, and slowly, as Sailo lifted his head and withdrew his fingers, my vision came back into focus.

"Jesus." I wiped a hand over my face. "That was…unreal."

He came up beside me and rested on his elbow. "So it lived up to your expectations?"

"Lived up to?" I laughed, sounding and feeling a little drunk. "More like blew past them."

He chuckled and kissed the top of my head. "Good. As it should be." He paused. "I mean it—I'm glad you came back. I've been thinking about the other night. A lot." He grinned, though there was a touch of shyness in his eyes. "I was hoping for the chance to fuck you."

"Didn't disappoint, I hope?"

"Not even close." He pressed a soft kiss to my lips before settling back onto the pillow. "It's been a long time since I've gotten to take my time like that."

"Really?"

He nodded. "That's half the fun of someone's first time—going extra slow and enjoying every minute of it."

Well, I didn't enjoy every *minute of it, but damn, once we'd crossed that line from* ouch *to* oh yes, *it had been well worth it.*

He sat up a bit and stretched. "I don't know about you, but I could go for another shower."

"Me too."

We started to sit up, but the room listed slightly, so I sank back onto the pillow.

"Okay, maybe in a minute."

He lay beside me. "You okay?"

"Yeah, yeah. A little dizzy."

"That's okay." He guided me back down and kissed my cheek. "We can lay here for a minute. I'm not going anywhere."

"Good." I wrapped my arms around him and pulled him down into a kiss. "Because I like you right where you are."

"Yeah? Me too."

Chapter Ten

By the time I left Sailo's apartment and made it back to Ethan and Rhett's, it was nearly four in the morning. Which meant I needed to get up and get ready for work, like, now. That might've been doable in my college days, but not anymore.

I left a little white lie in my boss's voice mail, claiming to have come down with some upper respiratory thing that I didn't want to share with the office. I assured him it was a mild one, that I'd most likely be back to work tomorrow. As it happened, my voice was probably pretty convincing too—for some strange reason, my throat was pretty raw.

Then I collapsed into bed, and that was it.

It was almost eleven when I crawled out of bed. Ethan and Rhett were long gone to work, so I had the house to myself. Sailo and I texted throughout the day, but he had his son for the afternoon and was working this evening, so I wouldn't see him until tomorrow night.

As long as I was playing hooky from work, I indulged completely. I took full advantage of the guys' Netflix password, which they'd given me the day I'd moved in, and lounged in their living room in a pair of sweats. I even ordered from one of the local sandwich shops that did home delivery. As my youngest son would put it—laziness level: expert.

Half an hour or so before Rhett was supposed to get home, I finally made myself presentable, texted him and Ethan to let them know I was making dinner tonight, and went to the supermarket a few blocks away. By the time they'd both arrived at home, I had some chicken cooking and a fresh six-pack in the fridge.

So, maybe it wasn't the best use of the company's paid time off, but it felt pretty fucking good to enjoy a day of doing absolutely nothing besides cooking for my friends. It was, I realized, the first time I'd done that since Becky kicked me out. Every day had been consumed with attorneys, moving, breaking the news to people, trying to go on as normal at work, and generally getting my feet under me. For the last twenty-four hours, though, it had been sex, sleep, and sloth.

I really need to do this more often.

~*~

By the time I returned to work the next day, I was well rested but still not terribly focused, because tonight I was meeting up with Sailo again. In between working and enduring meetings, we texted back and forth, and by the end of the day, we'd scrapped our plans to meet for drinks.

Screw it, he said. *Just come by my place. ;)*

Twist my arm.

The clock struck three, and I couldn't get out of the building fast enough.

And finally, God finally, I was back in Sailo's bed. Exhausted. Sweaty. Trembling. Wondering how the hell there'd ever been a time in my life when I wasn't experiencing sex like this.

We didn't say much for a while. As the dust settled and we caught our breath, my body was still achy, every muscle wrung out and completely spent, but I felt great.

Especially since my tired body was pressed up against Sailo's, his skin warming mine.

"Man." Sailo scrubbed a hand over his face. "I'm gonna fall asleep if we stay like this."

I yawned. "You too?"

"After the way you wore me out? Definitely." He turned to me, grinning. "I still can't believe I'm your first. First guy, I mean."

"You are."

"Well." He curved his hand over my thigh and slid a little closer. "You're a fast learner."

I laughed. "Isn't like I've never had sex before."

"Very true."

We shifted a bit, facing each other on our sides. As he moved, the intricate lines on his arm caught my attention.

"I didn't mention this before." I ran my fingers along the edge of the tattoo on his pec. "But your ink is *gorgeous*."

"Thanks." He smiled. "It's traditional pe'a."

"Pe'a?"

He nodded. "Samoan tattooing." He paused. "Well, I took a few liberties with this one." He ran his hand over his arm. "It's the traditional style, but there are some elements that aren't. But this one…" He gestured down at his legs. "Completely traditional. The design and the technique."

"How is the technique different?"

"The one on my arm was done with a modern tattoo needle. The traditional one was done by a master tattooist on Samoa with a thing that's like a little comb, and he taps it with a mallet." He pantomimed the technique on my arm, putting his fingertips on my skin and tapping the back of his wrist. "Like this."

"For…for the whole thing?" I craned my neck, peering at the tiny dots and fine lines.

"The whole thing."

"That must have been painful."

Sailo whistled. "Very. Some men in my family had theirs finished in a few months. Mine took three years." He laughed. "I doubt my brother will ever let me live that down."

"He had it done too?"

"Yeah. And his only took six months, the bastard."

I shuddered.

"To be fair," he went on, "I was in college and couldn't really fly to Samoa for weeks at a time like he could. Especially since, believe me, you don't want to fly home three days after getting this done." He patted his inked thigh emphatically.

"So you had it done in Samoa?"

He nodded. "The same artist who did it for my brothers, father, grandfather, and all my uncles. There are a handful of master tattooists in the States now, but the tradition for us means going back to him."

"Do you think your son will ever…" I waved a hand at Sailo's tattoos.

He shrugged. "Maybe. It's really up to him. His mothers know it's a tradition, and they know there might come a time where he decides to do it. But I won't make him if he doesn't want to. It was important to me, and I know my father was hoping for a long time that my brothers and I would do it. But after going through it—knowing how much it hurts—and also with something this big and permanent…it has to be his decision and nobody else's."

"That makes perfect sense. What does he think now? At this age?"

"He's seen my tattoos, and I've told him why I have them. Right now, he says he wants to have it. But he's six." Sailo shook his head. "It isn't something he needs to decide on right now, and I'm not going to let him make the decision until he's at least a teenager."

"How old were you?"

"When I decided? Or when I go it?"

"Both."

"I was fifteen when I told my father I wanted it done, and nineteen when we actually started the work."

"That young?"

"It's not unusual."

"Wow. You're a better man than me," I said. "My daughter got a small tattoo that took like half an hour, and the thought of even that…" I made a face. "No thank you."

He laughed. "They're not for the faint of heart." He gestured at the ink on his thigh. "Especially not something like this. If it hadn't been such a big tradition in my family, there's no way in hell I would have gone through that."

"I'm not even sure I could if it was a tradition."

"You'd be surprised." He draped his arm over me and smiled. "It isn't fun, but you just tell yourself it'll be worth it when it's over. And that it *will* be over. Eventually."

I shuddered. "I'll pass, thanks." I glanced at the tattoos. "But the result certainly is amazing."

"Thanks."

Our eyes met, and we both smiled.

Silence settled in. Slowly, I made the connection that we weren't just making idle conversation. We were making idle conversation in his bed. Naked. With sweat still on our skin and my body still tingling from the orgasm he'd given me.

Sailo's thumb traced a soft arc on my ribs. "You okay? You got kind of quiet."

"Yeah, I'm…" I hesitated. "I guess I was just thinking about what we're doing."

"Which part?" A cautious grin pulled at his full lips. "Talking about tattoos? Or sleeping together?"

"Both?" I rested my arm on top of his, curving my fingers over his elbow. "A month ago, I was still sharing a bed with my ex-wife. Then I was going to dip my toes in and see if I'm really into men. And now, we're together every chance we get."

His brow furrowed. “Is that a bad thing?”

“I don’t know. I’m enjoying the hell out of it.” I paused, trying to gather my thoughts. “So this isn’t, um, weird, is it? Meeting up again just to, well, hook up again?”

“Weird?” Amusement curled his lips. “Why would it be weird? We enjoy it, so why not enjoy it twice? Or more than twice?”

“So it’s not…moving too fast?”

“In what direction?” Sailo touched my face, then lifted his head and kissed me softly. “We’re doing exactly what I think we should be. We enjoy what we’re doing, so we do it again. If we stop enjoying it, we stop doing it.” He shrugged, settling back onto the pillow. “Doesn’t have to be any more complicated than that.”

“Fair point.” I laughed self-consciously. “I guess this is all just kind of new. I mean, I told you I’ve never been with a man before. I haven’t even dated anyone in almost thirty years.” I winced. “Christ, I just made myself sound old.”

He chuckled. “Well, you did marry young.”

“I did.” *Too young? Starting to think so.* “So, with all of that being said, I just want to put it out there that I have no idea what I want out of this.”

“Neither do I.” He traced my cheekbone with this thumb. “Let’s just take it a day at a time, and we’ll see what happens. For now, you seem to be enjoying the sex.”

“Oh yes. Very much.”

Sailo smiled. “Me too. So it doesn’t have to be more than that. If it is, well, we’ll deal with that when we get there. But this is good for now.” He slid his hand into my hair. “You’ve got a divorce to deal with. I’m juggling a lot of unpredictable gigs in between taking care of my son.”

“Sounds good to me.”

“And since neither of us has to be anywhere tonight…” He lifted his head again and kissed me lightly. “You’re welcome to stay here if you want to.”

"I would." I sighed. "But I have to be on the road to work way too early." I drew him down into another kiss, loving the way his thin goatee felt brushing against my chin. "Maybe this weekend, though."

He pushed himself up a bit, scowling. "My schedule's kind of a pain to work around, especially on the weekends. I'm at Wilde's on Friday night, and I've got a wedding on Saturday afternoon, but if you don't mind a late night on Friday and me rushing out by noon…"

"Sounds great to me."

"Good."

"And you're…" I hesitated, struggling to hold his gaze. "You're really sure about this?"

"Yeah, of course. Everybody has rebounds."

"But I feel like I'm…" I wrinkled my nose. "*Using* you."

"I know what this is, Greg." He trailed the backs of his fingers down the middle of my chest. "You're coming back into the game after a divorce. It's your first time with a guy. I don't have any illusions that this is—"

"But you're okay with it? With me using you to figure out if I'm into men?"

He laughed softly. "I think we've established that you're into men."

"Can't argue with that."

"And as for the rest of it…" He shrugged. "I'm enjoying the sex. You seem like a cool guy to talk to. So, what's not to like?" Before I could suggest anything, he kissed me softly. "If I decide I'm not okay with it anymore," he whispered, sliding closer to me, "you'll be the first to know. Deal?"

"Deal." I wrapped my arms around him. He pressed his lips to mine again. Holding him close, I coaxed his lips apart, and he opened to my kiss. I slid the tip of my tongue beneath his.

I wasn't sure who was in the lead, and I didn't care. His arms were around me, his tongue gently teasing mine, and it didn't matter who was in control as long as we didn't stop.

The exhaustion of a late night after a long work day couldn't compete with the way his touch brought my entire body back to life. I was going to regret this tomorrow, but I didn't care. I'd been waiting my whole damn life for this—a drowsy day at the office would be a small price to pay for the way I felt right now.

Sailo's hand followed my spine downward, and when he reached the small of my back, he pressed gently, drawing our hips together. His thickening erection brushed mine, and I held him tighter, kissed him harder.

He broke the kiss, and he was a little out of breath as he said, "You don't have to leave right now, do you?"

"No." I drew him closer. "I definitely don't have to leave right now."

Chapter Eleven

After work the next day, I wasn't meeting up with Sailo. He had somewhere to be with his son, and I had plans too. Tomorrow night, he didn't have anything going on, so we were meeting after I was off work.

But for tonight, it was just me, and a task I really wasn't looking forward to.

With my heart in my throat and a nervous flutter in my stomach, I followed the familiar side roads toward the house I'd lived in for so many years. All day long, this had been almost as distracting as my fantasies about Sailo. Though Becky and I had agreed that our marriage was over, and in the last three and a half weeks, we'd started going through the motions of dividing up twenty-five years of stuff and assets, those motions still hurt.

That wasn't the part I was dreading the most, though.

I took the last turn, and a moment later, I was…well, not home. But at the house. Becky's white Honda was parked in front of the garage, and I pulled into the empty space beside it. That in itself was strange—we'd never parked in the driveway, but the garage was now a staging area for everything I was taking with me. Once that was all gone—once I was gone—she'd probably go back to parking inside.

And it was fairly close to empty now. I'd moved the majority of my the big stuff out of the house the weekend I'd moved in with Rhett and Ethan, but a few things had stayed behind. Some seemed safer there than in my storage unit—a few family heirlooms, some electronics. There would be more, though. After all, we were still splitting things up.

I'd get the keys to my new place next weekend, and some friends were helping me move in the weekend after. In the meantime, Becky and I were slowly making our way through every room in the house, dividing everything we'd accumulated over nearly three decades. We'd already been through the bedroom, the kitchen, and my study. Today, we were tackling one of the storage rooms.

I took a deep breath, killed the idling engine, and stepped out of the car. I walked up to the porch, and paused on the Welcome mat. My stomach was twisted into knots, my chest tight with God knew how many emotions that had been cooped up there since the divorce bomb had dropped. I couldn't wait until this part of the process was over, and I could start really moving on instead of coming over here to pick at the wound.

I exhaled hard but didn't reach for the doorknob. I swore, nothing was weirder than ringing the doorbell of my own house, but I didn't live here anymore, so, gritting my teeth, I pressed the button with my thumb and waited.

Footsteps on the other side amped up my heartbeat.

A second later, Becky opened the door. She lifted her chin slightly, her lips pulling tight, and set her shoulders back. I swallowed. So did she. We'd seen each other a few times since she'd initiated the divorce. There'd been that first meeting with our respective attorneys. I'd been in and out to pick up belongings. We'd had the awkward sit-down with the kids. It was getting less comfortable every time.

Seeing her face-to-face less than twenty-four hours after I'd been between the sheets with a man? For the second time?

Yeah. Awkward.

Without a word, she broke eye contact and stood aside.

I came in and didn't speak either. As I toed off my shoes, I noticed there was a pair of sandals by the front door that definitely weren't mine and were too big to be hers. Even at a glance, I could tell they were the wrong size for any of the kids, and anyway, none of them would've been caught dead wearing Birkenstocks.

I didn't say anything, though. This was uncomfortable enough.

Becky set her shoulders back. "I, um, moved everything to the living room. I figured that would give us more space to sort it all out."

"I could've helped you with that."

She waved her hand, the gesture as taut as her features. "Mark and Kurt came over this weekend. They helped me move everything down from the storage room and the attic."

"Oh. Well good." I paused. "And they're, um, still doing okay with…"

Becky nodded. "They're stressed about it, but that's to be expected."

I forced myself not to wince visibly. "True."

"Anyway." She gestured for me to come with her, and we walked down the hall. In the living room doorway, we both stopped. The room was full of boxes. Some were old and dusty—likely the ones we'd stashed in the attic and forgotten about. Others were a bit newer, from cardboard boxes to plastic crates filled with shit I probably hadn't seen in years. I vaguely remembered putting some of them in the storage room, but couldn't recall what was in any of them.

There were also a couple of large empty boxes labeled Trash and Storage. I'd brought some with me, but they were still in my trunk—I'd bring them in once I knew how much of this I was actually taking.

Arms folded loosely across her chest, Becky surveyed the room. "There's probably a ton of stuff in here neither of us will want. So we might as well just toss it."

"Good idea." I rolled my shoulders. "Well, let's get started."

She nodded. I took the love seat. She took the one cushion on the couch that wasn't covered with stuff. In silence, we started cutting open boxes.

"So." She glanced at me. "How have you been?"

Now wasn't that a complicated question?

"I've been all right." I sliced the weathered tape on a box whose dusty label was too faded to read. "What about you?"

She didn't answer right away. "Still getting used to things, I think."

"Yeah. Me too." I opened the flaps on the box, and my breath caught. It was filled with folders containing schoolwork we'd saved from the kids' early years. Construction paper crafts. Dusty paintings. Faded certificates "Wow. Look at these." I withdrew a ceramic candle holder April had made in first grade.

Becky sat up a bit, laughing softly. "Haven't seen those in a while."

"No kidding. Some of these are…" I looked at the date written on a perfect attendance certificate. "Jesus. This is over fifteen years old."

"We could put them on Facebook." She smothered a giggle. "The kids would be mortified."

I snickered. "Yeah, they'd love that." I paused. "You think we should keep them? Or let the kids have them?"

Becky sobered. She gazed at the box for a moment. "Just, um, keep them in there for now. Next time they're over, I'll see if they want to keep anything."

Our eyes met.

So they'll stay here, then.

Her brow creased. I tightened my lips.

We both looked at the box again. It was one thing to separate our things. We'd both been grateful we didn't have to deal with custody of the kids, but I hadn't bargained for this.

The kids live on their own, but where do their memories live?

Without a word, I closed the box, resealed it, and toed it toward the stack of things that would go back into the storage room. In silence, we continued working.

After a few minutes, she said, "This is for the better, Greg."

I met her gaze. Who was she trying to convince? With a heavy half shrug, I shifted my attention back to the box in front of me. "It's…an adjustment. We'll be all right." Who was *I* trying to convince?

Becky didn't press the issue. Neither did I. We just continued going through everything we'd been storing for…what, exactly? It was impossible to say. There were boxes of tax papers and receipts that were well past the seven-year retention period. We'd even held onto an old VCR, for God's sake.

All the while, it was impossible not to compare this uncomfortable silence with last night's easy pillow talk. How was it so difficult to be with the mother of my children, and so effortless to be with a man I'd only known for a few days?

Of course, it made perfect sense. This thing with Sailo was shiny and new. We knew next to nothing about each other, so every conversation was interesting and full of revelations. When we weren't talking, we were making out and burning up the sheets, and then we were talking some more.

Becky and I had long ago stopped talking after sex. We were lucky even to have the energy to have sex in the first place, and when it was over, we were out cold. And then we'd stopped talking outside the bedroom too. Somewhere along the line, it seemed like we'd either run out of things to talk about, or we'd stopped caring what the other had to say.

We'd stopped doing a lot of things, I realized. Or else it would feel weird to be sitting this far from her, rather than this close to her.

I pushed another box to the storage stack, and started on the next one, all the while trying to tamp down my thoughts and feelings, but they wouldn't be ignored tonight.

What the hell happened? Or rather...*when?* They say you don't know what you've got until it's gone. Sitting there in uncomfortable silence with Becky, slowly dissecting the remnants of the life we'd built together, I understood that more profoundly than ever before.

There'd been a time when we were always cuddly, always chatting about something while we sat as close as we could. Even if we were watching a movie, my arm would always be around her shoulders and her leg would always be draped over mine. It wasn't sexual—just affectionate. Intimate.

And for the life of me, I couldn't remember how long it had been since that had faded into the rearview. Losing that closeness was what hurt, and I felt like an idiot for realizing way, way too late that we'd lost it a long time ago. I couldn't even remember when. I distinctly remembered that intimacy carrying us through those brutal early years with the kids. How many times had one of us fallen asleep in the other's arms after being up all night with a fussy baby or a sick toddler? How many years had it been since one of our preteens had wrinkled their nose at us and said, "Oh my God, you guys—gross!"? When had all that stopped?

I surreptitiously watched Becky sorting through a stack of old Christmas cards. I homed in on her hands. Long, elegant fingers. A little more weathered than they'd been in her younger days, and with a sinking feeling in my chest, I realized I had no idea what her hands felt like now.

Did her fingers still get cold? How long had it been since I'd enclosed her fingers in my hand to warm them up?

I shifted my gaze from her hands to her face.

How long have we been strangers?

I swallowed the lump suddenly rising in my throat, and turned my attention back to this box of junk that had come into our lives at some point. My knotted stomach sank, and I slowly exhaled. Now I understood why she'd insisted there was no saving our marriage. Her mind had been made up. Divorce was happening, and that was that, no matter what I had to say about it.

It made sense now. She wasn't ending things. They'd ended ages ago, and all she'd done was mercifully pull the plug.

"Looks like we need another trash box."

Her voice startled me. I craned my neck toward the trash box, and she was right—it was brimming with junk.

"Okay. Yeah. I'll take this one outside." While she set up another box, I carried the full one out to the garage.

As I set the box down beside the recycling bins, I did a double take. In the recycling bin, there were some empty brown bottles of some pretentious beer I'd never heard of. My gut tightened. Becky couldn't stand beer. I was more of a Budweiser man than a trendy microbrew guy.

I shook my head and went back inside. The Birkenstocks and beer bottles were painting a picture I wasn't ready to see but couldn't ignore. Thank God nothing of mine lived in the bedroom or the master bathroom anymore, and we'd already sorted through that part of the house. I really didn't want to see my replacement's razor or toothbrush.

Jealousy surged in my chest, but I tamped it back down. I had no right to be territorial. Hell, I was sleeping with another man, too, so I'd have been a colossal hypocrite to give her shit for it. In fact, she'd had more time to come to terms with our split than I had, since she had to have been planning it or at least thinking about it for a while before she dropped the bomb on me. So if it was okay for me to be with someone else at this point, it was definitely okay for her. She was moving on. So was I.

Did he close his hands around the ends of her fingers to warm them up?

That thought gave me pause. Hypocritical or not, I had to admit that it hurt to realize Becky was with someone else now. I was getting used to the idea of being divorced, of going through the motions of moving on with my life, but every now and then, something would take my breath away. Make me stop and realize this was really happening. Remind me of this massive upheaval in my life.

Seeing a new man taking my place? That was one of those things.

Outside the living room, where I was sure she couldn't see me, I closed my eyes and took a deep breath. I'd be okay. Becky would be okay. This was all part of the process, and in the end, we'd both be fine.

I just hoped that part came sooner than later.

~*~

"Well, I think that's the last of it." Dusting my hands off on my jeans, I nodded toward the boxes we'd added to the staging area in the garage. "We don't have anything left to go through, do we?"

Becky shifted her weight, thumbs hooked in her pockets. "I'm pretty sure that's it."

"Okay. If you find anything else, drop me a text, and I'll come by and get it."

She nodded. "I will. I think that's it, though." Squaring her shoulders, she held my gaze. "You're moving…the weekend after this one, right?"

"Yeah. So I'll, uh, come by that morning. Pick all this up."

"Right. Good. The code on the garage door hasn't changed. If we're not here, let yourself in."

We?

I didn't acknowledge it, though. "I will." I glanced around the garage, just in case I'd missed anything. "Okay. Well. I guess I'd better go."

"All right. You're sure you don't need help on moving day?"

"No, I've got some guys to help. I'll be fine."

"Okay." She swallowed. "What about…what about in general? Are you sure you're doing okay?"

"Yeah. I'm, um, adjusting. You?"

Her lips tightened and she nodded. "Same. Same."

We held each other's gazes, the silence feeling oddly like it needed to be filled, but I had no idea what to say. She didn't speak either.

Finally, I managed to murmur, "I should go."

"I'll see you later."

I nodded and headed for the door, and after I'd put on my shoes and made my way out to my car, I tried to shake off the conspicuous absence of "I love you" and "I love you too." Mostly because I couldn't remember when those had stopped being part of going our separate ways, whether one of us was getting on a plane or heading to work.

I turned on the engine and turned up the radio. As I backed out of the driveway, I wondered if her new man would be here soon. Parked where I'd been parked. And after next weekend, parked on my side of the empty garage.

Well. It didn't matter. We were moving on. This was our new life. Tonight, she'd be with the guy whose sandals and beers were slowly exorcising my ghost from the house I'd once lived in.

But tomorrow, I thought with a slowly forming smile, I'd be with Sailo.

Chapter Twelve

At the last minute, Sailo had to cancel, but promised we'd meet up the next night. So instead, since Ethan and Rhett had put me up for the time being, and they were going to help me move into my new place this weekend, I took them out to dinner. I planned to take out everyone who was helping me move—the guys, plus their friend Dale and his husband, Adam, and of course Sailo—but I owed these two bigtime. And besides, getting out with them was a nice diversion from the afternoon I'd spent with Becky.

Afterward, we lounged in their living room with beers all around.

"Thanks again," Ethan said. "That was an amazing meal."

"Seriously." Rhett groaned, rubbing his stomach. "Jesus. How had we never heard of that place?"

"Don't know, but we're going back."

I chuckled. "Glad you enjoyed it. I figured I owe you guys for putting me up and helping me out."

"Don't mention it." Ethan tipped his beer bottle toward me. "Happy to help, especially if there's food like that involved."

"Amen," his husband said.

"As much as you guys have been helping, I'll take you there every night of the week." I leaned back in my chair. "I will be fucking *thrilled* when this whole thing is over, that's for sure."

"I hear that," Rhett said. "My divorce was an epic pain in the ass."

"And our split was…" Ethan whistled. "Not fun. So, you have my sympathy."

Rhett nodded. "Mmhmm." He took a swallow of beer. "And as far as moving, are you sure one day is going to be enough? I could take Monday off if you need more help."

"Nah, one day is fine," I said. "I don't have *that* much stuff. I'm getting a head start this week too—Sailo's helping me get a few things from the storage unit to the new place, and then all that's left to move on Saturday is the big stuff." I paused. "Thanks again, guys. You've been a huge help all along, and it'll be great to have a couple extra pairs of hands this weekend."

"Hey, don't mention it," Rhett said. "We could probably snag Kieran and Alex too, if you think we'll need them."

"Nah." I waved a hand. "With Adam and Dale helping out, plus you guys, I think we've got it covered."

"Sailo, eh?" Ethan arched an eyebrow. "You've been seeing this guy pretty regularly, haven't you?"

"I noticed that too." Rhett winked. "Thought you were just hooking up and getting laid."

I chuckled. "There any rule that says I can't hook up and get laid with the same guy more than once?"

"Well, no," Rhett said. "But there's a reason they're usually called *one*-night stands."

"Watch out for him," Ethan warned with a hint of a smirk on his lips. "One minute, you're fucking him. The next he's got a moving van in front of your place full of his stuff."

Laughing, I gestured dismissively with my beer. "Yeah, I don't think so."

"Famous last words," Ethan muttered.

"Spoken from experience?" I asked.

Ethan chuckled.

Rhett rolled his eyes. "That is not how it happened."

"Okay." Ethan patted Rhett's leg. "We waited until the third date, but—"

"Oh, shut up." Rhett laughed. "He's full of shit."

I put up my hand. "I am not getting in the middle of an argument between you two."

"Smart man," Ethan muttered.

Rhett smacked his leg, and Ethan laughed.

"*Anyway*," I said. "Dating is a pretty foreign concept for me as it is. It's kind of been a while." I paused, thinking back. "In fact, the only dating I've ever done was in high school and the first part of college. Mostly with Becky."

"You guys married pretty young, didn't you?" Ethan asked.

"She was nineteen, I was twenty."

"I was around the same age when I married my daughter's mom." Rhett shook his head. "Oh, if I'd only known then what I do now…"

"Preach it," I grumbled into my beer bottle. After I'd taken a swig, I lowered the bottle and thought for a moment. "You know what's funny? I'm actually starting to wonder if I'm not bi at all." I fought the urge to wring my hands. "I think…I think I might be gay."

"Really?" Rhett asked. "So, you're not interested in women at all?"

I thought for a moment, then shook my head. "Can't say I've even thought about women lately. No woman's caught my eye either."

"Has any *man* caught your eye recently?" Ethan brought his beer bottle up, but stopped at his lips. "Besides Sailo, I mean?"

"Now that you mention it…"

"That's what I thought." He took a deep swallow, then set the bottle down. "It could just be because you're really into this guy. You might be so caught up in him, you're not noticing anyone else, regardless of gender."

"Valid point," I said.

"Wow, Ethan." Rhett elbowed him and grinned. "That was actually a mature—"

"Oh, shut up." Ethan rolled his eyes.

"Just saying." Rhett set his beer on the coffee table and folded his hands in his lap. "I wouldn't worry about it too much right now if I were you. Just enjoy being with this guy and putting your divorce behind you. There's plenty of time to figure out what it all means later."

"True."

"I mean, I'm bi," he said. "But it doesn't really matter because I haven't been with a woman since before Ethan and I—"

The doorbell rang.

Ethan and Rhett both turned their heads, then eyed each other.

"You expecting anyone?" Rhett asked as he stood.

"No," Ethan said. "You?"

Rhett shook his head. "I'll be right back."

"Well, while he's doing that…" Ethan collected the empty bottles. "You want another?"

"You know what?" I stood. "I think I will."

We moved into the kitchen, and Ethan pulled some fresh drinks from the fridge. He opened them and slid one across the island to me. He was about to speak, but Rhett's voice came from the hallway:

"Hey, look who's here."

Ethan and I turned as Rhett's daughter, Sabrina, and her husband, Tyson, walked in the kitchen with Rhett on their heels.

"Hey, kiddo!" Ethan hugged his stepdaughter. "This is a surprise." He kissed her cheek and let her go. Gesturing at me, he said, "You remember Greg, right?"

"Of course." Sabrina smiled. "Good to see you."

"You too." I sipped my beer. "Hey, Tyson."

"What brings you two into the neighborhood?" Rhett asked. "I didn't think we were going to see you until this weekend."

"Well, um." She glanced at her husband. He put his hand on the small of her back, and she faced her fathers again. "We just stopped by for a minute." She took a small gift bag from her husband and set it on the counter in front of Ethan. "We wanted to drop off your early birthday present."

"Birthday present?" Ethan cocked his head. "My birthday's not for another six months."

"I know." She pushed it across the counter. "But I wanted to give this to you now."

"But—"

"Just open it."

Something about her smile made my heart speed up. As Ethan and Rhett exchanged puzzled looks, I suppressed a grin because I was pretty sure I knew what was coming.

Ethan shrugged. He pushed the tissue paper aside, reached inside, and pulled out a bright yellow coffee mug. "World's Greatest—" His eyes widened.

Rhett craned his neck, turning the mug slightly so he could see it. His lips parted and his head snapped toward his daughter, who was now grinning so big she started laughing.

"World's Greatest Grandpa?" Rhett breathed. "Are you serious? You're…"

Ethan set the mug down, the quiet rattle as it touched the counter giving away the unsteadiness in his hands. "Didn't I tell you I'm not supposed to be a grandfather before I turn—" His voice caught, and he quickly cleared his throat. "Before I turn fifty?"

She pressed her lips together, shooting him an innocent look as she tried and failed not to smile. "Surprise?"

He laughed and hugged her tight, and though he was probably trying to be smooth and subtle, I caught him wiping his eyes just before he let her go.

Then Rhett gathered his daughter in a bear hug. "Congratulations, baby. Wow."

While he did that, Ethan shook Tyson's hand and exchanged smiles with him. "Congratulations."

"Thanks, Dad." Tyson beamed.

Watching Rhett and Ethan get choked up and excited over Sabrina's news was enough to bring tears to my eyes, and it wasn't just because I was thrilled for them. It was true, wasn't it—in the wake of a divorce, you just never knew where those reminders would come from, and how far they'd hit below the emotional belt.

My first grandchild had been announced with wringing hands and teary eyes, my daughter convinced we were going to hit the roof and that her life was over. Now that she was married—to my sent-from-heaven son-in-law instead of that useless deadbeat—there was some talk of more kids in the near future. And I hadn't realized until just now how much I'd looked forward to the announcement that number two was on the way. All of us together, my wife and me congratulating our daughter and son-in-law and making plans to spoil the kid rotten.

When my next grandchild came along, I'd be just as thrilled as I would've been before the divorce. But tonight, right now, I indulged in a moment to grieve that little scene I'd imagined.

Becky and I would attend our kids' college graduations and weddings, and we'd be cordial to each other because the divorce wasn't a bitter one. Even if it had been, we owed it to our kids to be civil and not make their important days about us. There would probably come a time when we'd bring new partners with us to those events. I'd meet her new boyfriend. She'd meet mine. There wouldn't be any drama—that just wasn't who we were—but I wondered if a part of me would still feel that little pang of sadness at one more reminder of our failed marriage.

I shook myself and took a deep swallow of beer. It was weird how the divorce reared its ugly head at the most unexpected moments. In bed with a man? Barely a peep from my subconscious. Watching two of my friends find out they were about to be grandparents? Hold on tight—here goes the roller coaster.

All part of the process, I decided.

All part of the shitty fucking process that was never going to end.

Chapter Thirteen

I met Sailo at his place and parked my car in one of the guest spots beneath his building. From there, we walked to a café a couple of blocks away.

"I've been here a million times," he said as he held the door. "I think you'll love it."

As soon as I stepped inside, I believed him. This was one of those places Capitol Hill was known for—kind of quaint, kind of hipster, with food that smelled utterly amazing. If it was anything like the rest of this neighborhood, the food would taste incredible too.

The hostess—who was probably my daughter's age and had at least half a dozen visible piercings—greeted us with a smile and showed us to a booth near the window.

It was hard to tell if I was just starving, or if the café's smells were fucking with my head—all I knew was everything on the menu sounded *amazing*.

"So what do you recommend?" I asked.

"Anything except the duck." He made a face. "This place can make anything, but that? No."

"Okay, that narrows it down to about three hundred options."

Sailo laughed. Furrowing his brow and pursing his lips, he scanned the menu. "Hmm. You vegetarian? Gluten-free? Any of that?"

"I'm not big on red meat, but otherwise, anything goes."

"Well, I guess that rules out the steak salad." He looked over the list again. "You a salmon fan?"

"*Oh*, yes."

"You'll love the…wait…" He turned the menu over and looked at the back, then the front again. "Aw, damn. They don't have it anymore."

"What?"

"The salmon filet." Clicking his tongue, he shook his head. "Those were to die for. But you really can't go wrong here."

"Aside from the duck?"

"Yes." He nodded sharply. "Definitely aside from that. Okay, let's see what else they have. The lemon chicken is good, pretty much anything they put hazelnuts on is good…"

As we continued looking through the options, I kept glancing at him. How weird was this? A few days ago, we were strangers. Now we were sitting in a restaurant, about to enjoy a leisurely meal together, with another night in the same bed a foregone conclusion. We'd already hooked up a few times, but this felt like an actual date. The kind people went on when they were sizing up a person for more than sex.

Too soon? The ink wasn't even dry on my divorce papers.

Right. And there was already a man practically living in my house, so it wasn't too soon.

But was it too soon for me? Was I ready for dating? Not just exploring this uncharted side of my sexuality, but…dating?

I looked across the table at the beautiful, tanned, black-haired man who'd been burning up the sheets with me lately. What did dating really mean? Spending more time with him. Getting to know him. More of that addictive sex.

Yeah. I was ready for this. Even if it *was* only sex and nothing more, I was ready. Because damn it, whether this thing was a brief rebound fling or stuck around for a while, it felt good to be with someone who was interested in being with me, in *or* out of the bedroom.

It sure beat the hell out of moping around at "home."

We finally settled on our meals and closed our menus. A moment later, the waitress appeared.

"What can I get you?" she asked.

Sailo handed her his menu, looking at her with sad puppy dog eyes. "You don't have the salmon filets anymore?"

She frowned and shook her head. "They just weren't selling very well, so it didn't make sense to keep them in the kitchen."

"But…but I liked them."

"I know." She smiled as sweetly as she could. "That's also why we took them off the menu."

I snorted, and he shot me a glares. Then, sighing dramatically, he looked up at her again. "Fine. I guess I'll settle for the beef tandoori."

She laughed as she jotted it on her notepad. "I'll tell the chef to half-ass it just for you."

He put his hand to his chest. "I'm offended, Lisa. I really am."

"No, you're not." She swatted him playfully with the notepad—obviously, they knew each other—and turned to me. "And for you?"

"How about the chicken bruschetta"

"Got it." She noted it and smiled. "Anything else?"

"No, thanks," I said.

"Not for me either."

"Wasn't asking you, dear."

They exchanged glares, then laughed, and she headed back to the kitchen.

"I take it you come here often?" I said.

"How'd you guess?"

"Call it a hunch."

He laughed. "Yeah, I'm here, uh, a lot. But it's really good food, so…"

"Can't blame you. I'm kind of looking forward to living in this neighborhood. Seems like the food up on Capitol Hill is amazing."

"For the most part, yeah." He rested an elbow on the table. "By the way, sorry I couldn't meet up last night. My son had a thing at school."

"Oh no, that's fine. I was taking care of some shit last night anyway." I poked at ice cubes in my drink with my straw. "I went out with some friends. And the night before, I had a nice uncomfortable evening of sorting through boxes with my ex-wife."

Sailo grimaced. "That sounds…fun?"

"It was awkward, but…" I hesitated. "I think I feel better about things now. With my ex."

"Yeah? How so?"

"I guess…" I thumbed the edge of the table to keep my hands busy. "I guess it really drove home that even though Becky didn't drop the divorce hammer until recently, we've been done for a long time."

He nodded slowly. "It's funny how often that happens. A breakup seems to come out of nowhere, but when the shock wears off—"

"You realize the engine's been knocking and the warning lights have been on for the past thousand miles?"

"Yes. Exactly." He paused. "How have your kids taken it?"

"They're not thrilled, but I think they're doing okay."

"Probably relieved, to be honest."

I winced. "You think so?"

"Well, if there was some tension brewing there, they might've picked up on it. Even if you didn't."

"Does that make me an oblivious idiot?"

"Nah. I think stuff like that's always harder to see when you're on the inside. Shit, a couple of my relationships? I thought everything was going great, and then when I looked back, I thought, was I drunk the *whole* time?"

"Still." I gazed out the window at people and passing cars, trying to ignore my own semitransparent reflection. "I feel like I really did miss some pretty big warnings."

"They're hard to see. I mean, if a plane's engines are on fire, it's easier to see from the outside than the inside."

I turned to him, eyes wide. "That's…kind of a morbid metaphor, but point taken."

Sailo laughed. "Well, think about it. You're in the plane, you know something's wrong, but you don't know what. Maybe it's just some turbulence. Maybe it's something worse. Can't really tell. If you're on the outside, you're like"—he pointed toward the street, as if he were gesturing at an imaginary plane—"whoa, dude. The wings are one fire."

I couldn't help laughing. "I definitely hadn't thought of it that way. But…I'm off the plane now. Ready to move on. And move into a place of my own *finally*."

"You found one yet?"

I nodded. "I get the keys tomorrow, and next weekend I move in." Rolling my shoulders, I exhaled. "After that, I think I'll feel more like I'm actually moving on with my life."

"Yeah, everything must feel really up in the air right now."

I nodded. "Big-time."

"Well, if you need some help moving, let me know."

"Are you sure?" I chuckled cautiously. "That isn't against gay dating protocols?"

He laughed. "Eh, maybe it is. But I know what a pain in the ass it is to move, and every extra pair of hands helps."

"Yeah, true. I, uh, just don't want to be presuming too much. About this. What we're doing."

Sailo smiled. "Relax. I'm offering to help you move, not asking you to move in with me."

"Okay, fair enough." I glanced toward the kitchen as the waitress emerged carrying two plates, but she continued past us. Facing Sailo again, I said, "Anyway, enough about my divorce." I waved the thought away like it was a mosquito. "The sooner it's behind me, the better. So how did you get into working as a deejay?"

His face lit up. Man, did I admire someone who was still that excited about his job. "I kind of stumbled into it. I mean, I was always into music, and one of my dad's friends was a deejay who did weddings. He needed some help during the summer, since that's his busy season, so I went to work for him to make some money when I was a kid." He laughed. "Doing weddings sucks, but I really enjoyed the deejay work, so I kept at it." Smiling broadly, he added, "Now it's all I do."

"What about Wilde's? Do you enjoy working there?"

"Oh hell yeah. That place is great. I go in, have an awesome time, and they cut me a check for a lot more than I'd charge for a freelance gig. I can't complain." He glanced toward the waitress, but again, she was taking plates elsewhere. "The people I work with are great too. The bartenders are a riot. So…" He shrugged. "I don't see myself giving up that gig any time soon."

"I don't blame you. Sounds like a fantastic job, especially if you still enjoy it after all this time. And you get paid well."

"Yeah." Some bitterness crept into his tone. "Tell that to my parents."

"What? I thought your dad helped you get into this business?"

"He did, but he didn't think it would be a permanent thing." He rolled his eyes. "Basically, my parents insist that especially now that I have a kid, I should be looking for more stable work." He quirked his lips. "Pretty sure they mean 'more respectable.'"

"I think respectable is seriously overrated. There is absolutely something to be said for spending your life doing something you enjoy."

"Right? And I do love it. Especially now that Mika, my son…*he* wants to learn how to deejay." Sailo beamed proudly. "Every time I'm packing up for a wedding or something, he asks to come along."

"You haven't brought him?"

"Not yet. He's not quite old enough. I'm teaching him at home, though. I've got an old turntable I don't use anymore, so I let him practice on that."

"Yeah? So you think he wants to deejay, or is he into music in general?"

"Hard to tell when he's this young, but he does seem to have some pretty strong musical aptitude. So his mothers and I, we figured in a year or so, we'll let him pick a basic instrument and take some lessons." He shrugged. "I don't want to put any pressure on him, but he's interested and seems to have some natural talent, so as long as he's enjoying it…"

"Good idea. By the way, I think I still have my son's trumpet and my daughter's clarinet. If he's interested in either of those, I can check. He's welcome to use them, since they certainly aren't."

Sailo nodded, smiling. "Thanks. I'll definitely keep that in mind. Were they into music?"

"They did band when they were in elementary school. They enjoyed it for a while, but they kind of lost interest. My youngest was the more musically inclined one. He started playing guitar in junior high and never stopped."

"That's great. Electric? Acoustic?"

"Whatever he can get his hands on. He's been in a few bands over the years. He says himself he doesn't think any of them will ever go anywhere, but he enjoys it."

"That's good. Very good."

Our waitress emerged from the kitchen again, and this time, she came right to our table.

"Here's the chicken bruschetta." She laid the plate in front of me.

"Oh wow," I said as I put my napkin in my lap. "That looks and smells awesome."

"Enjoy!" The waitress put Sailo's plate down too. "And the beef tandoori. Half-assed, of course."

"Of course." They exchanged playful glares, then she patted his arm and left us to our meals.

As I cut off a piece of chicken, I said, "So, you mentioned you got your tattoo while you were in college. What were you studying?"

"Business management, if you can believe it."

"Really?"

He nodded and took a bite of his beef tandoori.

"Decided it wasn't for you?"

"Mmhmm." He took a quick sip of his drink. "I'd rather work weddings every day than spend forty hours a week in a cubicle."

"Oh, I can't argue with that." I took a bite and nearly had to groan as the mix of savory flavors met my tongue. "You weren't kidding. This is great!"

"Told you." He winked, and skewered another piece of meat on his fork. "Just wait till you try Brew-Ha, down in Fremont?"

"Oh really? Better than this?"

"Better than anything you've ever tasted."

"Well, now you have my curiosity…"

~*~

After a lovely meal, and lingering until the waitress was starting to give us a less good-natured side-eye, we paid the check and walked back to where I'd parked.

"That was really nice," I said. "Thanks for introducing me to that place."

"Any time." He smiled, looking almost shy, which was strange—and insanely cute—on him. "I wouldn't mind doing this again. You know, just going out."

"Yeah, same here. Maybe we could try that place you told me about in Fremont."

"Tell me when, and we will." He put his hands on my waist and drew me closer. The shyness evaporated in favor of the devilishness that, without fail, turned my knees to liquid. "And, um, going out like this—that's not to say I'm opposed to everything else. Because I enjoy doing *that* with you too."

Goose bumps prickled beneath my shirt. "Well, as you say…tell me when, and we will."

He laughed. "Pity we can't tonight."

"Mmhmm."

"I'll see you soon, though," he whispered, and drew me in for a long, light kiss.

"Yeah," I murmured against his lips. "See you soon."

~*~

In a daze, I drove back to Ethan and Rhett's. They were watching a movie on the couch, so I said a quick hello and then slipped into my room.

Hands laced behind my head, I lay back on my bed and closed my eyes. Eventually, I'd get undressed, brush my teeth, and get ready to turn in, but for now, I needed a moment. And I wasn't sure I could concentrate on anything anyway. Not when my mind was all wrapped up in the evening I'd just had.

We hadn't even done anything physical beyond a couple of long kisses before parting ways for the night, but still. Spending the evening together, talking, enjoying the best meal I'd had in ages…

Smiling, I closed my eyes and sighed. What wasn't to love about this? And the best part was realizing that if nights like this still existed on this side of my divorce, then there was definitely hope.

My life wasn't over after all. If I wasn't mistaken, it was just getting started.

Chapter Fourteen

The next evening, I gave the storage unit's roll-up door a push, and it rumbled upward, revealing the stacks of boxes and plastic crates occupying half the bay.

"We moving all this tonight?" Sailo asked.

"No, no. I still have to get some of the bigger stuff from the house, not to mention the more expensive shit that I didn't want to leave here." I gestured at the stacks. "Tonight, I just wanted to grab a few things so I have some basics at the apartment. Dishes, stuff like that."

"Good idea."

"And it should all..." I glanced at a stack marked *move first*, and then at the open trunk of my car. "Yeah, it should all fit. I'd just as soon not make two trips if I can help it."

"I could've brought the van."

"Nah. This is fine." I picked up the first crate. "If it doesn't fit, I can probably live without it for a few more days."

"All right." He grabbed the second one. "And hey, if you need help with anything, just say so. I'll, uh, understand if you don't want me coming with you to get stuff from your ex's place, though."

That gave me pause. I hadn't even thought of how weird it might be to bring Sailo with me to the house I'd once shared with Becky. She had her boyfriend there, but showing up with mine might make things…weird.

I set the crate in the trunk, pushing it all the way to the side to make room for the others. "There really isn't much to take from there, so…shouldn't be an issue."

"Okay." He put a crate beside the first one. "Glad to help as much as I can, though."

"Much appreciated. I don't think you really want to get up close and personal with the remnants of a failed marriage, though. It can get a little awkward."

"Is it really a failed marriage?"

"Huh?" I turned to him. "Why wouldn't it be?"

He shrugged. "You've never said anything nasty about her, and it sounds like you get along. You had twenty-five good years, and when it ended, it ended."

"Which is…kind of the definition of a marriage failing. I mean, it was good, and then when it wasn't, we called it quits."

"But was it good for most of the time?"

I stopped, eyes losing focus for a moment. He had a point. Becky and I had shared a lot of good years—that was why the divorce had been such a tough pill to swallow. Our marriage *was* happy for a long time. "I hadn't thought of it like that."

Sailo picked up another box. "My aunt and uncle hate each other. They've been married for forty-two years, and I don't think they've been happy for at least forty-one of those. But they're still married." He put the box in the backseat and met my gaze. "So if they're miserable and hate each other, but you and your ex are amicably moving on with your lives, how is their marriage a successful one and yours is a failure?"

I quirked my lips. "Interesting way to look at it. I think you might be on to something."

He shrugged, a subtle smile on his lips. "I just think it's not as black-and-white, you know? Divorce isn't necessarily failure, and staying married isn't necessarily success." He gestured past me. "Do those all go on this trip?"

I turned around and scanned the boxes. "Not this stack." I tapped the top crate of a pile by the wall. "But these…"

We loaded up what was left, and then I shut and locked the storage unit. As I drove us out, I kept chewing on what he said. I really hadn't thought of things that way, and it…it made sense. A lot of sense. The feeling of failure I'd had since Becky dropped the bomb suddenly seemed…silly. Maybe it was a failure on paper, but was it really if we could both move on, start over, and be happy?

I pulled out on the main road. "You mind if I ask you something personal?"

"Shoot."

I rested a hand on the wheel and glanced at him. "Were you married before?"

"Me? Oh God, no." He paused. "Because of my son, right?"

"I'm…yeah, just curious."

"No, I've never been married. As for my son, basically, my friends are a lesbian couple who wanted a baby, but they weren't getting anywhere with the adoption process. We were all sitting around one night, and we realized that between us, we have, you know, all the necessary equipment to make one."

I chuckled. "That's one way to look at it."

"Right?" Sailo laughed. "So we spent a few weeks talking about it, and then…well, Mika."

"Ah, that makes sense."

"I mean, we *did* go the natural way. Which was kind of amusing since they're lesbians and I'm gay, but none of us owned a turkey baster that hadn't been handed down by a grandmother, so—"

I burst out laughing. "You're not serious."

He snickered. "Nah, I'm joking about that part. But we really did do things naturally. I guess…I don't know, every other option seemed so impersonal. And expensive, and unreliable."

"Not that the natural way has any guarantees."

"No, but it was a hell of a lot more fun than the alternative." He paused. "Once we'd had a couple of glasses of wine, anyway."

I burst out laughing. "Hey, if it works for straight couples…"

"Right?" He chuckled. "So, yeah, I know the whole thing is pretty unusual. People tell me all the time that the arrangement I have with my son's moms is going to screw him up. But he's got three parents who love him and have a good relationship with each other, so…" He shrugged again. "I guess I just don't see the problem."

I drummed my fingers on the wheel. "It sounds like it's worked out well? Being a single parent and all?"

"Oh yeah. It's been great." He rested his elbow beneath the window and leaned against it. "Before that, I never really saw myself volunteering to be a single parent, but to be honest, I don't feel like one. I'm not in a relationship with his moms, and we have joint custody, but everybody's amicable. We spend a lot of time as a family too."

"That's great. And if you all are happy, and he's happy…"

"We are." He gazed out the windshield. "I'm glad I did it. It's not how I imagined starting a family, but I really did want to be a father, and I'd always envisioned myself starting younger than I did. So, then I'm thirty and single, and I thought, well, at least this way I won't be rushing into a relationship just so we can have kids before I'm forty." He gave a quiet, somewhat bitter laugh. "Guess I was onto something—I'm thirty-seven, still single, but at least I have my son."

I glanced at him again. "Have you had any long-term relationships?"

He shrugged. "I had a boyfriend for a couple of years, but we didn't see much of each other toward the end. Mika was still pretty little, and my boyfriend and I were both trying to get careers off the ground, so there wasn't time, you know?"

I nodded. I thought about asking about his other relationships, but that faint bitterness in his tone suggested this wasn't a pleasant topic. So, I left the ball in his court while I continued down the road.

After a few blocks of silence, he asked, "Have you thought about coming out to your family? Not just your kids. Like, your parents?"

"I'm…pretty sure this would not go over well with my dad."

"Really?"

"Yep." Great. Now I sounded bitter too. "He's definitely from another generation. In fact, I'd say he's a huge part of why I didn't let myself even think of being interested in men until later in life."

"That bad?"

"Yep. He was the 'don't ever let me find out one of you boys is a sissy' kind of dad."

Sailo groaned, probably rolling his eyes. "Jesus."

"Mmhmm. As for, my mom and stepdad…" I thought about them for a moment. "It's hard to tell. They're from the same generation as my dad, but not complete assholes about it. Quite frankly, I have no idea what my mother thinks about gay people." I blew out a long breath, tapping my thumbs on the wheel. "They threw a fit over my daughter getting pregnant as a teenager. Except they were more upset about it after her boyfriend left. They'd have been fine if she'd married him, but the minute she was going to be on her own?" I clicked my tongue. "Suddenly she needed to think about giving the baby up."

"Of course," Sailo muttered.

"Once the baby got here, though, they were over the moon. I mean, seriously—show my mother a baby, and she'll forget any negative thought she's ever had."

He laughed quietly. "Sounds like my mom."

"Yeah?" I glanced at him. "She wasn't thrilled about your son?"

"Not at first. My whole family's had very mixed reviews about Mika. Some people think we were irresponsible, since I'm not married to his biological mother, or that I consider both of them to be his moms. There are people who are horrified over me 'letting' a couple of lesbians raise my kid." He laughed. "Like I'm not involved with my son's life."

"Everyone has an opinion about everything, right?"

"Especially when it comes to kids."

"Yes. Amen."

After a few more blocks, I pulled into the parking lot at the foot of my new building.

"Well." I put the car in park. "Here we are."

"Sweet." Unbuckling his seat belt, he flashed me a grin. "Let's go have a look at your new place."

His enthusiasm was infectious. I was actually a little excited now at the prospect of showing someone my new place.

My new place. My own apartment for the first time ever, since I'd lived in shared dorms right up until I'd moved in with Becky.

We each grabbed a box and headed upstairs. It took a few trips from the car—I really hoped the freight elevator was fixed by this weekend—but before long, we had everything stacked neatly in the hallway leading past the kitchen and to the living room. From there, we moved boxes and crates to their respective rooms, making sure there was plenty of space to bring in and set up furniture.

This was surreal. Even more than when I'd helped my kids move into dorms, apartments, and houses. The apartment had that sterile smell of a place that had recently been cleaned, and the fresh paint on the walls was still pretty fragrant. Kind of the "new car smell," but for apartments. The floors, walls, and counters were bare, and since the whole place was empty, it was difficult to imagine my furniture fitting in here. Intellectually, I knew it looked small because there was nothing in it, and my furniture absolutely would fit. Not that I'd brought in a tape measure and notebook or anything when I'd first come to look at the place.

I showed him around, but there wasn't much to see at the moment. A spare bedroom that I wasn't sure what to do with yet. A small but efficient kitchen. A living room that would feel much more enormous once it had furniture. The master bedroom, where I predicted I'd be spending a *ton* of time with Sailo.

And it was mine. Every inch of it would be to my taste. My rules.

Yes, I could get used to this.

I popped open one box and pulled out some of the various supplies I'd bought after signing the lease. I'd made a run to the grocery store for basic necessities—toiletries, laundry detergent, dishwasher soap, cleaning supplies—so I wouldn't have to try to remember everything as I was moving in. I'd bought a new coffeepot, which I plugged in next to the microwave, and coffee, creamer, and all that. Obviously.

I'd deliberately kept a stainless pot and a frying pan in the *move first* boxes, in case I wanted some real food before I'd unpacked. Aside from those and a couple of ceramic mugs, the only dishes for now were some halfway decent paper plates and plastic utensils.

As I put the sparse cookware away, Sailo held up a small, unmarked crate. "Where do you want this?"

"Just put that in the spare bedroom for now. I'll unpack it after all the furniture is moved in."

"On it." He took it back to the spare bedroom.

While he did that, I took the empty box into the living room, flattened it, and added it to the small pile to be taken down to the Dumpster.

Sailo came in a moment later, and paused to look out the bay window. "Not much of a view, is there?"

"I hadn't even looked yet." I joined him, and we stood in my empty living room, gazing out the window. He was right about the view. It wasn't great—mostly another building across the street—but there were glimpses of downtown and part of Capitol Hill.

Sailo wrapped his arms around me and kissed the side of my neck. "You're only a few blocks away from Wilde's. This is…convenient."

"It is, isn't it?"

"Mmhmm. Very."

I turned around within his embrace and decided I liked this view much better than the one out my window. "I guess I'll have to spend a bit more time at the club, won't I?"

"Or I can stop here on my way home from work."

"Hmm, I do like that idea. Especially once I have furniture."

He laughed softly. "Yeah, too bad your bed isn't here yet." He curved his hands over my hips. "We could christen the place tonight."

I pressed back against him, my own cock hardening as his thickened against my ass. "Do we really need a bed?"

"No, we do not. You have a shower, right?"

I gulped. "I do…"

He licked his lips.

Shower sex had never really been my thing, but without a bed, a couch, or really any flat surface besides the floor…

"Guess now's a good time to test the hot water, am I right?"

"Yes." He kissed me again. "I think you're right."

Chapter Fifteen

The next night, Sailo shut the VIP lounge door behind us, and before the latch had even clicked, we were all over each other.

"We should just reserve this place one of these days," I said between frantic kisses one night. "If we're gonna keep coming up here…"

Sailo laughed against my lips as he slid his hands under my shirt. "Yeah, but this place doesn't come cheap. And I don't think they rent it out for what we do with it."

"Has anybody figured out what we do up here?"

He dipped his head and kissed my neck. "You really think we're the only ones who use it like this?"

"Big shock."

"Right?"

"Do they actually *use* this room?" I panted. "Or do the employees just use it for, uh, private functions?"

Sailo laughed. "They have parties up here sometimes. But yeah, I think the employees use it more than anyone. I don't even know how many times one of the bartenders has been caught up here with his husband. But I mean, his husband's a bouncer, so they're both here. Can't really blame them for taking advantage."

"I'd say we could kick them out if they ever beat us to it, but if he's a bouncer…maybe not."

"Eh, he's a pussycat. Knowing them, they'd just ask us to join them."

"Oh?" I grinned against his lips. "Might be worth a shot."

"Mmhmm." He started kissing his way down my neck. "And I'm pretty sure plenty of people have been up here." He pressed a light kiss below my ear. "The shift manager and his husband had a fight a few months ago, and rumor has it, they had makeup sex up here and busted one of the tables."

"Wow. That's some serious makeup sex."

He laughed, sliding his hands up my back as he kissed beneath my jaw. "It was a pretty big fight by their standards."

"They still together?"

"Oh yeah. Jon and Liam will be together until they're dead. But you know how it is—sometimes people argue."

"For that kind of makeup sex, it almost sounds worth it."

"Right?" He lifted his head and met my gaze, his eyes gleaming with lust. "But I kind of like skipping the fighting and going right to the fucking."

"I love the way you think."

"Thought you would."

"Mmhmm. Come here." He led me to the booth and took a seat, gesturing for me to join him. I'd barely settled on the bench beside him before we were kissing again, arms around each other and bodies pressed as close as they could be with all these clothes in the way.

I cupped the front of his pants, and Sailo groaned into my kiss. He put his hand over mine and pushed on it, pressing my palm against his hard-on.

"Jesus," he breathed. "That feels…so good."

"Bet I know what you'd like better." I unbuckled his belt. He gripped my shoulders, kissing my neck in between hot huffs of breath across my skin. Not sure where this boldness was coming from, I ran with it, and drew down his zipper.

"God…" He squirmed against me. "Oh God."

"Did you really think I could wait until we made it back to your place after your show?"

He just moaned softly.

"Been thinking about this nonstop since the other night," I panted. "First time I've ever sucked cock. And I want to do it again."

He pulled in a sharp breath. "By all means, don't let me stop you."

I grinned. So did he. I kissed him quickly, then shifted as much as I could between the table and the back of the bench, and leaned down.

Sailo swore as I took his cock between my lips. He stroked my hair, his hand trembling slightly, and moaned as I ran my tongue down the hard shaft. The salt of his skin drove me wild as I took his cock deeper into my mouth. I wasn't sure if it was still the novelty of something so new, or if I was just that turned on by going down on a man, but sucking his dick aroused me more than I ever imagined it would.

I'd been fantasizing about him all damned day, and it was no surprise that the reality was even hotter. In no time, the pressure below my belt was getting unbearable, so I shifted a little, unzipped my pants, and stroked myself while I kept stroking and sucking him.

Oh. Shit. Wow.

The combination of turning him on and touching myself took me right back to the first few times we'd fooled around—overwhelming. Mind-altering. I didn't even care that it was a challenge to support myself with one arm and stroke him with the other hand. It was well worth the slight awkwardness just to listen to him moan as he kneaded the back of my neck.

The confines were cramped, reminding me of the backseat of a car, and somehow that made it even hotter. It brought back all those stolen encounters when I was a teenager, when we took advantage of whenever and wherever we could. Sailo and I were adults, and we could have all the time and space we wanted—within reason—for as much kissing, touching, fucking as we could stand. But here, tonight, we didn't have much time or much room, and someone could wander in here at any moment and catch us, and that…that was fucking *hot.*

He frantically combed his fingers through my hair, swearing under his breath as I licked and sucked him. The first night, sucking cock had been a novelty—something I was finally experiencing after years of wondering. Tonight, it was nothing short of addictive. I love the way his hard dick felt against my tongue and between my lips. The taste of his skin, the little sounds he made, the way his fingers twitched in my hair—I couldn't get enough.

"Goddamn," he breathed, his fingers tightening in my hair, pulling hard enough to sting my scalp. "Definitely…gonna fuck you later."

I groaned around his cock, and he whimpered. His dick stiffened between my lips, and his breath caught, and then I was coming a second before his semen rushed across my tongue.

"Shit!" he ground out. "Oh my…*God.*"

Yeah. What you said. Fuck.

Head spinning and eyes watering, I sat up, and he immediately grabbed me by the back of the neck and kissed me.

"I was gonna suck you off," he slurred. "You beat me to it."

"Couldn't wait." I kissed him in between catching my breath. "You turn me on too much."

"Likewise." He pulled back, meeting my gaze. "You're staying tonight, right? At my place after the show?" The hopefulness in his eyes made my heart speed up.

"I don't have to be anywhere tomorrow." I reached past him and pulled a couple of napkins from the dispenser. Wiping my hands clean, I added, "As long as you want me there, I'm happy to stay."

"Good." He laid his hand over my thigh. "Because I do plan to fuck you more than once."

"I should hope so."

"Why?" He eyed me. "You saying one time isn't enough to satisfy you?"

"Of course I'm satisfied. I just really, *really* like it when you fuck me."

Sailo fidgeted, as if suppressing a shiver. "Me too." He glanced at his watch. "Okay, I have to get downstairs. Soon as the show's over and I grab a shower, though? I am all yours."

"Looking forward to it."

We went back downstairs, and as he headed backstage, I found a seat at the bar.

When the show started, I ordered a Coke just to keep myself cool. That was becoming a necessity when I was watching the man who regularly took my breath away.

And I had to admit, I enjoyed the show. It wasn't my kind of music—was I getting too old for this scene?—but the beat was catchy, and I found myself tapping my foot and nodding along.

On the dance floor, men danced close enough to make me understand where the phrase "bumping and grinding" had come from. Others made out in booths or right there on the dance floor. It didn't take a brain surgeon to figure out that the majority of the men in this room would be getting laid before the night was over.

Any other time, I'd have been envious. Sitting here alone on a barstool, with no one's lips on my neck or hands in my back pockets, I'd have been wishing I had the nerve to find someone and break the ice.

But not tonight. Because my lips were still tingling from kissing Sailo and sucking him off. Because I could still feel his hands all over me. And watching him—watching the stage lights flicker across his bare, sweaty arms, playing with the lines of his tattoo and the contours of his muscles—I couldn't believe he'd be all mine later on.

But he would be. Because after his show was over, and everyone else either kept on dancing or went home with whoever they were bumping and grinding with, I was going home with the deejay.

The hot, insatiable, incredibly sexy deejay.

And I definitely needed to thank Ethan and Rhett for bringing me to Wilde's in the first place.

~*~

My body ached all over. Rolling over in Sailo's bed, I felt every last thing we'd done here last night. Every move ignited twinges in muscles that still weren't used to having this much sex anymore, and every twinge brought a grin to my lips.

We'd moved apart during the night, as we always did, and he was on his side, facing away from me and snoring softly. I slid toward him and molded myself to him.

He stirred a little, pressing back against me.

I kissed his neck. "Morning."

"Is it?"

"Mmhmm."

He stretched, and grunted softly. "Goddamn, I am sore."

"Tell me about it." I nibbled his earlobe. "You weren't kidding about getting as much out of me as possible before the weekend, were you?"

Sailo laughed, his stubble hissing across the pillowcase. "Did you think I was?"

"Nope." I kissed the back of his shoulder. "I was sure hoping you weren't."

He shifted a bit, so I drew back to let him roll over. As soon as he settled on his other side, facing me, I draped my arm over him.

"Too bad we can't just do this all day," he said.

"Mmhmm."

I'd suggest meeting up tonight, but I'll be home late. I'll probably just come in the door and collapse." He trailed his fingertips along my unshaven jaw. "So, I won't be good company. In fact, I won't be around much this whole week, unfortunately. But I *will* be here first thing next Sunday to help you move."

"I really appreciate it." I combed my hand through his hair. "I've got the rest of the guys helping bright and early, so don't feel like you need to be there as soon as the sun comes up."

"I'll be there." He smiled sleepily. "The sooner I get there, the sooner I see you."

"Well, I won't argue with that."

He lifted his head and kissed my forehead. "I guess we should get up. I have to load up the van and go pick up Evan."

I nodded. Groaning, I sat up. "I may just have to go home and sleep anyway."

"You're welcome," he said with a wink.

We both laughed, and, with some effort, got out of bed. After we'd both brushed our teeth and showered, we made our way out to the kitchen. Sailo had shaved. I hadn't bothered, since it was Saturday.

Leaning against the counter, I said, "Do you need any help today? With your gig?"

"Nah. I've got Evan." He sipped his coffee. "You'd probably be bored senseless anyway. Thanks for the offer, though."

"Any time."

"Of course, that's not to say I wouldn't enjoy having you there." He put his hands on my hips and smiled. "It's nice having you here."

"Likewise." I kissed him lightly. "I should get going, though. You've probably got things to do before you leave for the wedding."

"I do." But he didn't let me go. In fact, he moved his hands to the front of my shirt and pulled me closer. "They can wait a little while, though."

"Can they?" My lips brushed his. "How much time do you have?"

He kissed me, and as he did, tugged me toward him, leading me toward the kitchen door. "Probably as long as it takes to make you come again."

"Hmm." I let him pull me another step and grinned against his lips. "There enough time for me to make you come too?"

"You'll have to work fast." Another step. "Maybe we'll have to come at the same time. Efficiency and all that."

"Oh, I think we can manage that."

"We definitely can."

And we hurried back down the hall to Sailo's bedroom.

Chapter Sixteen

With the move coming up this weekend, I decided to take everyone who was helping me out to dinner. As luck would have it, despite his crazy schedule, Sailo said he'd make it, and promised to meet us there.

I drove Ethan and Rhett, and we planned to meet Adam and Dale at the restaurant. They'd all insisted we could just grab beers at a bar, but I refused. For one, I owed them better than that. But also, tonight was one of those nights when baseball and football were both happening, and Seattle crowds were enthusiastic to say the least. No way in hell were we walking into any place that had TV screens broadcasting anything, or we'd all be deaf before the end of the night.

So, we settled on one of the quieter places over in Queen Anne—still kind of a bar and grill atmosphere, but no televisions. Perfect.

As soon as we walked in, Dale waved at us from a table against the far wall. The place wasn't all that crowded, but I was glad to see they'd commandeered one of the few tables that could comfortably seat six.

We joined them, Ethan and Rhett sitting at one end, across from each other, with Rhett next to Adam and Dale, and an empty seat for Sailo next to me.

As we settled into our seats, Dale leaned toward me, dropping his voice to a conspiratorial whisper. "All right, Greg. I need you to level with me."

I straightened. "About…?"

Arching an eyebrow, he asked, "Is Ethan fucking with me again, or do you have a boyfriend?"

"Uh, well." I cleared my throat. "We just started seeing each other, so—"

"No shit?" His eyes widened. "How did I not know you played for our team?"

"Because I've been married to the other team for the last twenty-seven years?"

"Oh. Hmm. Yeah, true." Gesturing at the empty chair, he added, "And he's coming tonight?"

"Mmhmm. He should be here in"—I checked my phone—"five or ten minutes."

"Oh good." Dale flashed a mischievous grin. "I am really curious about this guy." To Rhett and Ethan, he asked, "Have you guys met him?"

"Not yet," Ethan said. "I've seen him, but I haven't actually met him."

Dale eyed him. "Meaning…?"

"He works at Wilde's," Rhett said.

Dale's jaw dropped. "No shit?"

I couldn't help grinning. "No shit."

"Nice one."

The waitress came by and took our drink orders, and while we waited for her to come back, Adam turned to me. "Hey, uh, sorry to hear about, you know, things with Becky." He shook his head. "I've been down the divorce road—it's rough."

"It is, but I think I'll be okay." I paused. "I'm just glad the kids are grown. It's still hard on them, but I think it would've been tougher if they were still young."

Adam nodded. "I don't have any kids, so I can't even imagine what that would've been like for them. They're doing all right, though?"

"Yeah, yeah." I waved my hand. "They're not thrilled, but they're doing fine." *I hope.* Right then, thank God, the restaurant's front door opened, and when I looked up, my heart skipped. "Oh, there he is."

"Oh, your new man?" Dale twisted around, craning his neck.

"Way to be subtle, Dale."

"You're one to talk." Rhett met my gaze, his lips quirked as if he were tamping down a smartass comment of some sort.

"What?" I asked.

He batted his eyes. "Nothing. Nothing."

"You're grinning about something."

"Me? I have no idea what you're talking about."

I would have pushed the issue, but Sailo was walking toward us, so I let it go.

He came around my side of the table and greeted me with a light kiss. "Hey you."

"Hey." I kissed him again and turned to everyone else. "So, I guess I should introduce you to the guys. Sailo, this is Ethan and Rhett. I'm staying with them for the time being. And this is Dale and his husband, Adam."

"Nice to meet you," Sailo said, and shook hands with each of them in turn. As he did, I cringed a little, wondering how wise it was to turn Dale and Ethan loose on him. At least they had their respective husbands here to rein their smartasses in if needed.

We all took our seats, and everyone focused on the menus for a moment. Once decisions had been made, we flagged down a waitress. She brought our various drinks and took our food orders, then disappeared into the back.

Dale sipped his beer. "Ah, that's what I needed." He raised the glass. "Thanks, Greg."

"Don't mention it. Thanks for agreeing to help me out this weekend."

"You know," he said, "most people don't take their movers out to dinner until *after* they move."

"I know." I grinned. "But this way I make sure you all actually show up to help me move."

"You bastard," he hissed into his glass.

Adam laughed. "Well, he bought you a beer. The covenant is sealed now. No bailing."

"Hey!" Dale scowled. "Whose side are you on?"

"Not picking sides." Adam lifted his own beer glass. "Just saying…beer's a sacred covenant. So, he's got you."

"Dick," Dale muttered.

I just laughed. That pair had always cracked me up. Dale was the smartass of the entire group, the one with no filter whatsoever, while Adam was a little more reserved. Still, he could throw a barb in there sometimes and render Dale speechless, which was impressive as hell.

As we always did, the group shot the breeze and took playful swipes at each other. We ate, we laughed, and damn, it was good to be with friends who completely accepted that the man beside me was my lover. Not that anyone at this table had a leg to stand on when it came to judging gay men, but given how long it had taken me to accept this about myself, I wasn't looking this gift horse in the mouth.

"Anyone else need a refill?" Sailo asked after a while.

"I'm good," I said.

Ethan gestured with his empty glass. "I could, if you don't mind."

"Me too," Dale said.

Sailo stood. "Ethan, you had a Fat Tire, and Dale, yours was…what again?"

"I'll take an Elysian Spacedust."

"Got it. Spacedust and a Fat Tire. Be right back."

"Thanks," Ethan and Dale both called after him.

After Sailo was more or less out of earshot, Dale turned to me. He shielded his mouth slightly and said in a stage whisper, "Well *done*, darling. He is a stunner."

I winked. "You don't have to tell me."

He laughed and patted my arm. "Never thought of you as a cradle robber, though."

"What?" I rolled my eyes. "Ten years is not robbing the cradle."

"Ten—" His head snapped toward Sailo. Turning back to me, he narrowed his eyes. "Bullshit. You've got way more than ten years on him."

I shook my head. "Thirty-seven if he's a day." I paused, glaring at him. "Or were you implying that I'm older than forty-seven?"

"Well." He shrugged. "I figured you had to be around Ethan's—"

"Hey!" Ethan elbowed him. "That's enough."

"Uh, actually," Rhett said. "You guys *are* pretty close."

Dale snickered. "Told ya."

Ethan and I both muttered curses and shook our heads.

A moment later, Sailo joined us again, distributing beers before sitting down beside me. "What'd I miss?"

"Just shit-talking about all of us being old men," I said.

"Except him," Rhett helpfully added.

Sailo laughed. "Hey, I don't get to be the youngest in the group very often. I'll take it."

"Yeah, I'll bet you'll take it," Dale mumbled.

Sailo waited until Dale was taking a drink, then shook his head and said, "Actually, I'm a top."

Dale nearly sprayed me with beer but clapped a hand over his mouth in time.

Adam howled. "Oh my God. Well done." He reached across the table to shake Sailo's hand. "Well played, Sailo."

Sailo snickered. "Kinda seemed like he was asking for it."

"He was." Adam patted Dale's shoulder. "He definitely was."

"As usual," Rhett said.

Sailo turned to me. "Is this normal with you guys?"

"Yep." I nodded. "We may all be old enough to be grandfathers, but none of us behave like it."

"Old enough to *be* grandfathers," Adam said. "But only one of us *is* one, so…"

"Yeah, yeah. Enjoy it while it lasts." I tilted my beer bottle toward Ethan and Rhett. "Won't be long before I can start firing grandpa jokes at the two of them."

Dale chuckled. "I think Sabrina knows better than to make them grandparents before fifty."

I started to make a comment, but paused, shifting my gaze toward Ethan and Rhett. Dale didn't know? Shit.

Rhett and Ethan exchanged glances, and they both grinned.

"Actually…" Rhett put his arm around Ethan. "Looks like we're going to be grandparents sooner than we thought."

"Oh really?" Dale's eyes lit up. "Congratulations! When is she due?"

"Not for another five or six months," Rhett said, beaming like only a grandfather-to-be could. "But I'm not sure if her mother knows yet, so just don't mention anything on social media."

"We should get something to celebrate." Sailo picked up one of the menus the waitress had left. "Do they have a senior menu on here?"

"Hey!" I elbowed him.

"What the hell?" Ethan clicked his tongue. "You need to keep that boy in line, Greg."

Sailo snorted. "Right. Because he's the one in charge."

Dale choked on his beer. Ethan's jaw dropped. Rhett's eyes widened. Adam just chuckled.

Sailo turned to me, his expression half amusement, half "did I go too far?"

I laughed, wrapping my arm around him, and kissed his cheek. "Something tells me you're going to fit into this group quite nicely."

"I don't know if I should take that as a compliment or an insult."

"Man, he is quick," Ethan said.

"Tell me about it." I put a hand on Sailo's leg. "But I'm sure he can slow down if you have trouble keeping up."

Rhett and Sailo both choked on their beers, and the rest of us burst out laughing.

"My God." Dale clicked his tongue, gesturing at Sailo and me. "You guys are a *scary* good match."

Sailo and I exchanged glances. He winked, and I grinned.

Yeah. Dale was right. We were a pretty fucking good match.

~*~

After I'd paid the bill, we all headed for the parking lot.

"Thanks again for agreeing to help me move this weekend," I said. "Seems like a much less daunting job with more people involved."

"Don't mention it," Rhett said. "We're always happy to help."

"Especially if there's beer and dinner involved," Dale said.

"Always the altruistic one, Dale." Ethan laughed. "Never change."

As Adam and Dale headed for their car, Rhett turned to me. "So, we all came together, but, uh…" He glanced at Sailo. "If you want to go with him, we can take your car back to the house."

I looked at Sailo. He gave a *your call* shrug.

"You don't mind?" I asked Rhett.

"Not at all. And I only had two beers, so I'm good to drive."

"Are you—"

He nudged my arm and smiled. "Go."

I hesitated, but really, was I going to say no to spending more time with Sailo? So I handed Rhett my keys, and judging by the grin Sailo flashed me, I'd definitely made the right decision.

We said our good-byes to Ethan and Rhett, and after more handshakes all around, they headed to my car, and I went with Sailo toward his van.

As we walked, I turned to him. "So, you had a good time?"

"I did."

"You didn't mind being the youngest in the group?"

Sailo laughed. "Not at all. Your friends are fun." He slid his hands over my waist. "And I get to be with you, so…"

"Likewise." I wrapped my arms around him. "You do realize I'm going to be physically useless this weekend, right?" I grimaced. "I don't see a lot of activity in the bedroom for a few days."

"Well." He drew me closer to him, until our lips were almost touching. "Then I guess I'll have to get as much out of you as I can before the weekend, won't I?"

"Jesus, I love the way your mind works."

He gave a quiet laugh and then kissed me. "Doesn't give us much time, does it?"

"Just tonight and…hmm, I don't suppose I can talk you into meeting me tomorrow night?"

He smiled. "I have to be at Wilde's at eight, but I would love to see you before that."

"Text me where, and I'll meet you."

The smile turned to a grin that weakened my knees. "I was thinking you could meet me *at* Wilde's."

Visions of the VIP lounge flashed through my mind, and my knees almost dropped out from under me. I gulped. "I…can definitely do that."

"What about tonight?"

"I don't have anywhere else to be."

"And I don't want you to leave." He ran his fingers through my hair. "I like having you here."

"I do like being here." I kissed him softly, but my heart sank a little. "Except…you probably won't like me getting up and heading out at four in the morning."

Sailo wrinkled his nose and playfully shoved me away. "Ugh. No. Get out."

We both laughed and pulled each other close again.

"I could stay a little while," I murmured. "Catch a cab back to Ethan and Rhett's."

"I'll split the cab fare with you, assuming I don't drive you myself."

"Deal."

~*~

It was almost midnight when I climbed into a cab and headed back to my temporary home. Aching, grinning, almost nodding off with postcoital fatigue, I felt amazing.

And it wasn't just from the sex. Sailo had an effect on me that I hadn't felt in *years*. Grinning like this, I probably looked like a complete idiot to anyone who happened to glance my way, but I didn't care. I hadn't felt butterflies in far too long. The thought of someone looking forward to seeing me as much as I looked forward to seeing them—amazing. Just amazing.

God knew where this was going. Was it too soon? Was it just a rebound fling to get me back on my feet after my divorce?

I didn't know, and I didn't care. I loved living from one date to the next. From one feverish fuck and sleepy workday to the next. There were still bumps in the road as I slogged through the motions of getting back on my feet, but being with him was enough to make me forget about all of that for a little while.

Because right now, with Sailo, I was living again.

Chapter Seventeen

On Sunday morning, the guys met me at the storage unit. Sailo looked a little tired, but he was there right on time with everyone else.

With six people, the job was much faster and easier than I expected. Despite the constant wise-cracking about some of us being way too old for this, we had my storage unit emptied and the U-Haul loaded in no time. Moving boxes from the truck up to my third-floor apartment? Easy.

The tricky part was getting the larger things up the stairs to my apartment. If a piece of furniture wasn't too heavy, then it was big and cumbersome and didn't want to make the turn in the stairwell.

"See, Greg?" Ethan grumbled as four of us maneuvered a dresser around the turn. "I told you a freight elevator is a necessity for an apartment."

"It has a freight elevator." I adjusted my grip on the bottom of the dresser. "It just happens to be broken right now."

"Of course it is."

"He did this on purpose," Dale muttered from beside me. "Any excuse to watch big strong men hump furniture up the stairs."

"Don't hump my dresser, Dale. You don't know where it's been."

Ethan snorted. Dale rolled his eyes. Sailo, who'd been quietly helping Ethan steer the top part of the dresser around the corner, just chuckled.

"Are you four taking a break or something?" Adam's voice echoed up the stairwell. "All I hear is jawing and no moving."

"You got any ideas?" Ethan opened and closed his hands gingerly. "Because I'm not sure anything short of a chainsaw's gonna get this around the corner."

Adam looked over the dresser and scanned the stairwell. "I think if you tilt it up a bit taller, it'll turn better."

"We tried that." I gestured at the ceiling. "It's a bit low."

"Nah. There's room. Can't put it all the way upright, but you should have enough clearance to get it around the corner. Might be easier to balance with a few more hands." He paused. "Dale, why don't you help them on that end, and Greg and I will handle it from down here."

Dale saluted playfully. "Yes, sir."

Chuckling, Adam muttered something and swatted his husband on the ass just before Dale squeezed past the dresser to join Sailo and Ethan.

"Ready?" I said.

"Ready," Ethan replied.

Right then, footsteps behind us turned my head.

Rhett set a box down on the landing. "You guys need a hand?"

"Sure," I said. "Join in the fun."

Between all of us, we managed to get the dresser tilted enough to clear the corner without scraping the low-hanging ceiling. Finally, the damned thing was around the turn so we could get it up the next flight.

"Awesome," Sailo said as we continued up the stairs. "Only two more turns to go."

All of us groaned.

Fortunately, now that we'd figured out how to steer the bulky bastard around the turns, the rest of the climb was smooth sailing. Not easy—why had I bought such a heavy fucking dresser?—but smoother. Once it was on the third floor, we guided it into my apartment, down the hall, and into its designated spot in my bedroom, where I vowed it would remain until the sun burned out.

"Whoever moves into this place after me can have it," I said as Adam and I pushed it up against the wall.

"Good plan." Adam dusted off his hands. "I'm starting to understand why someone invented inflatable furniture."

"Seriously," I said.

With the stupid dresser where it belonged, we broke for lunch. Sailo went downstairs to lock up the truck, and I ordered pizza. While we waited for the driver, we all lounged in my half-furnished living room, cracking open beers and resting our feet and backs.

And then, of course, it was back to the grind.

By mid-afternoon, after the heavy lifting was finished, everyone except for Sailo left. Together, we moved from room to room, emptying boxes and arranging furniture until my apartment vaguely resembled a place where a person might live.

In the kitchen, dishes and silverware found homes. Becky had kept the china from our wedding, and I'd taken the everyday stuff—she'd never been terribly fond of it anyway, and I didn't have any use for the china. I'd bought new pots and pans, measuring cups, silverware—all the shit people bought when they were just starting out. Admittedly, it was a little strange adding my new odds and ends to the old things I'd brought from my marriage. Stacking a new set of mixing bowls beside the baking sheets that had been a wedding gift? That would've been strange even if I hadn't been doing it with the help of the man I'd recently started dating.

"This is so weird," I said after a while.

"Hmm?" Sailo looked up from breaking down an empty box.

"Just…it's weird, you know?" I closed a cabinet and turned to him. "One day you're taking for granted you'll be with this person forever, and the next, you're moving into your own place."

Nodding, he put the box aside and came closer. "I've never been with anyone as long as you were with her." He rested a hand on the small of my back. "But I get it. It's always strange, starting over."

I wrapped my arm around him, grateful for his presence and the comfort of his touch. "It really is. I mean, I'm getting back on my feet, and I'm ready to move forward. But I do still kind of feel…"

"Shell-shocked?"

"Yes. Exactly."

He nodded again and kissed my cheek. "It always kind of reminds me of those old Bugs Bunny cartoons. When a bomb goes off, and Daffy Duck is standing there covered in soot, looking like 'what the fuck just happened?' That's about how I feel after a breakup."

I thought about for a moment, then nodded. "That's…pretty accurate, now that I think about it." I exhaled. "The most bizarre part is it's like there's two sides of me. One side is moving on, getting the hang of this new life." I squeezed him gently and smiled. "Seeing someone new."

He smiled back.

"And the other…" I sighed. "The other is stuck in the past and still standing there, covered in soot, wondering what the fuck just happened."

"But it's good that you're not just in the past. You're dealing with it, and you're moving on." He shrugged. "At this point, what else can you do?"

"Take it a day at a time, I guess." I touched his face. "And you've made a huge difference. Just so you know."

He covered my hand with his and kissed my palm. Meeting my gaze again, he said, "I'm happy to help."

"Thank you." I drew him in and kissed him softly, intending to keep it brief. Then I decided, to hell with it, and wrapped my arms around him, letting the kiss linger. Sex was the furthest thing from my mind, and I was pretty sure my body was too tired to get aroused, but this was too good to rush.

Sailo was apparently on the same page. He held me close and opened to my kiss, but didn't push for anything more. He let the moment be, and so did I.

Eventually, we separated, and when our eyes met, my heart fluttered.

Sometimes, as I sifted through all the emotions that came with my divorce, it was hard to imagine ever being completely back to normal. Moving on to the point that I thought of my marriage the way I did my school years and my past jobs—significant eras of my timeline that could be viewed objectively and without feeling like the whole world had tilted off its axis.

Moments like this—standing in my new kitchen with Sailo smiling up at me, his gentle kiss still tingling on my lips—made me believe that moving on was not just a possibility. It was inevitable. It was already happening. And for the most part, it felt pretty fucking good.

I kissed him once more, quickly this time, and we let each other go. "Guess we should get some of those boxes out of here."

"Yeah, good idea."

We got back to work, gathering up the empty boxes and carrying them down to the Dumpster. When we returned to the apartment, I decided the kitchen was more or less coming together, so we moved onto the living room. Like all the others, this room was still populated by boxes more than anything, but little by little, things were coming out and finding homes. A few books had found their way onto the newly assembled bookcase. Some framed pictures were leaning against the wall, waiting for me to hang them up.

The sofa didn't look quite right without the loveseat. The coffee table's glass top seemed bleak and bare without the shadows from the pine tree branches coming in through the window, and without that cluster of three purple candles I'd always hated.

The walls were completely bare at the moment, but the absence of the fading wedding photos prodded at my consciousness like a strobe light—undeniably there no matter how much I tried to ignore it. And little by little, that strobe illuminated the other things that were missing. The kitchen doorway didn't have that slightly uneven place where I'd had to replace the molding after my kids decided to ride their bikes in the house. The dining room table was gone, along with the books and papers and pencils spread out across it while we'd helped the kids with their homework. No more hash marks on the wall between the kids' bedrooms where we'd marked their heights from the day we moved in and on every subsequent birthday until they'd stopped growing. Or where we'd started doing the same for my granddaughter.

None of that was a surprise but damn, it took my breath away to see it all at once. Everything in this apartment and left behind added up to the sum I'd been trying to ignore all this time—she was gone. That life was over. Twenty-seven years, twenty-five of them with a ring on my hand, and it was done. Gone. Behind me. Reduced to the pieces I'd taken with me. All things I'd taken for granted, never thought twice about, and suddenly they were all that was left. The handful of household items salvaged from the rubble after a tornado. From nondescript thing to treasured keepsake in the blink of an eye.

"Greg?" Sailo's voice jarred me right to the core.

I quickly wiped my eyes and forced a smile before I turned. "Sorry, what?"

He furrowed his brow, tilting his head as if he could read everything I was trying to hide. "You okay?"

"Yeah." Why did it take so much effort to say one single word? I'd felt so good just a few minutes ago in this kitchen, and now…this?

I sank onto the sofa, ignoring that conspicuous emptiness where the loveseat should have been. Pressing my elbows into my thighs, I slid my hands into my hair and squeezed my eyes shut.

He sat beside me and touched my shoulder. "It's sinking in, isn't it?"

"Yeah. I guess I—" I cleared my throat. "I guess I thought I was over it. More over it than this, anyway."

"Over it?" He slipped his fingers between mine. "You said yourself you're still kind of in shock over it."

"I know, but…"

"Greg." He squeezed my hand. "Your marriage isn't even cold in the grave. How could you be over it?"

Eyes closed, I exhaled hard. "But I…"

He was right. Of course he was. And I knew damn well there was no reason for me to be over it yet, no reason I could fool him into believing it any more than I believed it myself. But if I let myself go down that road, he was going to see a side of me I'd had to fight hard to hide from everyone. From my ex, from my kids, from the friends who'd helped me pick up the pieces. The floodgates had held this long. Much more, and they were going to give, and God help me, I wanted to be alone when they did.

"I'm sorry," I whispered. "You've been so amazing today, and you didn't come over here to listen to me—"

"Greg," he said just as softly. "Look at me."

I turned to him, forcing my eyes to focus on his.

He touched my face. "You don't have to be strong right now."

And as soon as he'd said that, I couldn't be strong anymore. I rested my elbows on my knees, covered my eyes with one hand, and let go.

I'd cried the night she'd told me she was leaving. Or, rather, that *I* was leaving. Since then, I'd been wrapped up in moving on and keeping a stoic face for the kids. Focused on legal paperwork and finding an apartment and settling in and Sailo.

But now, it all came crashing down. The tears wouldn't stop.

Sailo wrapped his strong arms around me and stroked my hair, not saying a word but not letting go either. My God, I was grateful for him. By all rights, he didn't even need to be here helping me move, and this? Holding me up while it all came down?

"I'm so sorry." I wiped my eyes with a shaking hand. "Asking you to help me move was above and beyond. This…this is way too much."

"No. It's not." He took my other hand and kissed my fingers. "You're human, and so am I. You're going through some tough shit, and just because we're sleeping together doesn't mean I can't also be a friend."

"Thank you." I swiped at my eyes again. "God, I am *so* sorry."

"Don't be."

Slowly, I pulled myself together. Why did this have to happen now? Tonight? With him here? Though I was grateful for him, I could've done without him seeing me like this. But, it was done. Not much I could do about it. Hopefully he wouldn't run for the hills after he left tonight.

After a while, I exhaled and turned to him, running my thumb back and forth along his hand. "Ninety-five percent of the time, I swear I'm not like this."

"I know." He paused. "Do you, um, want me to stay?"

Please, don't leave.

I dabbed at my eyes. "I do, but I can't promise anything…you know…"

He put a hand on my leg and squeezed gently. "I didn't ask if you wanted to go fool around. I asked if you wanted me to stay."

"Yeah. I do."

"Come on." He rose, extending his hand. "Why don't we go relax where it's more comfortable?"

And get away from all these reminders of my past life? Yes, please.

I took his hand and stood, and we didn't let go as we walked down the hall.

Fully dressed, we lay back on my bed. As we settled, the bedframe creaked and groaned like they all did, but it had a different voice from the one I'd slept in for the past fifteen years, after my ex-wife and I replaced the one we'd had since we got married.

We met in the middle of the mattress, Sailo's head resting on my chest and my arm wrapped around his shoulders. I was exhausted—nothing like moving a house full of furniture to remind a man of his age—but wide awake, and we just lay there awhile, breathing in sync with our arms around each other.

A mix of sadness and relief tangled in my chest. I couldn't remember when Becky and I had stopped sleeping like this. When that tiny bit of space between us had started expanding until it became a gap, a canyon, and then a rift.

The worst part was realizing even more than before how long my marriage had really been over. How long it had been since Becky and I had touched like Sailo and I touched now. There was nothing sexual about the way he held me. It was all comfort and affection, the gentle warmth of one person keeping the other from coming completely unraveled. I missed her, but I'd missed this too, and realizing how much I must have deprived her of it, realizing how much I craved it myself, realizing how far gone our marriage had been before she'd finally dropped the hammer… It was too much.

It hurt to realize how long the divorce had been brewing, and how blind I must've been for it to catch me by surprise. The writing had been on the wall, clearer than our kids' names and heights between their bedroom doors, and I hadn't seen it.

And yet, there was relief, because even though all of that was hard to swallow, the fact was, I wasn't lying in bed with someone who was a million miles away. The last few weeks had been hell, but the silver lining was the man who'd suddenly come into my life. Without this divorce, without all this upheaval, I never would have known him. Whatever Sailo and I were doing, it gave me some hope I hadn't had in a long time. Like even if this wasn't love, and didn't turn into anything remotely resembling love, it gave me that little inkling of hope that love like that was still a possibility for me. Maybe, just maybe, I was still someone a person could fall in love with someday.

Sailo eventually broke the silence. "You all right?"

"I will be." I kissed his temple. "And thanks again. For being there."

"Don't mention it." He lifted himself and kissed me, gently pressing his lips to mine but not pursuing anything more. As he settled in beside me again, I closed my eyes and tried to think of nothing but the warmth of his skin against mine.

Yeah, I'd be all right. The divorce sucked. Starting over sucked. But the dust was settling. Maybe that was the hardest part. Not the shock, not the transition, but the realization that the book was closed and that piece of my life was now buried and gone. There was nothing left to do now but catch my breath, pick myself up, and move on.

He gently freed himself from my arms and pushed himself up on one elbow, gazing down at me. "I know it's not the same, but like I said, I've been through my share of breakups. None of them were as long as your marriage, and there weren't kids involved." He touched my face, his eyebrows pulling together as he held my gaze. "But I understand. It hurts, and it shakes up your whole life."

I nodded. "It really does. And I'm still worried as hell this is fucking with the kids more than they're letting on." I glanced at him. "Is it crazy that I really want to come out to them?"

He raised his eyebrows. "Do you?"

"Yeah. I guess…I don't know. I want them to know I'm moving on, and I also want to be honest with them. About who I am." I absently scratched the back of my neck, then rested my hand on his arm. "I've kept this side of myself a secret for so long, and now that I'm actually living it…"

"You want to tell people."

I nodded again.

"So, tell them."

"You don't think…" I moistened my lips. "You don't think that would be too much for them right now?"

His eyes lost focus, and he seemed to mull it over for a moment. "Well, if it were me, I'd want to know that my parents were getting back on their feet after a divorce. And I think if one of them could look me in the eye and tell me they were gay, I'd be happy they could be that honest with me." He gently rested a hand on my chest. "But you know your relationship with them better than I do."

I chewed the inside of my cheek. "They probably know their mother is dating again. I guess it wouldn't hurt to let them know I'm dating. Dating a man."

He smiled. "Well, you've finally had a chance to explore a side of you that you thought you never would. You have the opportunity now to be honest with yourself. So maybe this also means you can be open and honest with your kids about it too."

I swallowed. "I… God. I want to, and then I don't know if they could…right now…"

He squeezed my hand. "If they were little, then maybe they'd be angry and want you back with your wife because that's the family they're used to. But they're adults. Change is still hard for them, but they're mature enough to understand that their parents need to be happy too. It might take some getting used to, knowing their dad isn't straight, but it might be a sign to them that you're going to be okay after the divorce. Like you're going to move on and be all right."

"Assuming they don't think the divorce was because I'm gay. Or bi. Or…or whatever I am."

"Tell them," he said simply. "They're old enough to understand."

"True." I sighed. "I guess I'm just terrified of them hating me. Thinking I cheated on their mom, or…" I shook my head. "I'm overthinking it, I know."

"These are your kids. Of course you're worried. You don't want to hurt them or make them think you hurt their mom." He kissed my fingers. "Tell them the truth. If they don't understand right away, they will eventually."

"I hope so." I paused, then laughed dryly. "Why do I get the feeling this is going to be an awkward conversation?"

Sailo whistled. "It will be."

"Been there?"

He laughed. "Greg, I had my son with a lesbian couple. You don't think I've had a few awkward conversations with family members?"

"How did your families take that?"

"Eh, there were mixed reviews. My parents were happy to finally have a grandchild. Lea's family was iffy about the whole thing right up until the day Mika was born. And C.J.'s parents disowned her the day they found out she was a lesbian, so I don't even think they know about Mika. The rest of her family was thrilled, though." He ran his hand up my arm. "Your kids might have mixed reviews too. And, I mean, you know them, so you'd know better than I do if they're ready to hear this. But it could be a chance for them to see that you're moving on, and not wallowing in the divorce. It's good for kids to see that."

"True."

"Sleep on it tonight." He caressed my face with a lightly callused hand. "Settle into your place. When you're ready, *then* talk to them. But take care of you too."

"I will." I lifted my head and kissed him softly. "Thank you again. For everything."

"Don't mention it. I'm here if you need me."

I shouldn't need you as much as I do.

"Maybe…" I hesitated. "Maybe we should grab a shower and call it a night. I think I've had enough of unpacking things. You're, um, welcome to stay if you want to."

I was sure he was going to politely bow out and never look back.

But instead, he leaned down and kissed me again. "I'd love to."

Chapter Eighteen

Sitting in a coffee shop, I tore tiny pieces off an empty sugar packet and tried not to stare at the door. I hadn't seen much of my kids recently—they'd been busy with their lives, and I'd been busy restarting mine. We kept in regular contact via e-mail and texts, but hadn't had a lot of opportunity to actually see each other.

Now, I was waiting for my daughter to meet me for lunch, and I was nervous as fuck. More so than I'd been the day Becky and I had sat her and her brothers down to let them know we were separating. That day, I'd been pretty certain how things would go. There'd be some shock. Some questions. They'd probably need some time to process it, and maybe there'd be some anger or some tears. But they were resilient, always had been, and I knew they'd cope with this somehow. We'd all move on together—well, sort of—and we'd all be all right eventually.

And I'd been right. There'd been differing degrees of surprise. My eldest and youngest hugged us both before they left. My middle son didn't, but that wasn't unusual for him. In the days that followed, they'd approached us with questions. How long had this been going on? What happened next? Were we okay? It had certainly been a shock, and they were no more thrilled about it than I was, but they were adjusting. Yeah, we'd all be all right. Just as I'd guessed.

Today, as I ignored my untouched cup of coffee and kept mutilating the wrinkled sugar packet, I had no idea how things would play out.

I dropped the remains of the sugar packet beside my coffee and checked my phone. April was late, but that wasn't unusual. I was just impatient today because I wanted to get this over with.

Maybe I should've asked all three kids to be here for this, but I didn't have the courage for that quite yet. One at a time. And it was a no-brainer that I'd talk to her before her brothers because though I loved all my kids equally, I had very different relationships with them.

My youngest son Kurt and I had a much better relationship now than we had during his mid-teens. He'd been rebellious, as teenagers are, and there was a year or so in there where I was pretty sure he didn't say two words to me or his mother that weren't laced with "you fucking idiots" or "you're making my life hell." Somewhere around the beginning of his senior year, he'd leveled out, and by the time he graduated, the hormone-induced insanity seemed to have lifted, and the smiling young man was back.

When he was a kid, we'd hiked every trail in Western Washington. I'd carried him on my back until he could walk, and then there was no stopping him, and we kept up our regular hikes until he reached that phase where he wanted nothing to do with his asshole parents. This past summer, though, as we got him ready for college, we'd started again, and we'd promised to make a point of hiking whenever we could during the school year. We were even planning to go camping again come summer.

With Mark, my older son, I had a weird relationship these days. We weren't hostile, but we weren't all that close either. He'd been through some depression in his teenage years, and he was the most introverted of my three kids, so it was hard to crack through the walls he seemed to have put up around himself. I made a point of getting together with him as often as possible, texting him, e-mailing him, but he wasn't one to initiate contact. He was a closed book if there ever was one. I was thankful he still saw his therapist regularly—at least that meant he was talking to *someone*.

I made a mental note to shoot him a text later today and see how he was doing. I had no idea how the divorce was affecting him—as per usual, he hadn't shown many cards.

But this afternoon, I was meeting his sister, because of the three of them, I'd definitely been closest to her over the last few years. They say there comes a point when your kid becomes your friend, and April and I had absolutely reached that point. We talked frequently and candidly, and if I couldn't tell her about this, then I couldn't tell anyone.

It hadn't always been that way. We'd had a rather turbulent relationship all through her teen years. She'd been the hardheaded troublemaker, the reason we'd made a handful of trips to the police station in the middle of the night, and the one whose taste in boyfriends had been the source of many, *many* shouting matches from the time she was about fifteen. Looking back, it was no wonder she was convinced we were going to lose our minds when she told us she was pregnant. We'd even threatened her about that very thing before.

"The way you're going," we'd told her time and again, "you're going to wind up pregnant before you graduate. And how exactly are you going to take care of a baby? Because that will be up to *you*, not us." I'd known it was coming sooner or later, and was both angry at her irresponsibility and frustrated at my helplessness to stop the inevitable.

Then came the moment three months before she turned seventeen when she'd looked at me with tear-filled eyes and said in a tiny voice, "Daddy, I'm pregnant."

Instantly, I'd regretted ever threatening to leave her on her own if she found herself in this situation, and instead of shouting at her, I'd hugged her tight and promised her over and over that everything would be okay, and we'd help her any way she needed. It was the first time I'd seen her cry since she'd broken her arm when she was twelve.

The next year was hell for all of us. Stress and hormones were a vicious combination, and her pregnancy was a rough one. Her idiot boyfriend didn't last through her second trimester before he walked out and signed away his rights. The night my granddaughter was born, there were more than a few moments when we weren't sure she or April were going to make it, but thank God, they were both all right. Over the next year, Becky and I helped with the endless days and longer nights, and it was during that time that April and I really bonded for the first time. Even once she got back on her feet, finished school, and ultimately married the saint I called my son-in-law, we stayed close, and that hadn't changed to this day.

Now it was my turn to confess something to her, and hope like hell she didn't get angry. I wondered if what I felt now was what she'd felt that night seven years ago.

I can't change this. I need you. Please don't stop loving me.

Guilt twisted in my stomach. I still regretted ever making her feel that way. We'd only been trying to get her back on the straight and narrow, but the thought of my little girl ever being afraid I wouldn't love her anymore or that I'd abandon her—even after all this time, I still felt like the worst father ever. Especially now that I was scared to death she was going to hate me for the confession I needed to make.

The coffee shop door opened, and what little appetite I'd had was gone.

Here we go.

From across the room, she smiled, and as she came closer, I stood.

It amazed me how much she was looking like her mother these days. Ever since she'd had the baby, her features had been just slightly rounder, and her pregnancy had left her straight hair in tight curls that had never relaxed. Just like Becky. Sometimes it was weird to realize my kid was a mother herself now.

When the hell did you grow up, and when did I get this old?

"Sorry I'm late," she said. "My car keys grew legs again."

I chuckled. Yep, just like her mom.

We hugged briefly and then took our seats. She ordered coffee, and we made small talk, catching up on work and life in general.

"How's Kayla doing?" I asked. "Is she liking school?"

"Oh God, yes." She smiled. "Put her in a room full of other kids and construction paper, and it's a wonder we ever get her out of there."

Chuckling again, I said, "That sounds like her. Where is she today?"

"Nathan took her to a playdate, and then they're going to the zoo, so they'll probably both be sound asleep when I get home."

I smiled. Nathan was the only father Kayla had ever known, and he was the father *I'd* aspired to be when I was raising my own kids. He was also exactly the kind of spouse I'd hoped every one of my kids eventually found. A day didn't go by that I didn't thank God for bringing that man into my little girl's life.

April's coffee came, and after she'd mixed in some sugar and taken a cautious sip, she met my gaze across the table. "So, how are you doing?" Her eyebrows pinched together. "After everything with Mom?"

I wrapped my hands around my own coffee cup just for something to hold onto. "I'm doing okay, actually. On the upswing, I think."

She tilted her head. "But…?"

"But…" I hesitated. Well, this was why I'd asked her to meet me. Might as well cut to the chase and put it out there. "Listen, um…" I let go of the cup and folded and refolded my hands beside it. "I know the divorce hasn't been easy for any of us. And I don't want to add to that. But…" My mouth had gone dry and I was struggling to hold her gaze, so I broke eye contact and picked up my coffee. It was cold and nearly made me gag, but it was something to do besides try to stammer my way through this.

"Dad?" She tilted her head. "What's going on?"

"Well, let's put it this way." I set the cup down. "I'm seeing someone."

She sat straighter. "Already?"

I winced. "I know, it's probably too soon, but—"

"No, I think it's great." She shrugged. "Mom's been putting herself out there too, so…"

"Has she?"

April flinched. "Oh. Shit. I…probably wasn't supposed to say anything. I'm sorry."

"It's okay. I'm kind of glad to hear it, actually." I didn't need to tell her I'd already seen signs of another life around the family home. "How is your mother doing?"

"You haven't talked to her?"

"I have, but it's…" Exhaling hard, I thumbed my coffee cup. "It's hard to talk about things like that. And I don't want you going behind her back. Nothing like that. I just… Is she doing okay?"

April nodded. "I think she is."

"Good. That's good to hear." Why did it hurt to be reminded I'd been replaced? *Fucking hypocrite.* I took another sip of ice-cold coffee. "Well. So, like I said, I'm seeing someone." I took a deep breath and steeled myself. "I, um…"

"What?" She smiled cautiously. "You have a boyfriend or something?"

My stomach fell into my feet, and my breath hitched. "Um…"

The smile vanished. Her eyes widened. "Dad, I was joking."

"Right. But…"

Her eyebrows climbed even higher. "You do, don't you?"

I coughed into my fist. "Yeah. I…I do."

My daughter blinked. "You're serious."

I nodded, my stomach threatening to turn inside out as I waited for the shock to wear off.

"Is this…" She chewed her lip. "So, I mean, are you gay? Or…"

I studied her. "Or what?"

"Or is this some kind of rebound, midlife-crisis thing?"

"Midlife—" I laughed, shaking my head. "No, no, it's nothing like that. I…" I sobered and stared into my coffee cup, because I couldn't hold her gaze anymore. "To tell you the truth, I've known for a long time that I had some interest in men. So after Mom and I split…" I forced myself to meet her eyes. "I guess I wanted to see if I really was into men, or if it was just curiosity."

"Oh." She thumbed the side of her coffee cup. "Wow. That definitely wasn't what I was expecting."

"Are you mad?" *Jesus. Way to sound like an idiot kid instead of a parent talking to* his *kid.*

"Mad?" April stared at me. "What? Why would I be? You're a single man now." She shrugged. "I'm just happy you're moving on instead of dwelling on the divorce."

I exhaled. I was doing plenty of dwelling on the divorce, but she didn't need to know that. "We've just thrown a lot at you kids recently. I didn't want to pile onto that, you know?"

"This isn't really piling anything on anything," she said. "You being gay…" She paused. "Gay? Or bi?"

I waved a hand. "At this point, I'm not even sure. Let's go with bi."

"Okay, so you being bi, it's not exactly something for us to deal with. It's part of who you are, not like you committed a crime or something."

"So it doesn't bother you?"

"Of course not."

I shouldn't have been surprised. I really shouldn't have. And surprise might not have been the word to describe it. More like profound, all-the-way-to-the-bone relief. Confirmation that who and what I was didn't change things between us. The bond I had with April was hard-won, and few things scared me like the thought of losing that.

She absently tapped her fingers beside her coffee cup. "Can I be completely honest about something?"

I searched her eyes. "Please do."

"The divorce wasn't as much of a shock as you might think."

Good thing I wasn't taking a drink just then, or we both would've been wearing it. "What?" I sputtered. "What do you mean?"

"I mean I'm surprised you and Mom made it as long as you did."

"You are?"

"Yeah." She folded her arms on the table, the motion tense as if she didn't know whether she was trying to look casual or defensive. "It's hard to explain, but you guys always seemed like you were just kind of…there. Like you weren't really into each other. I mean, when was the last time you and Mom went and did something when it wasn't an anniversary or something?"

As I mentally ran through the last few years, I couldn't argue with her. If we weren't doing something with the kids, we were celebrating an anniversary, a birthday, Valentine's Day…

There was never any "just because," at least not in recent memory. And if I was honest with myself, I couldn't remember the last time there was. Or if there ever was.

I exhaled. "Maybe you're right. I don't know. I'll admit it caught me by surprise, but, well, you know what they say—hindsight is twenty-twenty."

Grimacing, my daughter nodded. "Tell me about it."

We exchanged uneasy glances. I didn't want to pick apart my defunct marriage with one of my kids, but I wasn't sure where to take the conversation now.

She sipped her coffee. "So, do I get to meet this guy?"

I blinked. "You want to meet him?"

"Well, yeah." She smiled. "He's dating my dad. Don't I get to, you know, approve him?"

I laughed, more relief rushing through me. "Let's not rush these things. I don't know if it's serious or anything. I mean, the divorce isn't even final yet. And he's, uh, quite a bit younger than me."

"Younger? How much younger?"

"Young enough that his son is the same age as Kayla."

"Really?" She smirked. "Well, I assume he didn't start quite as young as I did, right?"

"Not quite, no. For the record, he's thirty-seven."

"That's not *that* young." She waved a hand. "And even if you're on the rebound and you just met, I am kind of curious about this guy."

"We'll see. I'm trying not to pin too much hope on this. I haven't been single in years. He's the first man I've ever dated. Anything could happen. Or not happen."

"Still, you never know. Even if it's a rebound thing, sometimes those work out." She tapped her wedding ring. "If the right guy comes along, he comes along. Don't pass him by just because you're still on the rebound."

I released a breath. "Well, we'll see how it goes. We're still getting to know each other and all, so…"

April smiled, wagging a finger at me. "Is this where I get to lecture you about taking it slow, and how some guys have ulterior motives and—"

I burst out laughing, and so did she. "Very funny."

"Hey, I learned from the best." Her humor faded a bit, and she rested her chin in her hand. "So, are you going to tell Mark and Kurt?"

That sobered me right up. "I'm…not sure yet. I had to psych myself up to tell you."

"Really?" She arched an eyebrow. "Did you really think I'd be upset?"

"I don't know what I thought. It's been a weird thing to get my head around, and I guess I couldn't imagine what it would be like to find out one of my parents was gay. Bi. Whatever."

"That must've been tough for you. Being married one day, and rethinking everything the next."

"You have no idea," I said, barely whispering. "So, the boys…I don't know. Not yet."

"You should," she prodded. "I think the more open you can be with them, just like with me, the better."

"You're probably right. But give me a little time."

"Okay." She smiled, and then glanced toward the front of the coffee shop. "Should we order some food? I'm starving."

Now that she mentioned it, my appetite had come back, and suddenly I was aware of how little I'd eaten since last night when I'd asked her to meet me in the first place.

"Food sounds good." I pulled out my wallet and stood. "Let me know what you're having—it's on me."

"Are you sure?"

"I invited you, and you let me get this off my chest. Besides, I'm your dad. I'm buying. Don't argue."

She laughed, and didn't argue. After she'd told me what she wanted, I went up to the counter to order for both of us. And as I stood there, I rolled some of the residual tension out of my shoulders.

So this had gone much better than I'd expected. My daughter knew I wasn't straight, and she knew I was seeing someone, and she was okay with that. Completely okay with it. She even wanted to meet Sailo.

I smiled to myself. Maybe I wasn't ready for April and Sailo to meet, but just knowing that option was on the table gave me a little taste of the peace that had eluded me since Becky and I had split. Life was going on. I was moving on.

And for the first time in a long time, I really believed that whatever the future held, I was going to be okay.

Chapter Nineteen

The week after I came out to my daughter, Sailo had his son most evenings, and then he had a few deejay gigs over the weekend in between his regular appearances at Wilde's, so we didn't see much of each other until the following Monday. We kept up via regular texts, though, and since I was in the process of settling into my new place, I kept myself pretty busy, which made the time fly by. It would have been great to see him, of course, but I was doing okay on my own.

Finally, we were going to meet up for dinner. And not a moment too soon. Seeing him was going to be the bright spot in a day that was, otherwise, not great. It was "one of those days" at the office—people butting heads during meetings, higher-ups making unreasonable demands while the people I supervised made bullshit excuses—and it was capped off by a visit to my attorney. By the time I arrived at the restaurant on Broadway where Sailo and I had agreed to meet, I was sorely tempted to text him and bow out.

But I desperately needed that bright spot, so I took a shower to wake myself up, threw back some high-octane coffee, and headed over to the restaurant. I trudged in through the front door, and there he was.

Yes. Yes, this was definitely the bright spot in the day. One look at him—tan skin under warm lights, broad shoulders beneath a black T-shirt, that grin that made my spine tingle—and I had to smile. After the day I'd had, and seeing him now, I understood that expression "sight for sore eyes."

As I came up to the table, he stood and kissed me, which strangely didn't bother me in the slightest even though we were in public. Let people stare—I didn't mind if they knew I was with him.

We took our seats, facing each other across the small linen-covered table.

"Good to see you," he said as he closed his menu. "Sorry I couldn't get together the last few days."

"Oh, don't worry about it." I opened my own menu and quickly scanned it. "I've been keeping myself busy settling into the new place."

"Yeah? How's that going?"

"Not bad, so far. I'm getting used to the apartment. Liking it a lot, actually."

"That's great."

I nodded. "So how did that gig go yesterday? You said you were kind of worried about it."

"It was fine." He half shrugged. "Evan was still kind of sick, but he did make it, and between the two of us, we did all right. Mostly, it was a long day."

I grimaced. "And he made it through the day too?"

Sailo nodded. "Kid's tough as hell. I sent him home an hour or so before the end because he was starting to get woozy again."

"Working with a deejay after being down with a migraine?" I whistled. "I'd be woozy just thinking about it."

"Right? I paid him extra for yesterday. He deserved it."

"No kidding."

We chatted for a while about his various gigs, and the crazy shit that always seemed to happen when he worked at Wilde's. Never a dull moment at that place, apparently—if he and the bartenders weren't breaking up a vicious fight between two drunk boyfriends, they were breaking up the same two boyfriends having makeup sex in the bathrooms. Ironic, considering how many of the employees apparently used the VIP lounge the same way Sailo and I did, but at least there weren't customers up there while we were there.

After we'd ordered and given our menus to the waiter, I clasped my fingers loosely on the table. "So I came out to my daughter."

Sailo sat straighter. "Really? How'd that go?"

"Better than I thought it would. She was surprised, but she was okay with it."

"That's great," he said. "Can't ask for much better than that."

"No kidding. She, uh, thinks I should tell my boys, and she's probably right." I blew out a breath. "Just not sure I'm ready for that conversation. It took a lot to work up the guts to tell *her*."

"You think it'll be different with them?"

"Probably." I drummed my fingers on the table. "Kurt, my youngest, is pretty laid-back. And we're close. I don't know. He's got a lot on his mind right now. Settling into college and all of that."

"Freshman?"

I nodded. "So, I don't know. I'll have to gauge how stressed he is when I see him next, and go from there. As for Mark, my middle son…" My heart sank. "That's a bit more complicated."

Sailo tilted his head. "How so?"

"Well, Becky and I have been trying to get him to talk to us for a long, long time."

"About what?"

"Anything. When he was a teenager, he kind of clammed up, and that's never changed. We've been worried sick about him—we even put him in therapy because we were afraid he was going to hurt himself."

"Oh." Sailo's eyes widened. "Was he depressed?"

"Yeah. He has been for years. I mean, he seems to be on an even keel now. I think?" I sighed. "He still sees the therapist, thank God. And she promised us that even after he turned eighteen, she'd say something if she thought he was going to attempt suicide or something. So I trust her. I just…" I rubbed the back of my neck, wondering when the muscles had started tightening up like this. "I wish he'd talk to us."

"Well, maybe this is an opportunity." Sailo held my gaze. "If you can open up to him, maybe he'll feel safe opening up to you." He paused, then lifted his shoulder in a vague half shrug. "Or it could be that he's not an open book. Some people aren't."

I nodded. "I know. But it's…it's not easy being that distant from your own kid."

"I can imagine," he said, almost whispering.

I absently played with the edge of my faux leather placemat. "Does your son know you're gay?"

"Oh yeah. I mean, he's been raised from day one by a lesbian couple and a dad who has the occasional boyfriend." He chuckled, reaching for his soda. "Homosexuality wasn't exactly a shocker for him."

"I guess it wouldn't be. Wow. Talk about two different generations."

"Right?" He took a quick drink. "No way in hell it would've been like this when I was his age."

"Tell me about it. At the risk of aging myself, I didn't exactly grow up in a generation that embraced 'alternative lifestyles.'"

Sailo shrugged. "Isn't even aging yourself, really. My generation wasn't so hot about it either. It still kind of amazes me that it's no big deal with kids now. My son's friends know he has two moms, and it's so rare for anyone to give us the stink eye or make a negative comment, that it makes us all kind of pause and wonder what the big deal is."

"Well." I raised my glass. "Here's to a generation that will wonder why the hell ours thought being gay *was* such a big fucking deal."

He clinked his glass against mine. "I'll definitely drink to that."

~*~

After dinner, we walked down Broadway, and then followed Pike to one of the more colorful parts of Capitol Hill. I was very quickly falling in love with this area. There were some neighborhoods in Seattle that were on the hipster end of the spectrum, some that were so plain, they were painfully dull. Capitol Hill, though, was a mix of everything. The odd record store, endless bookstores, ethnic and eclectic restaurants, shops specializing in everything from mystic crystals to imported household items, art galleries ranging from extremely high end to things the average person could actually afford to put in their living room. There was even a community college and a funeral home right smack in the middle of it all. I was reasonably certain someone could venture no farther than a block off Broadway in either direction and be able to find literally anything they needed or wanted.

"You know," I said as we strolled along, "I had no idea there were so many shops and stuff up here."

"One of the best-kept secrets in Seattle."

"Seriously. I've lived in Seattle my whole life, but I haven't spent a lot of time up here."

"In the gay neighborhood?" He glanced at me, clutching his chest in mock surprise. "What a shock."

I laughed. "Well, okay. But it's not like that's the *only* reason people come to Capitol Hill."

"It's a reason for people to avoid it, though."

"Yeah, I guess it is."

"Which is kind of a good thing, if you think about it."

I turned to him. "How do you figure?"

"Keeps all the bigots out."

"Good point. Very, very good point."

We continued down the sidewalk, and a few doors down, a window display caught my eye, and I stopped dead. "What the…"

Sailo halted too, and burst out laughing. "Heat definitely knows how to get people's attention."

"Heat?" I looked up at the sign. "Oh, right. Ethan told me about this place." I lowered my gaze to the window again. Indeed, they knew how to get people's attention. A couple of mannequins had been dressed in wildly mismatched lingerie, with one arranged to be down on one knee, proposing to the other. Instead of an engagement ring, though, the kneeling mannequin offered a black box containing a pair of nipple clamps.

Beside me, Sailo chuckled. "I think they're trying to compete with The Oh Zone. The people at that place also seem to like having fun with their displays."

"So I see." I cleared my throat. "The sex shops in this part of town are certainly, uh, racier than the ones I've been to."

"Really?" He flashed me a grin. "You went to sex shops before?"

"Uh, well." I laughed self-consciously. "I've been to them before, but it's been a while."

"Want to go in?" He gestured at the door. "Maybe we can find something to play with next time."

I shrugged. "Why not?"

So, with my…boyfriend, for lack of a better term, walking ahead of me, I stepped through the door of Heat. Yeah, this was like most sex shops I'd been to—tons of lingerie, strange varieties of condoms, enough porn to sink a battleship. It was definitely racier, though. Behind the racks of lingerie was a wall covered in floor-to-ceiling shelves, and those were stocked with every kind of dildo imaginable. And I knew dildos now—God knew I'd browsed through every type, size, and style offered by The Oh Zone's website. Rubber, plastic, metal, even some colorful glass varieties that, if memory served, required a second mortgage to purchase.

Another set of shelves were buckling beneath the weight of lubes. There were literally dozens of brands, varieties, and…flavors? "Sampler" bottles were even set up so someone could put some on their finger and see if they liked it.

As we made our way past the lube and dildos, a twenty-something guy with "Kenny" on his name tag approached and cheerfully asked, "Can I help you gentlemen find anything?"

Sailo turned to me, eyebrows up.

I shook my head. "No, I think we're just looking around. Thanks."

"Okay," Kenny said. "Just holler if you need anything!"

"Will do," I replied.

He walked back toward the cash register. As he did, Sailo made a not-so-subtle gesture of checking the guy out, then turned to me and grinned. "He's cute. Nice ass too."

I glanced after him, and yeah, he was right—Kenny had a hell of an ass, especially in those snug leather pants. "Mmhmm."

A devilish grin formed on Sailo's lips. "Want to see if he's free after work?"

"Free?" I arched an eyebrow. "For…?"

The grin broadened.

The pieces fell together, and I nearly choked. "Are you serious?"

Sailo burst out laughing and patted my arm. "I'm just fucking with you. Relax."

"Okay, good." I chuckled, my cheeks burning. "Not…quite sure I'm ready for that."

"It's fine." He wrapped his arm around my waist and whispered in my ear, "As if I'd share you anyway."

I shivered. "I think you're all I can handle."

"Good. As it should be." He kissed my cheek and let me go, and we continued wandering through the shop.

I had to admit, his good-natured possessiveness fucked with my blood pressure. It was probably just as well we were in a sex shop—much more of this, and I'd have a visible hard-on, but that had to be par for the course in here.

Par for the course, but not terribly comfortable. I made a subtle gesture of adjusting the front of my pants, and hoped to God no one noticed. Sailo didn't. Kenny didn't seem to. Why was I so worried about it?

Because I'm a nervous, self-conscious idiot. That's why.

We turned a corner and found ourselves in the bachelorette party and novelty section. It was everything imaginable that could be used for a party—cups, hats, banners, cookware—but either shaped like a penis or covered in plastic penises.

Sailo put on a pair of sunglasses with a rubber penis sticking out from the nose piece. He turned his head one way, then the other, making the penis wobble from side to side. "How the hell are you supposed to see with these?"

I laughed. And, hell, I couldn't help myself—I found a hat shaped like a cock and balls and put it on. "Well? What do you think?"

Sailo stroked his chin thoughtfully. "Hmm. It's a little…lopsided."

I tried to straighten it, which made the whole thing sag in front of my eyes, and Sailo snorted. Then I snickered, and suddenly we were laughing our asses off. Okay, so it wasn't our most mature moment, but after the day I'd had? I wasn't going to bitch. Dinner with Sailo, wandering through Capitol Hill, and collapsing into fits of laughter over some dick-shaped merchandise—that definitely made up for an otherwise shitty day.

"We really should get a picture," he said, pulling out his phone.

"I agree."

We each put on a pair of the sunglasses with the penises on the nose pieces, and took a selfie together. As I put the glasses back on the rack, I turned to see him tapping something into his phone.

"Put that on Facebook," I warned, "and there will be hell to pay."

He laughed. "I'm not putting it on Facebook. I'm just sending it"—he tapped the screen—"to you."

And right on cue, my phone buzzed.

I pulled it out and looked at the picture that had just come through. Oh yes, this was one I'd need to keep to myself, but it was hilarious. And, I realized, the first and only photo I had of the two of us together. No way in hell was this getting deleted any time soon.

I pocketed my phone, and we kept wandering through the shop.

The next aisle was nothing but porn, so we skipped it. No point in spending forty bucks on a DVD when there was plenty of free stuff on the Internet. Not that I'd ever looked.

The aisle after that was…

Whoa.

I gulped as we turned down the aisle, and suddenly, instead of being surrounded by plastic dicks or gaudy DVD covers, we were in a jungle of stainless steel and black leather.

Floggers. Harnesses. Whips. Spreader bars. Cuffs. Paddles. Ball gags. Why were ball gags always red? I swore, every one I'd ever seen—in real life or in a porno—was red for some reason. As if they—

Something jingled, shaking me out of my feeble attempt to distract myself, and I turned to see Sailo pulling a long black whip off the rack.

My tongue stuck to the roof of my mouth as he ran his fingers along the braided leather.

Then his eyes flicked up and met mine.

"What do you think?" He held it up, grinning wickedly. "Ever tried something like this?"

"Um…" The truth was, I'd never given much thought to anything kinky besides the occasional playful swat on the ass or hands loosely tied to a bed frame. Now that I was diving headlong into sex with a man, I was suddenly curious about *everything*. What would it be like to use some of these toys?

What *would* it be like to bring something like that long, coiled whip into one of our bedrooms?

"Well." I coughed to get the air moving. "That might be a bit much, but…" I gestured at some of the other implements. "Maybe someday?"

He smiled and hung the whip back up. "Actually, I think that would be a bit much for me too. Some of these, though…"

"Maybe. They're certainly, uh, interesting."

He glanced at me and seemed to pick up on my nerves. Stepping away from the rack, he said, "We don't have to get anything tonight. It'll all still be here." He winked. "We can always come back if we want something."

I nodded, and as we continued down the leather-and-metal aisle, added, "Maybe they're one of the shops that does home delivery."

Sailo halted. "Wait, that's a thing?"

"Mmhmm. I, uh, had a few things delivered from The Oh Zone. When I was trying to figure out if I really wanted to bottom."

"Smart man. And what a genius idea. Sex toys delivered right to your door. Why aren't more people doing this?"

"I don't know, but they must be making a fucking mint."

"No kidding." He put his hand on my back and kissed me softly. "Well, if we get really adventurous one night, we can either come back here or order something."

"Sounds good to me."

"Want to head out for now?"

I nodded. As fun as it was to fantasize about the things we could do, I decided I was ready to get out of here for the moment. As he said, it would still be here. We could always come back.

For now…air.

We stepped out of the sex shop, and I took in a deep breath of air that didn't taste like leather and a few flavors of lube. What the hell was wrong with me? I'd been in sex shops before.

Never with a man, though.

But as much as I'd had sex with him, it shouldn't have bothered me to—

"You okay?" Sailo touched my arm.

"Yeah." I gestured over my shoulder and forced a laugh. "I, uh…haven't been into one of those places in a while."

He smiled warmly. "Well, if you want to get desensitized to them, we can go back *any* time."

I studied him and smirked. "If I didn't know any better, I'd think you were trying to subtly encourage me to come back so we could make a few purchases."

He shrugged. "I don't know about subtly, but okay."

We both laughed. Then we continued up the gently sloping sidewalk. As we walked down Pike, strolling past bars and bistros and wandering across the occasional rainbow-painted crosswalk, I didn't feel conspicuous in the slightest. There were other same-sex couples out here, and no one gave us a second look like they would've in other parts of Seattle.

And it was funny—after going into a sex shop together, I was certainly turned on, but not so much that I needed to drag him down on the nearest flat surface. Oh, we'd definitely have sex again soon, but for now, I was content just to walk beside him. Maybe someday, I'd even work up the courage to hold his hand or put and arm around him—things I'd never think twice about with a woman—but I couldn't complain about this.

So I didn't. I just walked alongside Sailo and enjoyed every second.

~*~

Eventually, we made our way to his apartment. It wasn't far from where we'd had dinner, so it would only be a short walk back to my car.

As we strolled into the parking lot, a mix of disappointment and giddiness swept through me. Yeah, I was a little bummed that the evening was coming to a close. But at the same time, I was thrilled about the evening we'd had. It had been relaxed and fun, and I hadn't even thought about my divorce all night. I hadn't once thumbed the place where my wedding ring used to be. And even thinking about it now, my mood didn't dim.

I felt better tonight than I had in ages. We'd had a lovely dinner. We'd goofed off in a sex shop.

For tonight, it had just been us. Just Sailo and me, without all the baggage and drama I'd been dragging around recently. We'd strolled through Capitol Hill, two guys out together—in more ways than one—with nowhere to be except wherever we were at that moment.

At the entrance to his building, we stopped.

"Well." He smiled. "I guess I'll see you tomorrow?"

I nodded. "Looking forward to it."

We held eye contact. I resisted the urge to rock from my heels to the balls of my feet, not sure what was prompting this sudden nervous energy.

Then Sailo glanced around us before meeting my gaze with uncharacteristic shyness. "I know we're kind of out in public, but…" He lifted his eyebrows.

"Aside from you, there's no one around whose opinion I care about." With that, I pressed a soft kiss to his lips. "You've been so amazing through all this. I'm sure it's not easy being with someone who's dealing with a divorce, and kids, and…"

"It's okay." He rested his forearms on my shoulders and held my gaze. "Everything you're going through is hard. Being with you?" He smiled as he shook his head. "That part *is* easy."

"Are you sure? Even with—"

"Yes." He grinned, gently cupped both sides of my neck, and kissed me again. "Everyone's going through something. I like being with you. The fact that you're dealing with a divorce doesn't change that."

"But if it does, or you get sick of hearing about my latest chaos, just say so."

"I will. Promise." He kissed me once more, then drew back a little, and his smile fell. "It's getting late. I guess I should let you go, since you have to be up early tomorrow."

"I know." I touched his face. "I wish I didn't, though."

"Me too."

"A few more minutes won't kill me."

His smile came back to life in one of those grins that weakened my knees. "You know a few more minutes is going to turn into…longer than that, right?"

"I'm willing to risk it."

"Do you want to stay longer?"

I hesitated. I was already getting into that window where every half hour I stayed awake was going to be costly tomorrow. But I could also be in bed with Sailo, his warm body against mine, our legs tangled beneath the sheets.

"Yeah." I grinned. "I can stay a little longer."

"Good."

"And I want tonight to be about you. Anything you want."

He grinned. "Well, there is one thing I want tonight."

"Yeah?"

"Mmhmm." He pulled me closer, and just before our lips met, he whispered, "You."

Chapter Twenty

Okay, so maybe I should've left Sailo's a little earlier than I did. Sitting at my desk the next morning, with three hours of sleep to my name, I was a fucking wreck. During my college years, I could handle that, but now? Not so much. Oops.

But was it worth it?

My body still ached, and I swore I could still feel his lips and goatee tickling my neck while we'd fucked just *one* more time before I'd left. Despite the fatigue, I grinned to myself as I reached for my coffee.

Oh yeah. It was worth it. And hell, I was getting used to working on less sleep than I needed. My coworkers didn't seem to notice. My work wasn't suffering. As long as I wasn't dozing off during meetings or fucking up paperwork, well, the only harm was a little extra yawning throughout the day. Totally worth it.

As I always did, I made it through the day, still functioning and still grinning like an idiot. Counting down the minutes until I saw Sailo again? Absolutely.

I was on my way home when my phone buzzed. Traffic wasn't moving, so I quickly glanced at the message. It was from Becky.

Have some papers from atty's office—come by or I can mail?

It was tempting to have her mail them. One less awkward face-to-face encounter. On the other hand, if I went over and dealt with it now, that would take us one step closer to things being finalized and over with. The sooner this was all over and behind me, the better.

I waited until I was home to text her and let her know I'd be there shortly. After a quick cup of coffee to wake myself up—*still worth it*—I drove the familiar route to the street I used to live on.

It was still weird and a little painful coming back to this place, but it was getting easier. The further I moved on, the more time I spent with Sailo and the new life that was feeling more like mine every day, the less I struggled to accept that this chapter was over.

I parked in the driveway and walked up to the front door. Before I could knock, Becky opened it.

Our eyes met, but only for a second. She stood aside and gestured for me to come in. "It's in the dining room."

"Okay." I ignored the unfamiliar jacket hanging by the door, and the hiking boots next to the Birkenstocks. She was moving on. That was good. So was I. Without saying a word about him, I followed her into the other room.

"Sorry to have you come over for something this small." She pulled the papers out of a manila envelope. "We both forgot to sign one of the pages, and my attorney said it would delay things if we sent it in like this."

"No problem."

She set the page on the table. Sure enough, two blank lines were marked with bright yellow sticky notes. She'd signed one already, and handed me a pen to fill in the other.

I uncapped the pen. "Not sure how we missed that, but glad he caught it."

"Yeah, he's pretty thorough."

"He is. Nice guy too," I said as I scrawled my signature across the highlighted blank. "Doesn't seem like the snakey lawyer type."

"No, he's not. That's exactly why Jase recommended him."

I tilted my head. "Jase?"

"Yeah, my—" She stopped abruptly and swallowed. "The, um, the man I've been seeing. Recently. Since you left."

Since I left*? Since you kicked me out.*

I capped the pen and set it on the form. "Anyway, I'm glad he caught it. Do you need me to take a copy to my lawyer?"

She shook her head. "He said he'll send it over once we took care of this."

"Great. Perfect." I chewed my lip. "Well, I should go."

"Right. Um. Thanks for coming by. I'll take it to his office first thing in the morning."

"Okay. I'll see you later, then."

With my ex-wife on my heels, I headed out. The jacket by the door, the Birkenstocks, the hiking boots—they were more conspicuous now. Throbbing at the edges of my peripheral vision, needling me and demanding that I turn and *fucking look at them.*

I kept my gaze forward, though, and got the hell out of there. On the porch, we exchanged quiet good-byes without eye contact, without touching. Then I walked away as she closed the door behind me. I got in my car, relieved that the awkwardness was over, but as I drove away, that taut, uncomfortable feeling—the one that usually followed me *to* my old house—set up shop in the middle of my chest.

Her *boyfriend* recommended her attorney?

My stomach tied itself in knots. Becky'd mentioned this attorney the day she'd told me we were getting a divorce. But she'd never mentioned this Jase. Not as a coworker. Not as a friend or a neighbor or some guy she knew from the gym. But they'd been close enough for him to recommend a lawyer before I even knew we were getting divorced?

I shifted uncomfortably. The pieces were falling into place whether I liked it or not. Mentally, I tried to push them apart, but it didn't work.

The man living in my old house wasn't a new addition like Sailo.

My wife cheated on me.

And as those pieces cemented themselves to each other, and the truth could no longer be denied, more questions emerged.

How long had it been going on? Was he the only one?

Did the kids know?

God, please, *tell me the kids don't know.*

No. She wouldn't have let the kids find out. She'd done a damn fine job keeping it away from me, and she wouldn't have been careless where they were concerned.

Oh, but now I knew. And holy shit, it hurt. Moving on had been difficult, but now it was like being dumped all over again. As if we were back to that moment when she'd said the words that threw my life off-kilter, only this time, there was someone standing behind her. A quiet, male presence. A reassuring hand on her shoulder while there was none on mine. Everything she said suddenly had new meaning.

"I want a divorce…so he and I can start our life together."

"I'd like you to move out…so he can move in."

"It's over, and it's been over for a long time…and you've already been replaced."

Wow. I laughed bitterly into the silence of my car. And I'd felt guilty about hooking up with Sailo so close on the heels of the divorce. Jesus Christ. At least I'd waited until we'd signed the papers, even if the ink wasn't dry yet.

At the end of our—her—road, I pulled over and put the car in park. Swearing into the silence, I rubbed my hands over my face. It was like the moment she'd pulled the rug out from under me in the first place. Suddenly I was running through the last twenty-five years, searching for signs and writing I should've seen on the wall. Was I blind? Stupid? Oblivious?

Not that it mattered. The divorce was still happening regardless of what had led up to it. In theory, I could bring this to my attorney and use it as leverage to get more from the divorce, but why? What would really be gained? The divorce would drag on longer. The bitterness would run deeper. The kids would probably find out, and they didn't need that.

So I'd let it go. I wouldn't bring it up to Becky. I wouldn't put this out there where the kids would find it. I'd tuck it into the bitter recesses of my memory, put it behind me, and just remind myself that the divorce was, in fact, for the better.

But goddamn, I wasn't happy about it.

Cursing under my breath, I shifted back into drive, pulled onto the road, and continued toward home as home faded in the rearview.

Chapter Twenty-One

I'd been home maybe an hour when Sailo came over. I was thrilled to see him—he was one of the brightest spots in my life right now, and I wasn't about to turn him away—but my enthusiasm was tempered by this afternoon's revelation. Even as we went out for a light dinner, and slowly strolled back to my place, and kicked back in the living room, it was always there. Like a quiet but annoying third wheel, it was there, tugging at me and pressing down on me.

I faked it as best I could, though. When I went into the kitchen to get us a couple of beers, I paused for a moment to take a few deep breaths, then cracked open the bottles and rejoined him on the couch.

"By the way, I forgot to mention—I'll be tied up most of the weekend," he said as I handed him one of the beers. "I'm doing back-to-back weddings on Friday and Saturday." He made a face. "At least I know the photographer on Saturday. We'll probably go out drinking afterward and commiserate."

"Commiserate?" I forced a laugh even though I didn't feel it. "That bad?

"Weddings? God, yeah. They can be fun sometimes, but man, when they're not?" He grimaced. "They're definitely not."

"I can imagine."

He looked at me, head tilted slightly. "Hey." He squeezed my arm. "You okay tonight? You've been kinda…elsewhere."

"Yeah. Yeah. Sorry about that. Just…" I met his gaze and waved a hand. "No, let's not. I've been bitching about all the craziness in my life and—"

"Because you've got a lot of craziness in your life." He took my hand. "What's going on?"

I shook my head. "It's nothing. I'd rather not think about it, to be honest."

"But you obviously are thinking about it."

My shoulders sagged under the weight of all this bullshit. As much as I didn't want to darken every moment we had together with talk of my divorce, this was going to eat me alive. So, I took a deep breath. "I was over at my ex's today. Getting some things I'd left behind. We did a little bit of talking, and long story short, I realized she was cheating on me."

Sailo exhaled. "Shit. That's rough. I'm sorry to hear it."

"Yeah." I rubbed a hand over my face. "Fuck. Talk about a kick in the balls."

He touched my arm but didn't say anything.

"I don't know why I'm worried about it. I mean, our marriage is over. We're done. Nothing is going to change that, so why the fuck do I care if…" I exhaled, running my fingers through my hair. "What difference does it make, you know?"

Sailo shrugged. "It doesn't have to change anything to hurt."

Wasn't that the truth? Nothing had changed, but damn it, definitely hurt. This was below the belt and beneath the skin, even if it didn't make a bit of difference to anything.

He squeezed my hand. "You gonna be okay?"

"Yeah. I…" I pressed my fingers into the bridge of my nose. "I just wish I could stop thinking about it."

"I'll bet. Is there anything I can do? To help you feel better now?"

I lowered my hand. "Honestly?"

Sailo nodded.

"Right now…" I closed my eyes and inhaled deeply. "Right now I just want to go in the bedroom and fuck until I can't see straight."

"Then what are we waiting for?"

I blinked. "What?"

He got up and took my hand. "You heard me."

Despite my disbelief, I rose, and I followed him. He led me halfway down the hall, and about that point, reality set in. That we were about to fuck each other senseless and get all this stress out of my system.

And I couldn't wait.

I grabbed him, shoved him up against the wall, and kissed him. Sailo didn't miss a beat. He held the front of my shirt, kissing me just as hard as I kissed him. I ground my hips against his, but he managed to slide a hand between us, and when he squeezed my cock, I broke the kiss with a gasp.

Immediately, he descended on my neck, kissing my skin so frantically, I was surprised he didn't bite me.

"Bed," he growled. "Before I fuck you right here against the wall."

I wasn't sure why that would be an issue, aside from my shaking knees, but somehow found the presence of mind to push myself off him and haul him toward my bedroom. Shoes came off, and my shirt disappeared, and then I dragged him down onto the bed by the front of his shirt, and he kissed me just as hard and deep as I needed him to.

Was this the right thing to do tonight? When I was still reeling from—

His teeth dug into my shoulder, driving a cry from my lips and jolting my focus right back to him. Oh, it was gonna be like that? Fine. I raked my short nails up his back through his shirt, and he groaned, throwing his head back. And a second later, he pulled his shirt off, tossed it on the bed, and came down to kiss me again, and I couldn't resist—I traced those same lines with fingernails. He swore against my neck.

"Like that?" I asked.

"I love everything you do." He kissed me hard, deep, pushing the kiss just to the edge of painful, and I did the only thing a man could do in that moment—wrapped my arms around him and kissed him back.

We didn't just take clothes off—we tore them off. A button came off something, and a seam ripped, and…whatever. I wanted his skin against mine. I wanted his tattoos beneath my fingers, the rough velvet edges seeming to spell out his name to my hungry nerve endings.

Sailo must've sensed every time my mind tried to drift to why we were here, why I needed this in the first place, because he always knew exactly when to dig his nails in, or sink his teeth into my shoulder, or stroke me just right to erase every conscious thought I had left.

After a while, he pushed himself up on his arms and met my gaze. "I think I know what you need tonight."

You. What I need is you.

"Yeah?" I swept my tongue across my lips. "What's that?"

He reached for the nightstand. Oh yes. Yes please. Fuck me until I can't—

He tossed the condom to me. "Put it on."

"Put—" I stared at the foil square in my hand, then at him. "What?"

Sailo stroked me lightly, just enough to make my breath catch. "I want you to fuck me. Good and hard."

My mouth watered. "You're serious? But you're a top."

"Mmhmm. But I told you that first night I wanted to see your face the first time you were on top. And I'm guessing tonight, you need to fuck more than you need to get fucked." His eyebrows rose. *Am I right?*

I hadn't thought of it like that, but he definitely wasn't wrong. I'd have been perfectly happy with him fucking me—God, I loved when he fucked me—but now that he'd brought it up, I sure as hell wasn't going to say no to being on top, even if it was just this once.

I tore the wrapper with my teeth. Good thing I'd practiced a little with my toy at home—at least I didn't make a complete idiot of myself as I rolled on the condom. "Hands and knees?"

"Oh hell no." He sat up and, in the same moment he kissed me, teased my balls with his fingertips.

"Fuck!" I gasped, throwing my head back as a shudder jolted through me.

Sailo laughed. He wrapped an arm around my waist and kissed my neck, still teasing my balls as he did. "To answer your question, I'm going to get on my back." He flicked his tongue across my skin. "So I can watch you."

I bit my lip, holding on to his shoulders for balance. "Then you'd…better get on your back so I can start. Or you're going to finish me off just like this."

Abruptly, he stopped. "Well, in that case…" Sailo put a pillow behind his ass, and lay back on the other pillows. Sobering a little, he met my gaze. "Start slow." He spread his legs wide. "It's been a while."

"Okay." I poured some lube on my fingers. Then, slowly, I ran my hand down his inner thigh, the bands of his tattoo acting almost like guidelines, directing me up as if I didn't already know what to do. "This—well, you already know. It'll be cool."

He laughed, nodding. "Yeah. I know."

I pressed my finger against him. He didn't jump. Didn't flinch. I carefully slipped my finger into his tight hole, and when he'd relaxed a little, added a second. Once he was easily taking my fingers, I withdrew them and poured plenty of lube on my dick.

And then I positioned myself between his legs. Heart pounding with both nerves and excitement, I met his eyes. "Ready?"

He nodded slowly. "Yeah."

I guided my cock to him. Pressing the head to him, I met resistance, and reminded myself that had happened when I'd used a toy the first time and when Sailo had topped me the first time. Just as he had, I paused there, letting the pressure remain but not trying to force anything.

Sailo took and released a long breath.

"You okay?" I asked.

He nodded and, with a grin, met my gaze. "Just been a long time."

"We don't have to—"

"I'm good." He hooked a leg around mine, drawing me forward. "C'mon. I want you to—"

We both gasped as he took the head of my cock. My vision blurred for a second. The condom was probably a blessing—I hadn't worn one in eons, but it dulled the senses just enough to keep me from going off too soon. As turned on as I was, watching my cock slowly slide deeper inside Sailo, that was a very real possibility.

Stroke by stroke, little by little, I worked myself into him. Every so often, my head would start spinning, and I'd remind myself that I still had to breathe during sex, and after a few gasps my vision would clear, and I'd still be there. Still kneeling on my bed, fucking the most gorgeous man I'd ever seen, running my hands along his tattooed thighs and staring down at him as he arched his back and bit his lip.

Swallowing, I met his heavy-lidded eyes.

He grinned. "I knew…this would be hot. Watching you."

I exhaled, rocking a little harder. "But does it feel good?"

"It…" He closed his eyes and squirmed. "God, yeah…"

I dug my teeth into my lip, my own eyes watering as I watched myself sliding in and out of him. "T-tell me what you want. Harder? Or—"

"Yes." He moaned. "Please."

Oh yes. I rocked my hips faster, and then even faster, until the bed frame was protesting and Sailo was murmuring pleas for more. My hips and thighs burned, and my dick felt amazing, and Sailo was clawing at the sheets beside him, so I fucked him as hard as I could.

He murmured something I didn't understand. Not that the words mattered. What mattered was how turned on he sounded, and how beautiful he was like this. He was jerking himself off as I rode him now, and Jesus, the sight of him—tan skin gleaming with sweat, muscles standing out beneath his tattoo sleeve, abs quivering beneath the V of his larger tattoo. And I was fucking him. Riding him. Driving myself into him as he gasped and arched.

"This is amazing," I said, my voice hoarse and shaky. "You're…fucking…"

"D-don't stop," he pleaded. Oh, I wasn't stopping. Not a chance. Not when every thrust drove me closer to an intense climax that promised to be utterly spectacular. And even better, a climax inside him. No wonder I'd had to wait my whole life for this—at this rate, it was liable to kill me.

"Ohh…" Sailo moaned. He clenched around me. His eyes flew open. "*Shit.*"

And then semen shot across his stomach, landing on bare and inked skin alike, and just like that, I was coming too, forcing myself as deep as he could take me and crying out things I didn't even understand as I fucking exploded inside him.

I slumped forward onto my arms. My elbows threatened to collapse out from under me, and I struggled to stay up, but then Sailo drew me down to him. I had just enough presence of mind to pull out, and then I closed my eyes and rested my head on his chest.

And just breathed.

~*~

We lay in bed for the longest time, letting the dust settle. I'd gotten up long enough to toss the condom and wash my hands, and then we'd both collapsed.

The physical release had helped. Lying here with Sailo in my arms probably did more than anything, though. My body felt incredible. Emotionally, though, there was something to be said for half dozing in the arms of someone who could still smile when he looked at me. Someone who still wanted me enough to come that hard.

Sailo fidgeted a little and winced.

"You okay?" I asked.

"Yeah." He rubbed his thigh gingerly. "Was starting to get a cramp earlier, and now it's coming back to bite me."

I grimaced. "Ouch. Did I do something wrong, or—"

"Not at all." He kneaded the muscle but met my gaze with an adorable smile. "Just the position. Don't worry about it."

"I'll remember that for next time." I paused. "Um, I mean, if you want a next time…"

He shrugged. "I could be persuaded."

"Really?"

"Mmhmm."

"So you're a top, but you like bottoming?"

"I prefer being on top." He turned on his side and faced me. "But if I'm with a guy who wants to be on top sometimes, I'll bottom. And yeah, when I do, I enjoy it. It's just not usually my thing." He paused. "You seem to like it, though? Being on the bottom?"

"I like it both ways. Bottoming is definitely new, and I really enjoy it."

"Good." He grinned. "We can switch now and then if you want to. Just say so."

"I'll remember that." I touched his face. "I think it's what I needed tonight. One hell of a distraction."

"So you feel better?"

Good question. I really hadn't thought being on top would make a difference in terms of distracting me from everything, but in hindsight, it had. It was something new. Something that had required extra concentration, and brought with it all new sensations that had pulled my focus away from anything and everything else. For those few minutes, I'd forgotten the rest of the world existed at all.

Mission accomplished.

Sure, it was all coming back now, and the tension I'd been trying to escape still existed behind my ribs, but none of it seemed as catastrophic as before. Did I feel better? Fuck yes, I felt better.

"I feel a hell of a lot better. Thank you." I touched his face. "I'm sorry this thing keeps coming up. My divorce and…" I shook my head. "I'd definitely rather be focused on you than the past."

He smiled and turned to kiss my palm. "Don't worry about it. I've been through breakups before. Even the ones that happen after a short relationship take time to get through."

"I know. I just…" I caressed his cheekbone. "I like being with you more than I like dwelling on her."

Sailo chuckled. He kissed the tip of my nose and, as he settled beside me, said, "Give it time. For right now, if she's on your mind, just say so, and I'll be happy to help you think of something else."

I laughed. "Deal."

We lay in comfortable silence for a while. Well, somewhat comfortable. The shock from this afternoon was wearing off. The painful sense of betrayal lingered, but now guilt was creeping in. Had I driven her to cheat on me? Had that slowly growing canyon between us been because of her affair, or had it caused her to cheat in the first place?

"Greg?"

I shook myself and turned to him. "Sorry, what?"

He draped his arm over me. "You were spacing out."

"Sorry." I sighed. "Just thinking about…everything I don't want to think about. I'm sorry. I shouldn't be dwelling on all that shit."

"You're not dwelling. You're processing." He pressed a soft kiss to my forehead. "Breakups hurt. Anybody who expects you to suck it up and move on overnight, even after you're already seeing somebody else, is fucking clueless."

I closed my eyes and exhaled. "Yeah. I know. Thank you again, by the way. You've been amazing through all this."

"You're welcome."

Propping myself up on my elbow, I studied him. "Why do I get the impression you've had your share of shitty breakups?"

"You noticed?" he laughed bitterly.

"Sorry to hear it."

"It's life. Hell, the last guy I dated…" Sailo whistled. "*That* ended in disaster."

"What happened?"

He stared up at the ceiling with unfocused eyes. "We'd been dating for about six months, and everything was just…God, it was amazing. The sex. The conversations. I was even starting to think this was it, that he was the guy I was going to spend the rest of my life with. And then one day, he realized he could do better." Sailo's lips twisted, and bitterness dripped from his tone as he added, "So he did. He left, found some personal trainer with a six-pack and a pretty face, and…well, that was that."

"Jesus. That's cold."

"Tell me about it." He blew out a breath. "Took me almost as long to get over that as I dated him in the first place. Which is kind of pathetic, but—"

"No, I don't think so." I laced our fingers together. "Somebody hurt you. Getting over that takes…as long as it takes."

He turned to me, and a hint of a smile pulled up the corners of his mouth. "Says the man who keeps apologizing for trying to get over his divorce."

Well. He had me there, didn't he?

"Fair point, fair point. If it looks like it's going to take twenty-five years to get over that, though, please smack me."

Sailo chuckled. "I think you've got your head on a bit too straight for that, but just in case…deal."

We shared a quiet laugh, and then we settled on the pillows. He rested his head on my shoulder, and that comfortable silence set in again.

I couldn't have asked for a better person—male or female—to help me bounce back after Becky. He was wise beyond either of our years about relationships and their aftermath, and he knew just how to get my mind off things when I'd dwelled on them too long.

It was bizarre to imagine that if one devastating conversation in my old house had never happened, I wouldn't be here. I wouldn't be reeling from a divorce and the discovery of an affair, but I wouldn't be *here*.

The question that haunted me more than anything…

Did the end justify the means?

I ran my fingers up and down Sailo's tattooed arm. Without the divorce, the cheating, the hurt, the upheaval—I wouldn't be here. I would still be curious about what it would be like to be with a man, instead of insatiably hooked on the way Sailo kissed me, touched me, fucked me. Things would still be the same as they'd always been, and this wouldn't exist except in the fantasies I didn't dare tell anyone about.

I could have done without all the heartache and headache surrounding my divorce. At the same time, I felt like I wasn't just starting my life over again—I was starting to *live* again. After going through the motions, gritting my teeth and telling myself we'd fix things eventually, I was free. So was Becky. We'd broken out of that miserable stagnation, and for the first time in a long time, I finally felt like I was…*me*. Like I wasn't putting on a smiling face for Christmas cards, or pretending everything was fine while I was dying inside. Instead of wondering where my life was going, I was *living* my life.

Maybe all this stress and pain were what I needed. Having the rug pulled out from under me wasn't *fun*, but I was starting to think it was necessary. Growing pains, as it were. Something to shake me up and *wake* me up.

One thing was for sure—it was time to start letting go of Becky and focusing on Sailo.

Slowly, so I didn't disturb him, I turned toward him. The streetlights illuminated just enough of his face to hint at his familiar features. Watching him now, listening to him breathe, I smiled in the darkness.

A year ago—hell, a few weeks ago—I couldn't have imagined being here.

Now, I couldn't imagine being anywhere else.

Chapter Twenty-Two

Throughout the workday, there were landmarks that signified that quitting time was getting closer. The first break. Lunch. Second break. All I had to do was make it from one of those milestones to the next, and eventually, it would be time to hurry out to the giant parking lot and hope I made it out ahead of my thousands of coworkers.

Lately, there'd been another marker that gave me something to look forward to each day—the first text from Sailo. He usually woke up around ten in the morning, so partway between my breaks. It wasn't quite like clockwork—sometimes he rose earlier to see his son off to school, and sometimes he slept in after a particularly late gig the night before—but once that first message came through, my day went by so much faster.

Days like today, when I still felt lost and hurt over what I'd learned about Becky, I lived and died by those little milestones. They were something normal, something to remind me that, yes, life was continuing and everything would eventually be fine.

I'll get through this, I reminded myself while I sucked down coffee at my desk. *She cheated. We're divorced. It's over.*

And I had Sailo now. The thought of him brought a smile to my lips. As tough as things had been recently, I couldn't really complain because all the chaos and heartache had made it possible for us to cross paths. Everything happened for a reason, apparently. The pain would wear off. This new life? It would be worth it. It was already worth it.

At a little past nine one morning, my phone vibrated. I flipped it over, surprised he was awake this early, but the message wasn't from him.

Can we have lunch?

The message was benign enough. I just hadn't expected it from Mark, my middle son. He wasn't one to make contact out of the blue like that. Immediately, I started imagining every possible worst-case scenario that might've made him reach out when he normally wouldn't. I tamped them down, though, and replied: *Sure—when?*

After a second, though, I added, *Everything ok?*

He responded almost immediately: *Everything's good. Just want to get lunch.*

That didn't do much to settle my stomach. This was not like him at all.

Through a series of short texts, we made plans to meet for lunch. Then he had to get to class, and I tried to concentrate on the report I was working on, but my brain was a million miles away.

What had prompted this? *Was* everything okay? We didn't have a bad relationship per se, but we weren't as close as April and me. We hadn't been in a long time, especially from the time he was twelve or thirteen. All his life, he'd been a little shy, but lively once he warmed up to people. Then around seventh grade or so, he'd started putting up walls. While both his siblings had fought and rebelled their way through their teenage years, he'd quietly avoided us. He was the kid who came home from school with one-word answers about his day, stared at his plate all through dinner, and disappeared to his room or with his friends whenever he had the chance. Now that he was in college, he dutifully visited on all the holidays, and had occasionally shown up for Sunday dinner or to join his younger brother and me for a hike, but he always seemed…elsewhere.

Becky and I had been worried sick that he was depressed or something, and we'd put him in therapy as a teenager, but the counselor hadn't been able to pry anything out of him. He had what seemed like a healthy social circle, so we'd eventually decided he just preferred the company of his peers.

Still, I worried about him, and this text out of the blue didn't help.

The morning crawled by, but finally, it was time to go meet him. As soon as I could, I ducked out of my office and headed down to the brewery we'd agreed on. It was a sports bar, but since there were no games today, it was relatively quiet, and I immediately zeroed in on Mark at a booth near the back.

He was hunched over a glass, both hands wrapped around it, and gave me a slight nod when he saw me. Then he dropped his gaze and shifted a bit as I approached.

I sat across from him and tried not to let my nerves show. "Hey." I smiled. "This is a surprise."

"Yeah." He smiled back, but it seemed forced. "Just, uh. Hadn't seen you in a while."

"Well, it's good to see you."

"Yeah. You too."

And…silence.

We perused the menus, placed our orders with the waitress when she came by, and quietly sipped our drinks, but I struggled to find a way to break the silence. I was still uneasy, still uncertain about why we were here. At the same time, I didn't want to pry at him to the point that he decided meeting up for no reason was grounds for suspicion. Especially if he really was just trying to spend more time together.

It was Mark who finally spoke. He took a long swallow from his soda, then pushed the glass away. "So I talked to April the other night."

Well, that was a surprise. He and his sister had never been all that close. "Oh. How's she doing?"

"Good." He watched himself fold and refold his fingers on top of his untouched menu. "She's, uh…she's good."

I studied him, not sure what to say.

Abruptly, he lifted his gaze and looked me in the eye. "Is it true that you're gay?"

I nearly choked. "What?"

"April said…she told me…"

I winced. "Oh. She did?"

He nodded slowly. "So, is it true?"

He held my gaze, and I had no clue what answer he was looking for. His tone was flat, his expression blank. How would he react if I told him the truth? I couldn't lie to him, though. And if April had already tipped my hand, then there was no point in hiding it anyway. Shit. This is what I needed. First I'd found out my ex-wife cheated, now my son knew I was seeing a man.

"Well…" I hesitated. "I'm not sure if I'm gay, to be honest."

His eyebrows pulled together. "Huh?"

"I mean, I guess I'm bisexual? Maybe?" I shook my head. "I'm still kind of working it out, I think."

"Oh." He lowered his eyes, wringing his hands on top of the menu. "So is that why you and Mom split up?"

Ha. No. Someone *had a boyfriend, but it wasn't me.*

I swallowed the bitterness and shook my head. "No. I think Mom and I just reached a point where…" I tapped my thumb on the edge of the table as I searched for the words. "Sometimes people just don't…" Christ. How was I supposed to explain this to him when I didn't fully understand it myself? Why *were* we divorcing? Why *had* she cheated? Finally, I sighed. "I don't know, to be honest. I guess we both just realized we weren't as meant to be as we thought."

He lifted his gaze again and studied me for a long moment, as if searching for a sign that I was bullshitting him. I didn't break eye contact. I wasn't bullshitting him. That was the best answer I could come up with, and in the absence of any other explanation, I believed it.

"So, what?" he asked finally. "You and Mom broke up, so now you're gay?"

"Well, no. I've known for a long time that I was attracted to men. So after we separated, I…" Decided to go get laid? Decided it was time to hook up with a dude? How the fuck was I supposed to word this?

"And now you have a boyfriend."

I swallowed. It was hard to think of Sailo as my boyfriend—weren't we just friends and fuck buddies?—but that wasn't something I wanted to explain to my son.

"Yeah," I said quietly, bracing for his response. "I do."

He held my gaze for a long moment, his expression offering nothing, until he finally whispered, "Me too."

I stared at him. "What?"

"Me too." His shoulders slowly sank as he softly said, "I…have a boyfriend too."

I leaned forward, resting my arms on the edge of the table. "You're gay?"

My son nodded, and when his eyes flicked up and met mine, he released a breath, one he seemed to have been holding since *long* before today. "Yeah."

"Oh. I…I had no idea." I paused. "How long have you known?"

"Since junior high. Seventh grade."

I swallowed. "All this time?"

Eyes down, he nodded.

"Why didn't you tell me?"

"I don't know. I guess I didn't want to disappoint you."

"Mark. My God." I reached across the table and squeezed his arm. "Disappointed? No, not at all. I—" I paused, my mind flashing back to all those years when he'd been so quiet and distant. How he'd withdrawn…right about the beginning of seventh grade. When he apparently figured out he was gay. Barely whispering, I asked, "Did I ever give you any reason to believe I'd be disappointed if you were gay?"

Cheeks darkening, he lowered his gaze. After a moment, he shook his head. "No. But I guess…I mean, how many dads want their sons to be gay?"

My heart clenched. "Jesus, Mark. I don't think I ever gave it much thought, to tell you the truth. I just wanted you kids to be happy." I cleared my throat. "The hardest thing in the world was seeing you unhappy when you were a teenager, and not being able to do anything about it. There's no way in hell I'd have been upset about you being gay—I just wanted you to be all right."

Mark swallowed hard, as if pushing back a lump. "I feel stupid for never saying anything."

I shook my head. "No, there's no reason to feel stupid." I squeezed his arm again and then withdrew my hand. "I don't think it's easy for anyone to come out to their parents."

"No, it's not. And I didn't want to be gay. I didn't want to think about it. So I guess I started pulling back from everyone." He ran an unsteady hand through his dark hair. "And then when I got to where I accepted it about myself, I didn't want to tell anyone." He sighed, shaking his head. "It's stupid."

"No. I…kind of had the same thoughts."

He met my gaze. "You did?"

"Well, yeah. When I realized I was interested in men, I was already married to your mother, so I couldn't really tell anyone anyway. Not without hurting Mom, or making anyone think I was planning on cheating on her. Which, for the record, I never did."

"I know." He shrugged. "I never thought you did."

"Just making sure that's clear. I don't know why I'm so worried anyone will think I did, but…"

He laughed dryly. "But part of coming out seems to be thinking everyone will think you're the worst person on the planet?"

"Yeah. Kind of." I exhaled. "I'm sorry you had to go through that."

"You're going through it too. Sucks, doesn't it?"

I nodded. "And you know, I don't envy you for all that hell you went through when you were a teenager, but I do envy you for figuring this out about yourself now. Instead of when you're, you know, my age."

He watched me silently for a moment. "But you knew? When you and Mom were still married?"

"Sure." I shrugged. "I'd been in denial for a long time, I think, but finally admitted it to myself, even though it was a moot point. Or, I *thought* it was a moot point."

"So, you and Mom…" He gnawed his lower lip. "Be honest—*is* that why you split up? Because you're gay?"

I shook my head. "No. It was never an issue." *Was it?* "I loved your mom, and I always will. After we decided to separate"—*after your mother threw me out*—"I just decided it was time to see if I really am interested in men. And it turns out, I am."

"Oh."

Silence set in again. I wanted to bat it away, physically chase it off with my hands like a cloud of smoke in the air between us. I'd been hoping for way too long that Mark and I would find a reason to open up to each other—I wasn't ready to let it go now.

And once again, it was Mark who finally spoke.

"I was going to come out to you and Mom," he said. "I'd been thinking about it for a while. But then you guys separated, and I didn't want to make things worse."

"Worse? My God, no. To be honest, this is a huge relief."

"Really?"

"Well, yeah. I've been worrying about you for years. We knew about the depression, and Jesus, we tried everything we could to help with that. But—"

"You and Mom helped a lot," he said quietly.

"But you were still afraid to tell us you're gay?"

Mark sighed, his shoulders sinking a little. "It…was a little more complicated than that."

"What do you mean?"

"I mean, it wasn't just you and Mom." Mark took a deep breath and, with what seemed like a lot of effort, met my eyes. "I was afraid to tell you guys, but it wasn't because of anything you or Mom did. My therapist said a lot of it was the depression talking."

"The depression was that bad?"

"Still is."

I reached for my drink, needing something to moisten my parched mouth. "I had no idea. I mean, I knew you were struggling, and—"

"Nobody knew," he said. "Dr. Sandler was the only one. Because I didn't tell anyone. I felt stupid and helpless, but that was the depression talking too. That was one of the things she and I worked on for a long time. Knowing when the depression was telling me lies." He sighed. "She thinks being in the closet made the depression worse, and the depression made being in the closet worse, and it was just this awful cycle. I didn't want to be gay, and the more I tried to tell myself I wasn't…" Mark shook his head. "So it was rough."

I swallowed, my mouth suddenly dry. "I can't even imagine. And you're still struggling?"

"I probably always will," he said softly. "But she's got me on some antidepressants. And they help. I still have bad days, but it's not like it was before."

"Good. Good." I paused. "Listen, if it gets bad, you know you can call me any time. Day or night. Come by my place, call me, text me."

He nodded. "I know. I've always known that."

"But you've kind of shut us out the last few years. Did I…did we make you think you couldn't come to us?"

"No. It's hard to go to anyone. I mean, do you have any idea how hard it is to tell someone that your own brain is telling you you're a worthless slug?"

I flinched. "I can't imagine."

"Most people can't."

"Can I ask you something about the depression?"

He nodded.

"Were you ever…" My throat tightened around the words, but I forced them out. "Did you ever think about hurting yourself?"

Mark avoided my eyes for a moment, and then nodded slowly. "Sometimes. I never did. But…the thoughts were there." He stopped, but I had a feeling he wasn't finished, so I didn't say anything. After a while, he went on, "I was mad when you guys sent me to Dr. Sandler. I thought you thought I was crazy or something. But she made me realize there really was something wrong, and that it wasn't my fault, it was just something I needed help to work through." He paused, swallowing. "You and Mom gave enough of a shit to send me to her. So yeah, you helped."

"Of course we gave a shit," I said. "You're our son. We love you."

"I know." He smiled faintly. "I wasn't trying to shut you out. I promise."

"I can see that now." I watched him for a moment, and then cautiously asked, "And Dr. Sandler knows, right?"

"That I'm gay?"

"Yeah."

He nodded again. "I didn't tell her for a long time because I thought she'd tell you and Mom, but when I realized she'd only tell if she thought I was going to hurt myself or someone else, then yeah. I told her."

"Good." I swallowed. "I'm glad you were able to tell someone." I couldn't even be upset with April for outing me to Mark. Though I'd asked her to give me time, since I wasn't ready to talk to my sons about this, she'd gone ahead and told him. If she'd known about him—that he was gay, that his sexuality was the reason for so many of these walls between us—then she must've known what she was doing.

"Does Mom know?" I asked.

"No." Mark shook his head. "How do you think she'd react?"

"I can't imagine she'd react any differently than I did. If anything, she's been as worried as I have about you."

He winced. "I'm sorry."

"Don't be sorry. I just wish we'd made it clearer that you had no reason to hide this from us."

"Does she know about you?"

"No. I never told her, and I don't think she knows I'm seeing anyone."

"Think you'll ever tell her?"

I pursed my lips, then shrugged. "Haven't really gotten that far, to be honest. Maybe someday."

He seemed satisfied with that answer and didn't push the issue. Right then, our food came, and as we ate, we continued into lighter subjects. The whole time, though, my mind kept going back to everything we'd admitted since we'd sat down. It killed me to know just what he'd been suffering through all these years, but in a way, it was a huge relief to hear it. To be having a conversation like this at all, listening to my son open up to me about things that were difficult to hear, was a big improvement from trying to chip away at the stubborn silence.

After the waitress had taken our plates, Mark laid his napkin beside his drink. "So, um." He drummed his fingers rapidly on the table. "Maybe we could meet up for dinner or something. With both of our guys. I'd kind of like you to meet Devon."

"Yeah, we can do that." I paused. "I mean, let me see how Sailo feels about it."

"Sailo?" A faint grin played at his lips. "That's his name?"

I nodded. "He's Samoan."

"Cool. What does he do?"

"He's a deejay."

"A deejay?" Mark laughed. "That doesn't seem like your type."

"Oh yeah?" I raised my eyebrows. "What kind of 'type' do you think I have?"

"I don't know. Before April said something, I didn't think you'd be into guys, so I guess…I don't know. But…a deejay? Really?"

I shrugged. "You just never know who you'll stumble into, right?"

"Yeah, that's true."

"What about yours? What does he do?"

Mark smiled shyly. "He's a musician."

"What kind? He in a band or something?"

He chuckled, shaking his head. "First chair violin at the university."

"Oh. *That* kind of musician."

"Yeah. That kind. He's going to school on a full ride." Mark beamed with pride. "He's really talented."

"Wow. He must be. So, that's what he's going to do professionally?"

Mark nodded. "I mean, he's doing a double major, and he's planning to get an MBA so at least he has a fallback."

"An MBA is a pretty ambitious fallback plan."

"Right? But he figures if he's got that, he'll be in good shape if he can't land a symphony gig that pays well enough."

"Smart man."

Mark grinned. "He is."

"How long have you two been dating?"

"About a year."

"Wow. I had no idea."

"I know." Mark's good spirits dimmed a little. "I wanted to tell you and Mom about him, but…"

"No, I understand. I'm just glad you're telling me now." I smiled. "He obviously makes you happy."

Once again, his face lit up with a shy but heartfelt smile, and he nodded. "He does."

"Good. I'm, um, assuming this is pretty serious, then?"

"Yeah. We've talked about getting a place together. Probably this summer."

I smiled. "Well, if you need help moving, give me a call."

"Really?"

"Sure."

"Cool. Thanks."

"So how did the two of you meet, anyway?"

"Well, we were taking a history class together…"

As he told me the story of how a study group turned into missing class because they were too busy talking over coffee, I couldn't help getting an odd little thrill out of casually chatting with Mark about our respective boyfriends. Just having a candid conversation like this, talking happily about boyfriends as if neither of us had ever had a reason to hide who we were from each other, was such an enormous relief, I was almost giddy from it.

I studied him for a moment. "How long has your sister known? About you?"

"A few years. Kurt knows too."

"Oh. Good. Good, I'm glad you were able to be open to them." I just wish you could've been open with me. "Have they met your boyfriend?"

"April has." He laughed. "She keeps joking that Nathan is going to leave her for Devon—get the two of them together, they never shut up about music."

"We might have to pry him and Sailo apart, then. He's pretty passionate about his music too."

"Cool. Can't wait to meet him."

"Likewise."

I paid for lunch, and we left the table. Outside, we paused. This was where we'd normally have a tense, muttered good-bye, but the air between us had shifted dramatically since I'd sat down at the booth. I wasn't sure what to expect now.

"Well, I should go," he said finally. "Thanks for lunch." And then, for the first time in years, my son hugged me.

I held him tight, willing myself not to break down despite the tremendous relief. "I'm sorry if I ever made you feel like I'd be disappointed in you." I forced my voice to remain even. "I mean it—all I've ever wanted is for you kids to be happy."

"I know," he whispered. Drawing back, he said, "Let me know about dinner?"

"Absolutely. I'm looking forward to it."

"Me too."

We exchanged smiles, and then he headed toward his car. Halfway to it, he paused, looked back, and waved.

I returned it and started toward my office, my head spinning as I thought about everything we'd discussed. Of all the scenarios I'd played out in my head before we'd sat down, this was the furthest from what I'd expected. I'd never guessed he was gay. And I'd sure as hell never guessed he had any reason to believe I'd be disappointed in him if he was.

All the way back to my office, I was grinning like an idiot. We hadn't talked that much in ages, and it felt good not to be so far away from him anymore. It would take time to knock down the rest of the walls, but it was a damned good start. Even knowing how serious his depression was felt like a positive step—maybe now that I knew, I could help somehow. At least be there for him. And for God's sake, he was talking to me about it.

Opening up. Not ashamed of his depression or his sexuality, despite what the demons in his head told him.

It was a start. I'd take it.

At my desk, I pulled my phone out of my pocket and was about to put it beside my computer where I always left it when I was working.

But then I paused. And pulled it back.

I pulled up April's number. After a long moment of hesitation, I wrote out a text:

Thank you for telling Mark. Love you.

Chapter Twenty-Three

The night of our double date, I picked up Sailo, drove us to the U-district. A few blocks away from the restaurant where we'd meet Mark, I parked, paid for a few hours just in case we decided to stay late, and we strolled up the road to the agreed-upon place.

As the restaurant came into view, its bright blue sign standing out from the overcast sky, I slowed, then stopped.

Sailo turned to me. "What's wrong?"

"I…" I glanced at the restaurant, then faced him. "Are you sure about this?"

"Sure." Sailo started to reach for me, but then looked around and withdrew his hand. "We both know what it's like, trying to come out. If this makes it easier for your son to come out? Hell yeah, I'm in."

"I appreciate it. But I don't want to ask too much of *you*. We just started seeing each other a little while ago, and—"

"Relax. If you'd tossed this at me the night we met? Yeah, that might've been a bit much. But we've been out a few times. We're getting to know each other. Meeting each other's kids… I'm okay with that." He chewed his lip.

"Maybe not my kid yet. He's a bit young to understand how all this works."

"He knows you date men, though, right?"

"Oh yeah, yeah." Sailo shifted his weight. "But I prefer to wait until I've been with someone for a while. So he doesn't get, you know, attached."

In case things go to shit, I thought with a pang of dread in my gut.

"That makes sense," I said quietly. "My kids are old enough to understand. Plus they've already been through the divorce, so…" I waved a hand. "Anyway. I really do appreciate you coming tonight. As long as you really are comfortable with it."

Sailo smiled. "Completely."

"Okay." I took a deep breath and squared my shoulders. "Well. Let's do this."

"Let's do it."

We exchanged one more long look and then continued up the sidewalk.

The restaurant—apparently one of Mark's favorites—was as bright on the inside as it was on the outside. Nearly everything was some shade of blue, aside from the multicolored tablecloths and the matching aprons worn by the staff. The second I walked in, I was greeted by a warm gust of about half a dozen different spices. A little bit of garlic, a little bit of rosemary, and several others, all combining for a pleasant, aromatic air. I couldn't remember if I'd been hungry before we arrived, or if I'd been too nervous for that, but I sure as hell was now.

As my eyes adjusted to the slightly dimmer lighting, I saw Mark waving from a few tables away. Sailo and I made our way over, and I introduced them.

"Sailo, this is my son, Mark. Mark, Sailo."

They shook hands over the table, and Sailo and I took our seats.

"Devon should be here soon." Mark checked the time on his phone. "He had class this afternoon, and that prof always runs late."

"No problem," I said. "I don't think we're in any hurry."

"Definitely not." Sailo picked up one of the blue leather menus. "But we may need to order whatever I'm smelling as an appetizer or something, because goddamn."

Mark laughed. "I've had almost everything on the menu. It all tastes as good as it smells."

"Yeah?" Sailo glanced at him. "Anything you recommend?"

"Well…" Mark gestured at the menu. Sailo laid it down and turned it so they could both read it, and they hunched over it, analyzing and discussing every appetizer.

For my part, I just watched them in disbelief. My boyfriend and my son? Chatting easily over menu items? Somehow, I'd convinced myself they'd be standoffish and awkward at first, but so far, so good.

I was absolutely grateful for Sailo's presence, though admittedly, I still wasn't sure how I felt about tonight's arrangement. This was something I'd never imagined in a million years—having dinner with my son and both our boyfriends.

But…so far, so good.

While we perused the menu and discussed the various items Mark had and hadn't tried, his eyes kept flicking toward the door. Whenever it opened, he sat up a little. Then a second later, he'd relax.

Shortly after we'd ordered our drinks and a plate of bacon-wrapped dates, he glanced at the door, but this time, his face lit up with the brightest smile I'd seen on him in years. "There he is."

I turned, and immediately homed in on the guy in question. A gorgeous African-American guy was striding toward us, eyes locked on Mark with the same smile on his lips. And I had to say—my son had damned good taste in men. Devon's black hair had been divided into braids, the longest of which were loosely tied together at the base of his neck while some of the shorter ones hung beside his face. He was tall, fit, and he had a warm, infectious smile.

As Devon approached, Mark said, "So, um, this is Devon. Devon, my dad, Greg, and his boyfriend, Sailo."

Everyone shook hands. As Devon sat beside Mark, they shared a quick peck on the lips before Devon turned to flag down the waitress.

With our drinks on the table and his on the way, we all faced each other.

Okay. Here goes. Same-sex double date. With my son.

Devon leaned forward, peering at Sailo's arm. "That's some great line work. Who's your artist?"

"A friend in California." Sailo pulled his sleeve up, revealing more of the intricate tattoo.

"Polynesian, right?"

Sailo nodded. "Samoan."

"It's great work."

"Thanks."

While they scrutinized Sailo's ink, I turned to Mark. "So, how long before *you* start getting tattooed?"

His cheeks colored, and he sheepishly lowered his gaze. "Uh…"

I chuckled. "You already have one, don't you?"

Avoiding my eyes, he raised three fingers.

"Three?" My jaw dropped. "This from the kid who broke out in hives at the sight of a needle?"

"Well, to be fair," Sailo broke in, "they're not quite the same thing."

"Exactly," Mark said.

"And to be even fairer"—Sailo smirked—"those silly tattoo needles they use here have nothing on the ones they used on me." He leaned back and lifted his shirt just enough to reveal a few lines of his big tattoo. "*This* was a painful tattoo."

Mark gulped, eyes widening.

Devon craned his neck. "Wow. That is some sick work. How long did it take?"

"A long, long time." Sailo pulled his shirt back down and reached for his drink. "A lot of very long sessions over the course of a few years."

"And they do that the traditional way, right?" Devon made a gesture like he was holding a pencil and poking the air with it. "One dot at a time?"

"Yep." Sailo took a drink, and I thought he shuddered. "One. Dot. At a time."

"*No* thanks," Mark said. "Mine were painful enough."

"Speaking of." I shot him a playfully scrutinizing look. "What tattoos do you have?"

He twisted slightly and pulled up his T-shirt sleeve, revealing a hand of playing cards—a royal flush—about the size of his palm on his upper arm. "Got that one last year." Then the turned the other way and pulled up his other sleeve to show an elaborate Celtic design. As he fixed his shirt, he met my gaze uncertainly. Gesturing at his back, he said, "And then I have an eagle between my shoulder blades, but it isn't done yet."

"What I've seen so far is nice work," I said. "When were you going to show your mom and me?"

"Uh, well." He cleared his throat. "Eventually?"

I laughed. "Fair enough. They are pretty nice, though."

"So you don't disapprove?"

"Does it matter if I do?" I raised my glass. "You're an adult."

"Sometimes," Devon muttered.

"Hey!" Mark elbowed him. "You're not helping."

They tried to glare at each other but burst out laughing. Devon patted Mark's hand on the table, and then kept it there. They laced their fingers together, Devon's dark skin and Mark's fair skin contrasting dramatically on top of the multicolored tablecloth. Neither seemed the least bit self-conscious about showing affection in public. For that, I envied both of them.

"So," Sailo said to Devon. "Greg says you're a musician?"

Devon nodded. "Since I was seven."

"Oh really?" Sailo said. "My son's six, and I think he might have some aptitude. I'm just worried about starting him too young."

"I don't think you have to worry about starting music lessons young," Devon said. "Just don't *push* him at that age. I know a lot of kids from my music school who were burned out by fourteen because they had to practice three hours a day." He scowled, shaking his head, which made a couple of his braids bounce against his cheek. "They probably hate music now."

"Your parents didn't push like that?" I asked.

"Nah. They made me practice, but I still got to go play with the other kids, do sports, all of that. I stuck with the music because I enjoyed it, not because they made me." He turned to Sailo. "Any idea what instrument he might want to try?"

"Don't know yet." Sailo shrugged. "Maybe I'll let him try a few and see if he likes one better than the others."

"That's how Dad did it with us," Mark said. "The music shops that do rentals will let you try them out."

"Good idea," Sailo said.

As they continued talking about various instruments and difficulty levels, I slung my arm across the back of Sailo's chair, resting my hand on his shoulder, and for a while, just watched the three of them interacting. The conversation still registered, and whenever anyone asked me something, I responded without missing a beat, but for the most part, I was watching. Taking it all in.

Sitting here at a café table with our boyfriends was mind-blowing. Even when neither of us were speaking, just being here like this—my arm behind Sailo, Mark's fingers loosely intertwined with Devon's between their menus—was the most open and honest my son and I had been with each other in years.

Every time Mark stole a glance at Devon and smiled, my heart sped up. That was exactly the way April had looked at Nathan when they were first together, and I caught myself hoping and praying Mark had found someone as amazing as the man his sister had married. As far as I was concerned, all my kids deserved nothing less than the best partners, and especially after all the hell Mark had been through—hiding his sexuality, battling that godawful depression—I hoped he'd found the man he deserved.

They were young, I reminded myself, and they'd only been together a year. Even if there was talk of moving in together, things like this didn't always last. But for the moment, they really did seem deeply, genuinely happy. What more could a father ask for?

A close relationship with his son, for one thing. But that was finally happening. Out of nowhere, prompted by the last thing I'd expected, we were here. He was smiling. He was *talking*. I tried not to think about how many more years he would've stayed distant and silent if his mother and I had stayed married. What would have finally pushed him to come out and tell us he was gay. He'd kept it quiet all this time. How much longer could that have gone on?

Though my divorce still hurt, I was thankful for it today. I'd found my way to Sailo, and that had brought me closer to Mark.

Absently stroking Sailo's shoulder through his shirt, I couldn't help thinking that maybe the divorce had been a blessing in disguise after all. Sailo was in my life now. My son and I had found some common ground I'd never imagined we'd have. I was being open and honest with myself about who I was attracted to. About who I was.

Though it still scared me to be starting over a whole lot later in life than I would've liked, maybe this would all work out for the better after all.

After dinner, we left the restaurant and lingered outside for a few minutes. I wouldn't have objected to staying until the place shut down, but everyone had places to be early in the morning, so we called it a night. Mark hugged me again. We shook hands with each other's respective boyfriends, and then headed off in separate directions.

A few steps from the door, I paused and turned back. For a moment, I watched them walking away, hand in hand on their way down the thinly-crowded sidewalk. Admittedly, I envied them. Though Mark had been nervous about coming out to me, he and his boyfriend obviously didn't mind people knowing they were a couple. The way they kept smiling at each other, I wasn't even sure they were aware there were other people around to notice them in the first place.

"You okay?" Sailo asked.

I turned to him, and the instant our eyes met, I smiled like Mark had been smiling at Devon. "Yeah. I'm good."

He didn't question. He just returned the smile, sending shivers down my spine and adding to that giddiness in my stomach.

I gave Mark and Devon one last glance, and then we headed toward my car.

As we walked, neither of us said anything. The silence was comfortable and pleasant—two people enjoying each other's company without the need to fill the space with anything. My heart was still going a million miles an hour.

Our fingers brushed, sending a tingle right through me. I glanced at him, and when he met my eyes, he smiled. Without a word, I slipped my hand into his. He splayed his fingers, letting me lace mine in between, and we both gently closed our hands.

We glanced at each other. Smiled.

And, holding hands in public for the first time, continued down the sidewalk.

Chapter Twenty-Four

From the time we left the parking lot until we made it back to my apartment, everything was kind of a blur. My mind was beyond overwhelmed, and I was lucky I remembered how to drive.

We made it in one piece, though, and the silence that had been between us since we left the restaurant stayed with us all the way up to my third-floor apartment.

In my narrow kitchen, we cracked open a couple of beers and leaned against the counters on opposite sides. The silence lingered, but it was comfortable. Contemplative, not awkward.

"Thinking about your son?" he asked after a while.

I nodded. "How'd you guess?"

"Had a hunch. He seemed pretty happy tonight."

"Yeah." I released a long breath. "He really, really did." I reached up to rub my neck, wondering how long it would stay this tense now that the evening was over. "I know he's still dealing with depression, and he always will, but damn, it was good to see him that happy tonight."

"I imagine this was a huge weight off his chest."

Rolling my stiff shoulders, I sagged against the counter. "I just wish I'd known about it. I hate that he had to carry it by himself all this time." My heart clenched just thinking about it. Swallowing hard, I met Sailo's gaze. "He's got enough to deal with, you know? Feeling like he has to keep that kind of secret from his parents…"

"You couldn't have known." Sailo slid his hands over my waist. "You'll just drive yourself crazy trying to change the past, but the good thing is, the future's going to be better."

"Yeah." I swallowed hard. "Better late than never, right?"

"Absolutely."

"And it really, really was good to see him like that. Devon seems like a pretty good guy."

"He does. That must be a huge relief."

"God, yes." I smiled. "There's nothing better than realizing your kid's found a good partner. My daughter's husband is amazing, and so far, Devon is checking all the right boxes."

"I can only imagine." He laughed. "I don't think I have to worry about it for a few years."

"No, I guess you don't. But, uh, when you get there—buckle up. That's a hell of a ride when your kid starts dating."

He shuddered. "I don't even want to think about it. I think I'm still traumatized from realizing my boy is old enough to be in kindergarten."

"Yeah. Just like my granddaughter. So, tell me about it."

He chuckled, drawing me in closer. "I haven't dated many guys who can commiserate about parenthood."

"That makes two of us. This is, um, my first time dating someone who's already a parent too."

"First time for both of us, then." He tipped up my chin, and when our eyes met, he smiled. After a second, I did too. Then he gathered me in his arms and pressed a soft kiss to my lips.

I had a feeling he'd only meant for something short and sweet, a show of gentle affection and nothing more, but he made no move to pull away, and neither did I. For a moment, it was only our lips. Before long, though, he tilted his head and parted his lips, so I did the same and was rewarded with the tip of his tongue. Holding him tighter, I let him deepen the kiss.

We separated at one point and met each other's eyes. My pulse was thumping, my knees shaking, and what a relief when he drew me back in and picked up right where we'd left off.

"Didn't think you'd be in the mood for anything," he whispered breathlessly against my lips.

"Didn't either." I slid my hands over his ass and pulled him to me. "But you're here, so…of course I'm in the mood."

Sailo laughed softly and kissed me again. "In that case"—he pressed his hardening dick against mine—"maybe we should go someplace more comfortable."

"Good idea."

I lost track of time and hands, of what we were doing besides kissing and holding on to each other. One minute we were making out in the doorway. The next, we were naked beneath my sheets.

I was horny as hell, but not in the slightest hurry. I was never in a hurry with him. How could I be? I ran my hands over his ass, his sides, his thighs, my fingertips tracing the raised lines of his distinctive tattoo, every bump and contour of which seemed to spell out his name in my mind. Somewhere along the line, the novelty of having sex with a man had diminished, replaced by the thrill of having sex with *this* man. With Sailo.

"Why would I be in any rush?" I remembered him saying that first night. *"I've already got what I want."*

"Do you?"

"Yeah. You in my bed."

Likewise, Sailo. My God.

Oh, but even if I wasn't in a rush, that wasn't to say our kissing and touching lacked any sense of urgency. I was hungry for him, desperate for him, and having his naked body and rock-hard erection against me aroused me to the point I wanted to beg him for release, except that would mean I'd have to stop kissing him.

He stopped kissing me, though, and pushed himself up. "I didn't think you'd be in the mood tonight," he panted, "but I am really glad you are." He pressed his dick against me for emphasis. "Because I really want to fuck you."

I licked my lips. "Then why aren't you?"

His eyebrows flicked up. For a split second, I thought that might've come out as too demanding or too needy or…something, but he grinned and leaned down to brush his lips across mine.

"Turn around," he ordered as he lifted up again and reached for the nightstand. "I gotta fuck you before I go crazy."

Before you *go crazy?*

Didn't matter who was going crazy first. He was putting on a condom, and I was getting on my hands and knees as ordered, and now he was going for the lube…

I gripped the sheets, digging my fingers into the mattress and my teeth into my bottom lip. *Hurry up. Please. God, I want you.*

Finally, he knelt behind me. The lube bottle clicked, and the cool, slippery contact of his fingers made me grind my teeth with frustration.

C'mon…

He didn't waste much time, thank fuck. I was used to bottoming now, so he didn't have to do near as much prep anymore. Without the nerves, without anticipating pain, I relaxed much more easily. All he had to do with his fingers was put on a little bit of lube, just a few gentle strokes to make sure there wasn't enough friction to be unpleasant, and then he started pressing his cock in, and I…

Sweet Jesus.

I was in heaven.

His thick cock, slippery with exactly the right amount of lube, slid in and out, turning my vision white and electrifying every nerve ending in my body. Times like this, I didn't care if he never let me top him again as long as he kept topping me.

With his body weight, he guided me all the way down to the mattress. Yes. Oh yes. This was rapidly becoming one of my favorite things, when he pinned me down so I couldn't move, not with his body molded to mine, but he didn't have that problem. He rode me with slow, gentle strokes, holding me close and kissing the side of my neck as he moved inside me.

I was pressed too hard into the mattress to stroke my cock with my hand, but this—rubbing against the sheet with every motion of his hips—was almost better than what I could do for myself anyway. Gripping the headboard, squeezing my eyes shut, I just lay there, and he drove himself into me again and again and again, and I could do nothing but enjoy the ride and building orgasm.

"Gonna come," I breathed.

"I know." He thrust just a little bit harder. "I can…feel it."

I suddenly remembered the way he'd felt when our roles had been reversed, and he'd clenched around my cock just before his climax, and that was all it took.

"*Oh God!*"

He cried out too, and he fell apart, and I fell apart, and his rhythm fell apart. He fucked me painfully hard now, driving my orgasm on and on and on until I was pretty sure I blacked out for a few seconds.

As he shuddered to a stop, panting against my shoulder, my vision started clearing. With a shaking hand, I wiped my eyes. Jesus. He'd made me come so hard, I'd teared up. As the spinning room slowed around me, I was actually a little surprised he hadn't made me break down sobbing—it was just so damned intense, so amazing, I was *that* overwhelmed.

"Fuck," he breathed against my neck, pausing to press a soft kiss below my ear. "I didn't think I could come that hard."

"Makes two of us." I was amazed I could form words. Turning my head toward him, I added, "Funny what happens when you started fucking me."

He laughed, the rush of cooler breath giving me goose bumps, and he kissed me once more. Then he withdrew carefully. As he got up to get rid of the condom, I rolled onto my back.

God. This man. The sex we had. I closed my eyes and grinned like a fool. If this didn't make up for some of the recent bullshit in my life, I didn't know what did.

As his soft footsteps came back from the bathroom, I turned my head and smiled up at him. He returned it, settling into bed beside me, and without a word, we wrapped our arms around each other. Like we often did, we lay there for a while, just kissing lazily and enjoying the delicious afterglow. No wonder I was hooked on him—I'd forgotten what it was like to be affectionate and cuddly after sex.

Eventually, we rested our heads on the pillows and gazed at each other.

"So, you feel better about things?" he asked. "After this evening?"

"Definitely." I smoothed his hair. "About everything. My son. Getting over the divorce." I smiled. "You."

He lifted himself up on his arm. "Me?"

"Yeah." I let my fingers drift down the side of his face and neck. "I just…I don't know. Feel like I have a better handle on things these days. My relationships with my kids. Who I am. And, yeah, what we're doing."

His Adam's apple bobbed, but his expression registered nothing. "What exactly *are* we doing?"

I thought about it for a moment, then shook my head. "Hell, maybe I don't really know. I guess I just feel less like

I'm flailing my way through this than I did in the beginning."

He pursed his lips and shrugged. "Fair enough. It is still a rebound, though. And something completely new for you."

"I know." I traced his jaw with my thumb. "But I don't think any of that is the kiss of death. Some things just…work."

His eyebrows rose slightly. Some unspoken thought creased his forehead and tightened his features.

"What?" I asked.

He took a breath. Hesitated. Then clasped my hand gently and kissed my palm. "You're right. Some things do work."

"That first night I came to Wilde's," I whispered, lacing our fingers together, "I just wanted to see if I really was into men. I didn't expect…this."

Something flickered across his expression, but it was gone so fast I might've imagined it. He gently freed his hand and rested it on the side of my neck. "I keep wondering, though—what *is* this?"

"Like I said, I don't know." I swallowed. "I don't feel like I'm flailing anymore, but everything we've been doing since day one has been pretty new to me."

Sailo's lips pressed together, and he nodded. "I guess it would be. Since you hadn't dated anyone in so long. And you'd never dated a man."

"Yeah. But it's…" I held his gaze as I searched for the words. How did I explain that this wasn't just different from what I expected, it was more. So, so much more. It had quite by accident brought me closer to my kids. It had given me hope that divorcing this late in the game didn't mean I was out of luck. But there were all these feelings too. The way my heart fluttered whenever I was around him. How his text tone was enough to shake me out of a bad mood, and how much I just plain looked forward to being in the same room with him.

I swept my tongue across my lips and whispered, "It's just better than anything I expected when I walked in that night."

He smiled, a hint of shyness in his expression. "Glad it hasn't been a disappointment."

"Not at all." I ran my fingers through his hair. "When I went to Wilde's that first night, I had no idea what I was getting myself into."

He laughed softly. "Guess you picked the right door to lean against."

"Guess so."

We held each other's gazes for a moment. Then he said, "We should get some sleep. You have to be up early."

"Unfortunately." I cupped his face and pressed my lips to his. "Good night."

"Good night."

Sailo rested his head on my shoulder as he often did when we first went to bed. He was out cold in no time, and I wasn't far behind. As fatigue kicked in and I started fading, I kissed the top of his head, lay back on the pillow, and closed my eyes.

I knew eventually we'd separate and wind up on opposite sides of the mattress, but for now, he was snoozing peacefully with his head on my chest, and I was in no hurry to put a stop to that.

I loved this. I loved everything about it.

And couldn't wait to see where things went from here.

Chapter Twenty-Five

I was tired as hell at work the next day, but it was worth it. Fortunately, everyone was always dragging at the office because we had to be there so damned early, and Monday mornings were especially brutal.

During lunch, Sailo texted me as he often did.

Have to be at Wilde's at 8—drinks at 5?

As if he had to ask. I always loved meeting him before work. Even if we didn't have time to fool around—though we sometimes did—just seeing him was enough to make my day.

We agreed on a wine bar a few blocks from Wilde's. Wine bars were a little hoity-toity for my taste, but the place was quiet and the drinks were decent, so at five o'clock sharp, I met him there. When I walked in, I immediately zeroed in on him at a high table near the back. He met my gaze, but only for a second, and the faintest smile just barely registered on his lips before it vanished without a trace.

My stomach tightened. That was unusual. But hey, he was entitled to off days just like the rest of us. Maybe he was tired, or he'd had a long day. So I tried not to worry about it as I crossed the floor and took the seat opposite his.

Neither of us said much. I ordered a drink. He already had one. After mine came, we still stayed quiet, and the longer that went on, the more restless I became.

Throughout my marriage, I'd avoided breaking uncomfortable silences. Too often "What's wrong?" turned into a fight over something stupid. Looking back, it was my own damned fault for letting the quiet linger until the frustration had festered. She could've come to me when she was upset, but I should've seen the signs sooner too.

Though there was no changing the past, I could at least try not to repeat the same mistakes in the future.

Steeling myself, I put my hand over Sailo's. "You okay? You're kind of quiet tonight."

He watched our hands for a moment. Then, slowly, he pulled his back and released a long breath. "I think we need to talk."

My gut clenched. Those six words had been the start of my marital supernova, and nothing about his tone suggested that this conversation was going to be any more enjoyable. I wanted to reach for his arm, but the tension in his shoulders made me wonder if he'd recoil. "Okay. What about?"

"Us. What we're doing." He kept his eyes down. "Whether or not we should keep doing it."

My throat tightened. "Should we?"

"Well, I…" Sailo looked away for a moment, fixing his gaze on something across the room before he finally faced me again. "Look, you're a great guy. Really. And we've definitely had some fun together. But I think…I think I need to call time on this."

"What?" My heart dropped into my feet. I sat up. "Sailo, we—"

"Listen to me," he pleaded softly. "This isn't going to work."

"But…how can you know that? We just got started."

"I know, and it's…I mean, it's a rebound, and things like that, they…" He pushed out a long breath and met my eyes. "I've had a few rebounds, and I've been a rebound a few times myself. Sometimes it works, but usually, they go too fast, they get too intense, and then they blow up." His brow pinched slightly as he added, "And it's your first time with a man. You haven't played the field. How can you possibly know I'm what you want in a man?"

I stared at him. "How…I…"

"I'm glad I was able to introduce you to gay sex," he went on. "I'm glad I was able to make your first experiences good." He'd been rehearsing this, hadn't he? "But that doesn't mean this is going to last forever. And I can't just throw myself into relationships that I know aren't going to work. I've got a kid to think about."

"I've got kids to think about too."

He shook his head. "Mine is too young to understand relationships. He gets that I like men, and that his moms like women, but he's way too young to get his head around this kind of thing."

"What kind of thing exactly? I'm not following."

Sailo pursed his lips and lowered his gaze. Then he said, "I don't want him to get attached to you—to us as a couple—only to have me turn around and explain to him why you're gone."

"Why *I'm* gone?" I blinked. "You're the one putting on the brakes here, if I'm not mistaken."

"Because I have to," he whispered. "I'd rather end it now than after we're both in over our heads."

Oh, it's too late for that.

I blew out a breath. "This is so out of left field. I…I don't even know what to say."

"I know. And I'm sorry. I…to be honest, my first thought was that we didn't need to stop. We could just, you know, take it back a step. But…" He swallowed. "I'm sorry, Greg. I'm not doing this to hurt you. I just… I need to protect myself. And my kid." He set his shoulders back, as if steeling himself. "I can't take the risk that I'm your red sports car."

"My red—what?"

"Your midlife crisis. Your experiment. The red sports car you buy so you can have your twenties back, and you sell by winter because you realize…" He shifted, his features tightening as he looked away. "Because you realize how impractical it is, and sell your toy for something more mature and reasonable."

I gaped at him, barely comprehending what he was trying to say. What he thought I felt about him. "Sailo, you were a fling and an experiment…maybe for the first *week*. It's been different ever since then." *Hasn't it?*

He didn't speak. I didn't know what to say. Panic surged through my veins—what the hell *could* I say to stop this? How did I explain to him that this was like nothing I'd ever experienced? I couldn't change the way I felt about him.

Maybe I was in over my head, but I liked it.

"We can't keep doing this," he said.

"Have I done something wrong?" I asked. "Is it… I mean, did—"

"No. No." He put up his hands and shook his head. "Honestly, you're a great guy. Anyone would be lucky to have you. But this… It's just too fast. Too intense. It's going to blow up in our faces."

"Isn't that what it's doing right now?" More venom than I intended slipped into my voice, and I quickly added, "We can slow things down, can't we?"

"I don't think it works that way."

I paused to collect my thoughts. After a deep breath, I looked him in the eye. "Look, I get it. I know rebound relationships usually don't work, but sometimes they do. You don't want to give this a chance to—"

"I don't want to give it a chance to crash and burn like I'm ninety-nine percent sure it will." He set his jaw and sat a little straighter. "The odds are just not in our favor, and I don't want to get hurt like that again."

"Sailo, I don't want to hurt you."

"I know you don't. But, I mean, you said yourself you're not sure if you're gay or bi." His brow pinched as he shook his head. "How can you be sure of what's going on between us? You don't even know who *you* are, Greg."

"No, but I know I love you."

We both froze. His eyes widened, and I cringed, instantly regretting the words.

"Shit, I—"

"This is exactly what I'm talking about." He deflated a bit as he sat back. "We met, what, two or three *weeks* after your wife kicked you out after twenty-five *years*? And not only that, I'm the first man you've ever been with." His eyebrows knitted together as he looked me right in the eye. "Do you really think something like this is going to last?"

"Is there any reason why it can't?"

He exhaled hard, lowering his gaze as he reached up to rub his neck. "I've been someone's rebound before. And I've been someone's first before. It's never ended well." Sighing, he met my gaze again. "Being a rebound *and* your first? That deck is stacked against us. Has been from day one."

I opened my mouth to speak, but Sailo continued.

"I was perfectly happy being your rebound and showing you what it's like to be a man, but I don't think either of us had any illusions about this turning into more."

"Because I didn't know it was possible to feel like this," I said. "About anyone."

Sailo flinched, breaking eye contact. "You're not in love with me. You're in love with your new freedom and with everything we've done together." His lips were tight, his eyes pained, as he looked at me and whispered, "You're in love with being alive again."

"What? How the hell can you tell me what I'm feeling?"

He rubbed the bridge of his nose, sighing heavily. Lowering his hand, he met my gaze again. "It's obvious from where I'm sitting. You're infatuated with me because you've been able to have something with me you didn't have before. But when you figure out that I'm too young, or you're not over your ex-wife enough for a real relationship—where does that leave me?"

"Couldn't any relationship blow up in your face? Or mine?"

"Of course." He slid his thumbs into the pockets of his shorts. "But I don't like to play unless I think the odds are at least slightly in my favor, and this…" He exhaled hard. "Look, I was okay with this turning into a relationship eventually, but it's gotten too intense too fast. And that's never a good sign. So, I need to stop before it crashes. Because I don't want to be there when you wake up one morning, realize this is a rebound and a midlife crisis, and send me packing."

For a moment, I couldn't even pull in a breath. My brain frantically tried to make sense of everything he'd said in between panicking that he was ending things. "Do you really think that's what's going to happen?"

"Do you really think it isn't?" He put up a hand. "We agreed at the start to take things slow and see what happened. And they've…happened a lot faster than they should have." He grimaced. "Too fast for me to believe this has any kind of staying power."

That hit me in the balls.

"Sailo—"

"I don't doubt for a second that you're sincere. What you feel… I know you're not just blowing smoke. But you're not in love with me. You're in love with getting over your wife. You'd feel the same about any man who happened to be in my place right now." He shrugged tightly, maybe a little apologetically. "And I just don't want to wait around for you to figure that out and kick me to the curb."

"So you're kicking *me* to the curb?"

"I'm nipping this in the bud before we both get hurt." He put up his hands. "I can't do this. I'm sorry."

"Sailo…"

"I'm sorry," he said again. "I need to go."

My throat tightened.

He reached for me like he was going to touch my arm, but then apparently thought better of it and pulled his hand back. Folding them tightly in his lap, he said, "This is going to hurt. And I really am sorry. I'm not doing this because I want to hurt you. But give it some time, and you'll understand why I can't stay, and why we can't keep doing this."

"My ex-wife said something similar as she was showing me to the door of my own house," I said through my teeth.

Sailo's brow creased. "This is kind of my point, actually. You're not over her. And you're not in love with me." He inched away, paused, and then rose. "I'm really sorry. I have to do this, though."

He got up and started to go.

"Wait."

He turned around, eyebrows up, but didn't speak.

I swept my tongue across my lips. "Are you really telling me this is all…me?" I tried to keep the anger and hurt out of my voice, but it was a struggle. "You don't feel anything?"

Sailo met my gaze, and the intensity in his eyes nearly drove me back a step. "Don't put words in my mouth. I never said I didn't feel anything."

Before I could make sense of it, before I could extract a response from my stunned brain, he turned again, and he didn't stop this time. As he walked away, I stared at his back, my mouth dry and my mind reeling as I tried to come up with some argument to make him stay.

But nothing came. All I could think was what if he was right? What if this was just a midlife crisis? Maybe a rebound-induced need to reinvent myself from the ground up?

The door opened.

Closed.

And he was gone.

I slumped back against the back of my chair, all the breath leaving my lungs at once. My head spun as I stared at the empty glass and the empty seat and the empty space between here and the door.

No. No way. He was completely wrong.

Wasn't he?

If I wasn't in love with him, then what the hell was I feeling?

My heart sank deeper in my chest.

What if he *was* right? Sure, the attraction to men had been there all along, but I'd never been unhappy being with a woman. Was I just doing this to get over my divorce?

Was Sailo my red sports car? My much-younger rebound?

And if he was, why did it hurt so much to watch him go?

Chapter Twenty-Six

I didn't sleep that night. At work the next morning, I was a zombie—physically there, mentally elsewhere. Even as I went through the motions of my day, Sailo's departure was never far from my mind, and I couldn't get past it.

Every time I replayed my last conversation with Sailo, it made less sense than before. The words all made sense, but the ending didn't. Going our separate ways. Calling this thing a disaster waiting to happen.

No. No, this was the wrong ending. There was no telling if our relationship had the legs to last forever, but now? No. Too soon.

Or maybe I was just out of my fucking head? It had taken time to accept that my marriage was over, so why not this?

By the time I was home from work, I barely remembered anything since that morning. I was vaguely aware that I'd driven to the office, made a valiant attempt to be a decent employee, and slogged through traffic to get home. Now I was here, and still flailing as badly as I'd been last night.

The next day, same shit. The next, again. The one after that, I was up, out the door, and halfway to work through unusually thin traffic before I realized it was Saturday. I didn't even have the energy to feel like an idiot. I just drove home, took off my shoes and tie, and collapsed in bed again.

My ex-wife hadn't turned my world on its head like Sailo had. Maybe this was just because Sailo's departure was so close on the heels of hers—insult to injury, salt in the wound, whatever.

But that didn't make sense. I wasn't thinking about her. I'd more or less made peace with the divorce. I was settling into the life that came after Becky.

After Sailo, though…

God. What do I do?

One thing was for damn sure—I needed some advice from someone whose head was screwed on a little straighter than mine right now. So, I pulled out my phone and scrolled through my contacts, searching for someone wiser and saner than myself.

And the minute I saw Rhett's name, I didn't hesitate to send him a text.

You busy tonight?

He didn't respond. After ten minutes, I decided I'd had my answer. Time to see what Netflix had to offer tonight. Something funny? Maybe a horror movie?

A good twenty minutes later, though, Rhett texted back:

Sorry, didn't hear my phone. Free tonight. What's up?

Oh, thank God. After a few back-and-forth texts, we agreed on a bar a few streets over from his place, and an hour later, Rhett slid into a booth across from me.

"Hey," he said. "How are you doing?"

"I'm all right." *Liar.* "Where's Ethan?"

Rhett chuckled. "Sabrina dragged him out shopping for baby stuff."

"Ethan? Really?"

"Yeah." He shook his head, still laughing. "He made the mistake of telling her he can spot shoddy furniture construction from a mile away, so now he's been recruited to help her furnish the baby's bedroom."

"Poor sap."

"Yep. Teach him to open his big mouth." Grinning wickedly, he added, "I've done my time going to Babies 'R' Us and all that. It's his turn."

"Smart move." I chuckled, but it took some effort.

And judging by the way he eyed me, his grin fading, Rhett heard it.

"Something going on?" he asked. "I get the feeling this isn't just a friendly beer."

"I could, um…" *Why do I feel like such an idiot?* "I think I could use some advice."

"Sure. What about?"

"Well…" I hesitated, struggling to even put the words together. "Sailo and I split up."

"Wow. Really? Shit." He held my gaze for a moment. "What happened?"

"That's the part I'm still trying to figure out." I sat back and told him about Sailo dropping the bomb on me. "Up until that night, everything was great. Shit, we even went on a double date with Mark and his boyfriend the night before."

"With—" Rhett blinked. He put up his hands. "Back up, back up. First, your son is gay?" He lowered his hands again. "And second, you went on a double date with him?"

I nodded. "And then the next day, Sailo…" I gestured in the air, as if to say, *do the math.*

"Out of the blue?"

"Out of the blue." I drew lines in the condensation on my beer glass. "Everything seemed great that night. I mean, it was an awesome night. Not just dinner with my kid, but me and Sailo afterward. It was…" Remembering the sex we'd had prickled my neck with goose bumps and twisted my stomach with renewed sadness. "I thought everything was fine."

"Did he say why?"

"Yeah, he…" A mix of guilt and shame knotted in my gut. Everything was fine? No, it wasn't, and I only had myself to blame. Shoulders sagging, I said, "He said things were moving too fast. That it was doing what rebound relationships do—getting way too intense, way too quickly, which—"

"Inevitably ends in disaster," Rhett said softly.

I nodded again.

He watched me for a moment, absently thumbing the side of his glass. "Was it going too fast?"

"I…" I rubbed my eyes. "Fuck, I don't even know. It *was* moving fast. I just don't know if I agree with him that it was too fast." Lowering my hand, I asked, "How do you even know if it's really too fast?"

Rhett shook his head. "You've got me. Falling for someone usually happens on its own time. Some people take years. Some people take one date."

"And some people think they're falling, but they're really just getting over the person who just dumped them." I lifted my beer glass almost to my lips, and right before I took a deep swallow, grumbled, "Fuck knows how I'm supposed to tell the difference."

"I don't think anyone can tell," he said with a shrug. "The only time you know for sure about a relationship is when you're looking back after it's over."

I raised my eyebrows. "That's a cynical way to look at it."

"Think about it." He wrapped both hands around his beer, his wedding ring clinking quietly against the glass. "How many people are blindsided by divorces and breakups? We all think we've got our shit together, but there's no guarantee that any of us are going to make it to the next anniversary." His shoulder lifted slightly. "I firmly believe Ethan and I will be together until we're dead, but I thought that before we almost called it quits for good. If that separation taught me anything, it's that we can't take a damned thing for granted."

I chewed on that for a moment. "How do you know when to give up and when to try again, though?"

Rhett shook his head again. "I wish I knew. Sometimes you're beating a dead horse. Sometimes you're bringing something back to life that will probably last." He held my gaze. "I guess what you have to think about is what you had before you split. Is having that again worth the risk of another round of feeling like you are now?"

"Yeah," I said without hesitation. "It is. Right now, I just…it doesn't feel *right*."

"That's rough. So are you guys still talking, or…?" His upraised eyebrows finished the question.

Shaking my head, I ran my finger around the rim of my glass. "I don't think so."

"That's a shame."

"It is, and it's…" My shoulders were suddenly as heavy as the ball of lead in my gut. "Can I be completely honest? Even if I might sound pathetic?"

No judgment in his eyes, Rhett nodded. "Sure."

"To be honest…" I swallowed. "This hurts more than when Becky kicked me out. Shit. Maybe Sailo's right. Maybe I was in way too deep."

"Or maybe you'd checked out of your marriage."

"I…" Had I?

Rhett sat up a little, resting his elbows on the table and clasping his hands loosely between them. "It seems like you've figured out a lot about your marriage after the fact. Stuff you didn't see or know about before the divorce." His brow creased, and he softly added, "Maybe you and Becky need to sit down and talk some of those things over."

"Like what? We're done. Why pick at the scab?"

He shrugged. "Maybe there's stuff you both need to work through so you can move on completely. I mean, when Sabrina's mom and I split up, we could barely talk to each other for like five years before we finally decided enough was enough. Then we hashed a few things out, buried the hatchet, and now we get along fine."

"I'm assuming it's easier said than done."

He whistled. "*Oh*, yeah. But by then we'd been apart for a while, and we'd started seeing other people. I was already with Ethan by then. And I guess enough time had gone by for us to be objective about it. We could see the things we'd each done wrong, and I mean, maybe hindsight really is twenty-twenty, but it was a lot easier to see that our marriage had been coming apart long before we broke up." He picked up his drink. "Something about that, it made it easier to put the whole thing to rest. Like, it really was something that needed to end because we just weren't meant to be, not because one or both of us were horrible people."

I sat back, exhaling. "That was a few years later, though. We're not even out of the same calendar year."

"And it would've been a hell of a lot better if we'd done it sooner." He sipped his beer and muttered, "Trust me. And sometimes after you split with someone, the best way to make peace with it is to bury the hatchet with them, and then move on. Without them."

I winced.

He pushed his glass away. "The thing is, you've raised your kids. It isn't like you have to do a custody switch every other week. If you can't see eye to eye, then maybe…" He held my gaze, his brow pinching slightly, and his tone was soft as he added, "Maybe a clean break is what you both need."

Fuck. Splitting up with Becky had been painful enough. The thought of not having her in my life at all, of moving on alone without the woman who'd been there for better than half my life, was a tough one to swallow.

"It's hard to imagine life without her."

"I know. But if you two have to close the book on each other, maybe you can do it peacefully. You'll always have all the good memories of her. You'll always have the kids you raised together."

"That's true. Still…"

"It doesn't mean either of you failed, or that you're bad people. It might mean you're just ready to move on." He held my gaze for a moment, then added, "And I'm not saying it's easy. It's never going to be easy to let someone go after you've spend that much of your life with them." He grimaced. "Believe me—I get it."

"I appreciate the advice," I whispered.

Silence fell, but it didn't last long. "It might not hurt to talk to Sailo too."

His name hit me in the gut. I pushed back the lump rising in my throat. "What's the point? It was a fling. It's over."

Rhett tilted his head, eyeing me as if he saw right through me. "I don't think that was a fling, and I don't think you do either."

I squirmed under his scrutiny and held onto my cold glass for dear life. "What makes you say that?"

"Well, for one thing, how quickly you said you'd be willing to risk hurting like this again if it meant giving what you had another shot."

"That could just mean I'm not good at letting go."

"It could, but…" His eyes lost focus for a good minute. Then he looked at me again. "Do you remember when we all went to dinner with you and Sailo? Before you moved?"

"Yeah."

"You remember when he walked in, and you looked at me and asked what I was grinning about?"

I nodded.

Rhett idly ran his finger along the rim of his glass. "The thing is, I knew Sailo had walked into the restaurant before you said anything. The minute he was in the room, you changed. You just…came to life in a way I'd never seen before."

An image flashed through my mind of Mark's eyes lighting up when Devon had walked in for our double date, and I shivered at the memory of my heart speeding up when Sailo walked in the night Rhett was talking about.

"I was infatuated," I said. "He was…the first guy…"

Rhett's eyebrow arched.

I looked away and sighed. "I think I'm better off just letting him go. He's probably right. It went too far, too fast, and I…"

"Who are you trying to convince?" he asked softly. "Me? Or yourself."

I didn't have an answer.

"I think you need to talk to him."

So I can listen to him tell me why I'm an idiot and this is a disaster and—

"Greg." Rhett's voice was gentle and soft. "Talk to him. He might not be willing to give it another shot, but you won't know unless you *talk to him*. Trust me—I know what I'm talking about." A strange undercurrent worked its way into Rhett's tone, like a mix of hurt and desperation. "Ethan and I were well on our way to moving on without each other, and *one* conversation put us back on the right path." He swallowed. "Don't think for a second I wasn't scared out of my mind going into that conversation, because I had no idea what would happen. But I can't even put into words how many times every day I'm thankful we had it, because now I know exactly what I would've lost if we'd kept walking away."

"You guys had so much more history, though."

"Doesn't matter." Rhett dismissed the idea with a sharp wave. "You and Becky had twenty-five years of history, and you've said yourself there was no salvaging it. Time guarantees nothing. But…look, just talk to him. It's better to say your piece and walk away empty-handed than to leave it unsaid and still be empty-handed."

I tamped down the emotions aching in my chest. "I'm just having a hard time believing there's a chance of not being empty-handed when it's over."

Rhett nodded. "It's a risk. It's not easy, but…is what you and he had worth that risk?"

I swallowed. "I don't know. I don't… I just don't know."

"Just think about everything we've talked about," Rhett said. "Don't give up on him."

"I'll think on it. Thanks."

We finished our beers, and after I'd paid, headed out for the evening. In the parking lot, I sat in the driver's seat for a while, just staring out into the night and trying to make sense of…hell, everything. In a matter of weeks, everything I knew had changed. I'd had to get used to saying "ex-wife." I'd come out to my kids. One of my kids had come out to me. I'd been with a man, fallen for a man, and lost a man. Things were different now.

But maybe Rhett was right. Maybe I still had more to do before I could leave the past behind and move on in peace.

So I finally texted my ex-wife:

Can we meet for coffee? I'd like to talk about a few things.

~*~

Becky didn't respond to my texts until later that evening, but when she finally did, she suggested meeting at the house instead of a coffee shop. Admittedly, I was grateful we weren't going to do this in public. It just seemed like something better handled in private.

It seemed like a good idea until I was walking up the familiar porch steps the next morning.

I paused with one foot on the bottom step and gazed up at the house.

We needed to do this. I needed to do this. Didn't mean it was going to be fun or easy, but what *had* been recently?

Besides being with—

Yes. Besides that.

I took a deep breath and continued up the steps. Becky let me in, and in silence, led me through the living room. The house seemed bare, semi-skeletal, without the furniture I'd removed. There were some new pieces now—a new sofa and coffee table, a different TV stand, even though I hadn't taken the original. Had she gone shopping? Or was someone else moving in?

I didn't let that thought stick and continued into the dining room with her. At the familiar table, where there were still two placemats set at the adjacent chairs at one end, we sat down. She brought us coffee, and we sipped it in silence for a couple of uncomfortable minutes.

Her brow pinched as she watched me over the top of her coffee cup. "How are you doing?"

"Better. I think." Sighing, I shook my head. "I don't know. I was seeing someone, but we…"

She stiffened slightly. "Oh. It didn't work out?"

"No. I guess I shouldn't be too surprised. This soon after the divorce, I mean." I hesitated, wondering how far to tip my hand. Finally, I decided that as long as we were going to be honest with each other… "He didn't want to be someone's rebound."

Becky's eyebrows flicked up. "He?"

Swallowing hard, I nodded. "Yeah."

She lowered her coffee cup and clutched it in both hands. "When did *that* happen?"

"I've known for a while. A few years." I sat back and folded my hands beneath the table. "I guess after we split, it seemed like as good a time as any to figure out if I was just curious, or if I'm really into men."

"I see. And…are you?"

I absently stroked my jaw with the backs of my fingers. "Yeah. I am."

"So you're gay."

Part of me wanted to correct her and say I was bisexual. At the moment, though, there was only one person in this world who stood a chance of turning me on any time soon, and he was a man, so… "Yeah. I guess."

"Oh." She clicked her nails rapidly on the table. "This might be difficult for the kids to hear. They're still dealing with us breaking up."

I shifted in my chair. "They know."

Her eyes widened. "They do?"

"Well, Kurt doesn't. He's been so stressed with school and the divorce, I didn't want to add to it. But April and Mark know."

"You told *Mark*?" She exhaled sharply. "Greg, for God's sake, you know damn well he has a hard time dealing with things. Why would—"

"Just trust me, okay?" I said. "We talked. The subject came up. And he knows."

She scowled. "How did he take it?"

Better than you could possibly imagine.

"He took it well. Really well, actually." I wrung my hands, watching them instead of looking at her. "It gave us a reason to really sit down and talk about things."

"Things…like?"

I gnawed the inside of my lip. I wasn't about to out my son to his mother, so this subject was rapidly turning into a minefield. "Just life in general. I guess opening up to him gave him a chance to do the same with me."

"Oh." She went quiet again, the silence stretching on for an uncomfortably long time. "So." She met my gaze, and her expression hardened slightly. Walls going up, maybe? "Well. We're here. You wanted to talk?"

"Yeah." I ran my toe up and down the chair leg to get rid of some nervous energy. "I'm not even sure. I guess…I don't know, maybe I'm looking for some closure."

"Okay. What kind of closure? I mean, what else can we say that we haven't already?"

Nervousness prickled my spine and twisted my stomach. I pulled in a deep breath. "Well, for one thing, I'd kind of like to know..." I hesitated, forcing my voice to be soft, nonconfrontational. "How long have you and Jase been seeing each other?"

She bristled, her fingers tightening around her coffee cup. "What does that have to do with anything? You've been seeing someone too, so—"

"Becky." I didn't raise my voice. Didn't snap. I was too damned exhausted for any of that anyway. "Just tell me the truth."

She leaned back in her chair and pushed out a long breath. "Greg, I'm sorry. I thought about telling you the truth, but by that point, I was hurting you enough by telling you I wanted a divorce. It didn't seem necessary, and definitely not kind, to throw that in your face too."

I wrung my hands in front of me. "That doesn't answer my question."

She turned her head, setting her jaw as she gazed out the window. "I met him last year. In a...on a forum."

All those hours of sitting on the couch watching television while she used her iPad beside me...had they...?

"We met in person in November," she went on. "And we..." She shook her head. "Look, there's no point in dissecting it. We were friends, and then we were more."

"For how long?" I asked as calmly as I could.

She pressed her lips together. After a long, long silence, she whispered, "About six months."

More heavy, uneasy silence.

Finally, I asked, "Why?"

"Why?" She tilted her head. "Why him? Or..."

"Why anyone?" I struggled to hold her gaze, but managed. "What changed between us?"

Becky looked away and focused intently on something outside the window. "I don't know. Honestly. All I know is that it did change."

"But…why didn't you say anything? If I had known…"

"I tried, Greg. I… God, I tried." Jesus, but she sounded exhausted. As if the words took all the energy she had.

"You did?"

She nodded, slowly turning her head toward me again. "I tried to talk to you. I suggested going to counseling."

"But, when I said we should see that counselor—"

"I know." She sighed. "There was always something else. One of the kids. The baby. It…" Another sigh, and this time, her shoulders sagged as if under a real, palpable weight. "We just never made it happen. I don't know whose fault it is. Or if it even matters. But I just… I realized one day I didn't want to make it work anymore."

She might as well have punched me in the chest. And the worst part was, I believed her. Looking back now, the pattern was there. The fights were fewer and farther between. The suggestions of seeing a counselor dropped off around the time we were down to one kid left in the house. She'd checked out. I'd checked out.

"I'm sorry," she whispered. "The affair, it…it wasn't what I should have done. And I didn't tell you about it because I didn't want to hurt you more than I had." She swallowed hard. "I do still love you, Greg. But what we had, it's over."

Hesitantly, I reached for her arm and rested my hand on it, making contact with her for the first time in weeks. "I know it is. And I still love you too. I guess I just…wanted to know."

She nodded. "I'm sorry."

"Me too."

~*~

I'd been driving this car for four years, and I couldn't help but stop and stare at it now, parked in the driveway in front of my ex-wife's house. It was the same plain old sedan with the dent below the door handle where Kurt had smacked it with the passenger door of his mother's car during one of those teenage emotional blowouts. It didn't look quite right between the slanted white lines of my apartment complex's parking lot instead of tucked into the two-car garage that always seemed to need cleaning.

It was things like this—the things that hadn't changed at all—that made me realize how much my life had changed recently. I had the same old job, which I drove to via a whole new route in the same old car.

Numbly, I drove back to my place, parked, and trudged up the steps to my empty apartment. Inside, I lounged on the couch with a cold beer but didn't taste it. I wasn't even sure why I was drinking it. For something to do? Some alcohol to make my muddled brain even foggier? Something cold? Fuck, I had no idea. Couldn't think of a reason *not* to drink it though, so…bottoms up.

So this was my life now. My marriage hadn't been what I thought it was. My sexuality wasn't what I'd always believed it was.

Though everything had changed, it was all settling. The ink was drying, and the shock was rapidly turning into old news.

But the one thing I couldn't accept was the empty space that would be beside me in my bed tonight.

And it wasn't Becky I was missing right now. She had pulled the plug on something that, I realized after the fact, had died a long time ago.

But what Sailo and I had, it wasn't dead. My feelings for him sure as hell weren't. Being with him meant tearing open emotions that were tied to my ex-wife. Feeling them with him and letting go of them with her. And yet it meant all new feelings that were for him and him alone. And they were completely different. Completely alien.

The easiest thing would be to write off our fling as a rebound, an experiment, some infatuation gone bad, and move on. It was quick, it was intense, and now it was over. In the past. Done and dusted. At least then I wouldn't have to risk hearing him say good-bye twice.

Except I didn't want to walk away. I wanted to walk right back to him, even if all these emotions threatened to tear me to ribbons like no other feelings I'd ever had.

All these years later, I still remembered what it was like to fall in love with Becky. Time had done nothing to fade the memories of staring at the ceiling at night, with a stomach full of butterflies and a mind full of that gorgeous woman who I couldn't wait to see again.

And yet, that had nothing on what I felt for Sailo.

Falling for Sailo…*hurt*. Maybe because he was gone, but I could've sworn it was already painful before he'd said good-bye. It hurt in the way I imagined getting a tattoo hurt. Intense, almost unbearable, but exhilarating at the same time. Like a temporary sting that would be over soon, but the mark it left behind was there forever.

If this had been a rebound fling like he thought, then the pain would be over and the endorphin rush would be gone, and I'd be able to see clearly that he was right. But the pain was the only thing that remained. That endorphin rush was long gone. Sailo hadn't been a part of my world long enough to feel so permanent, but his absence was driving me insane. Like everything else could smoothly assimilate into this new reality except the lack of his body heat beside me, the absence of his tattoo beneath my fingertips, the low timbre of his voice in the darkness.

In my empty apartment, in between wondering how drunk I should get tonight, I went through the conversation I'd had with Rhett, the one with Becky, and the last one I'd had with Sailo. Rhett was right. Becky was gone. And Sailo…

I pressed my drink against my forehead. Well. What was I supposed to do? Sit here and think about how fucked up this was, or try to do something about it?

Couldn't hurt to try, I supposed.

I pulled out my phone. Hesitating with every letter, I wrote out the message, and then my thumb hovered over the Send button for a solid minute. This was pointless, wasn't it? Sailo had made up his mind and said his piece. And he was right that rebounds and first times were nearly always doomed to failure, so I was probably deluding myself if I thought I could convince him this was any more than a novelty. Anything more than stupid infatuation.

But Ethan and Rhett were right too. If I didn't talk to him, then I'd never know. If I did talk to him, there was a good possibility nothing would come of it, but at least I would know.

So I steeled myself, held my breath, and hit Send.

Can we talk?

Chapter Twenty-Seven

I checked my phone constantly after that. All evening. A few times throughout the night. During my stop-and-go drive to work. At all those points during the workday when his texts usually broke up the monotony.

Nothing.

The message was clear—he wasn't interested in talking.

Maybe texts and phone calls weren't the way to handle this. He'd given me the courtesy of letting me go face-to-face.

Fine. I'll go down to Wilde's. And we'll talk.

Or not.

I cringed as I picked up my keys off the kitchen counter. It was entirely possible he'd tell me to leave, or have one of those ex-Legionnaire bouncers pass the message along. Or maybe sic that surly assistant on me—Evan hadn't been thrilled with me the night Sailo and I crashed into each other, and he probably wouldn't mind telling me to get lost.

Still, I had to try. It was worth a shot. *One* shot. I wasn't going to be that asshole who kept coming back again and again when it had been made abundantly clear that the relationship was over.

One shot. I'd say my piece, or at least try to, and be done with it. If he wouldn't talk to me tonight, then I'd call it a loss and move on. Delete his number, stay away from Wilde's—done. Of course it wouldn't be that easy, but it had to be done or else I'd drive myself insane trying to win back someone who wanted nothing to do with me.

So, I got in the car, drove up to Broadway, and parked outside the club.

Wilde's, I thought as I walked up to the tinted glass front door. *We meet again.*

Hand on the door, I hesitated. One shot. It wasn't unreasonable to ask him to hear me out *once*. Right?

Here goes nothing…

I took a deep breath and went inside. After I'd paid the cover, I walked past the intimidating bouncers and up to the bar. The bartender wasn't one I recognized—Chris, according to the tag on his shirt.

I leaned across the bar and shouted over the music, "Is Sailo here tonight?"

The bartender glanced at the stage where another deejay was performing, and then looked at me. "I'm not sure. You want me to pass a message along to him?"

I hesitated. It would be easy as hell for Sailo to send back a secondhand *fuck off*, but at least then I'd have my answer. "Could you tell him Greg needs to talk to him? For like ten minutes?"

"Sure." Chris shrugged and headed toward the back of the club. Well, that was promising—Sailo hadn't given all the bartenders instructions to tell a guy named Greg to kick rocks.

The bartender disappeared into the back. I gulped, wondering if I should've had him mix me a drink first. I wanted to believe I was ready for whatever happened. Just like when I'd sat down with Becky, and moving on separately had been a possibility from the start, I was strong enough to take anything that might come from this conversation. Even when she'd hit me with a gut shot, admitting to the affair I'd never once suspected, I'd been all right, and I'd be all right this time too.

And then he appeared out of the crowd, materializing as if from thin air, and it was all I could do not to run for the door.

No. I came here to talk to him, and I was going to see this thing through, no matter how hard it was to face him.

He stopped an arm's length or so away, eyebrows up. "This is unexpected." Was that sarcasm? Or an actual observation? He was impossible to read, and the noise around us wasn't helping.

"I just want to talk. For a few minutes."

Sailo scowled. He opened his mouth to speak, but then glared at the crowd around us. Meeting my gaze again, he sighed as his shoulders dropped, and he gestured for me to come with him.

Well. That was promising.

I followed.

And two steps later, I knew exactly where we were going.

God. No. Not there.

But yes…there. He led me into the back, up the stairs, and to that familiar door. His keys jingled like they always did, and the lock clicked. In tense silence that seemed to thump harder than the bass downstairs, we stepped through the door.

Did it have to be here? Of all places, did we have to do this in the Wilde's VIP lounge?

"All right." He faced me, leaning against a table and resting his hands on its edge. "You wanted to talk."

"Yeah." I gulped. "Look, I think you might've been right about a few things. I know things moved too fast. And that was my fault. And yeah, you're right—I was in love with being alive again. But…that doesn't change what I feel about you."

He stiffened, lips pulling tight. "The ink isn't even dry on your divorce."

"No, it isn't. And yeah, I've still got some shit I need to work through." I paused, certain with every breath that he was going to run for the door at any moment. "I get why you left. I do."

His eyebrows rose a little.

"It was too much too fast. I get that." I hooked my thumbs in my pockets just for something to do with my hands. "Something finally felt right, and I pushed it until it went wrong. I own that, and I'm sorry."

He shifted his weight, but didn't say anything, and his expression still offered nothing.

I cleared my throat. "I know the timing is shit. And there's nothing I can say to convince you that I can give this what I'd give a relationship that didn't happen right after a divorce like that. The only thing I can do is ask you for the chance to prove it."

"Do you hear yourself?" He pressed his hip against the table and folded his arms. "You want me to take a gamble like that? You didn't even know for sure if you were gay until recently—you don't even *know* what you want yet." Expression hardening, he added, "And I don't want to be there when you realize it isn't me."

"That's just it. Yes, I'm still finding my footing. And myself. Yes, my divorce still hurts." I took a deep breath. "But the whole time you've been gone, I've been thinking about you. Not finding some other guy. Not my ex-wife. Not…not any of that. *You.*"

His lips tightened, but he didn't speak.

I closed my eyes, exhaled, and met his gaze again. "The night we met, I was just looking to get laid and forget about my divorce. I wasn't even thinking about getting into another relationship. And then I quite literally stumbled into you, and…I haven't been able to stop thinking about you since."

"Because I was the next thing that came along." He sounded exhausted, as if it took all the strength he had to speak loud enough for me to hear him. "That doesn't mean there was anything between us besides some sex and being friends." He exhaled. "How can you know you love me when you don't even know who you are?"

I flinched. "Look, you're right. I haven't figured out who I am yet. I'm not sure if I'm gay or bi. I just don't know. But what I do know is that I love you. Whether or not I'm attracted to women doesn't matter, because I know I'm attracted to men, and I know—" My voice tried to crack, but I quickly cleared my throat again. "I know I love you, Sailo."

He started to speak, but I put up my hand.

"Please," I said. "Let me finish."

His lips tightened, but he nodded.

"I don't know if this will work out," I went on. "There's no way to know. But the way I feel when I'm with you, I've never felt like that with anyone." I hesitated. "Not even my ex-wife. With you, it's this feeling like…like I can take whatever life throws at me, and I can roll with anything, because at the end of the day, it's going to be you, me, a couple of beers, and whatever stupid movie is on TV."

He lowered his gaze.

"I know I love you," I said. "The thing is, they're feelings. They are what they are. But it doesn't mean we have to speed things up or start talking about moving in together or any of that. I don't want to force anything from this. I'm not after some kind of commitment. All I want is to be with you, give this a chance, and see where it goes." I swallowed. "Because I've never felt like this for someone. And even if it means taking the risk of falling flat on my face down the line, it seems…it seems like whatever this could turn into in time is worth taking that risk."

Sailo held eye contact for a long moment. Then his shoulders sank, and he lowered his gaze. "This does feel pretty different from anything I've ever had too. I won't argue with that. I think that's what scares me." Still avoiding my eyes, he rubbed the back of his neck. "The last time I got this close to someone…"

I watched him, and abruptly, the pieces fell together. "The one who left. For someone else."

He winced, but nodded. "I'm terrified of getting close to you like I did my ex. There are just so many ways this thing could fall apart, and then when it all goes to shit, having to put on the strong face for my kid when all I want to do is break…"

My throat tightened around my breath. I fought the urge to reach for him. "Was your relationship with your ex a rebound?"

"Not for him, no."

I raised my eyebrows. "So…it can happen even when it's not a rebound relationship?"

"Of course. But the odds aren't that great when it is."

"The odds aren't great anyway," I said gently. "It's a gamble no matter what. There are no guarantees. And that's coming from a man who had his marriage pulled out from under him after twenty-five years."

Sailo chewed the inside of his cheek and avoided my eyes again.

"I know this is terrifying," I said. "Believe me, I know." Cautiously, I took a step closer to him. "We have two choices."

He looked at me through his lashes. "Stay or go."

"Yeah. But it's a bit more than that. We can walk away now and wonder for the rest of our lives if anything might've happened. Or we can give it a shot." I pushed my shoulders back and took a deep breath. "I know damn well there's a chance we'll get hurt if we try it, and I'm well aware of how much it could hurt. But the only thing that scares me more is what we might miss out on if we walk away."

Sailo lifted his gaze. "It's not that I don't want to. But I don't think you realize what you're asking for."

"I do," I said. "I'm not asking for a commitment. We're not moving in together. Or meeting each other's parents."

"What exactly *would* we be doing?"

"We keep doing what we've done so far." I tentatively touched his face, worried he might recoil. "We have sex. We talk. We go out. We be friends." He didn't pull away, so I rested my palm against his cheek, the warmth of his skin raising goose bumps all over mine. "And we see where this thing goes."

He still didn't pull away, but he didn't come closer either. "But…you're dealing with your divorce. And we've both got kids to think about."

"Yeah, and I'm pretty sure our kids want us to be happy." My heart jumped into my throat. "And I don't know about you, but when we're together, I *am* happy."

Sailo's gaze was intense, as if he were searching mine for something, anything, to tell him I was wrong. Or right. Or somewhere in between. My heart was going crazy as I waited for him to speak.

Are we? Aren't we?

Am I walking out of here alone tonight?

He didn't say a word, though.

He closed the space between us.

Put his arms around me.

And kissed me.

Chapter Twenty-Eight

We must've stood there for hours, holding on and letting that kiss last and last. Eventually, though, we had to come up for air.

I broke the kiss and touched my forehead to his. "I missed you."

"Me too." He held the back of my hand, fingers twitching against my skin. "I'm sorry. You know I didn't want to hurt you."

I nodded. "I know. I never doubted that for a minute." I ran my thumb along his cheekbone. "Maybe it's what I needed, though. To make me really dig in and think about this."

"Still." He combed his fingers through my hair. "It was never about whether or not I wanted to be with you. I just… I'm scared to death of this. I know how rebounds and first times can both end in disaster."

"There's still a chance this could end in disaster." I smoothed his hair. Drawing back a little, I met his gaze. "But the way it feels now…kind of seems like it's worth the risk."

Sailo nodded, a smile slowly forming on his lips. "Yeah. It does." He pulled me back in and, just before our lips met, murmured, "I love you." Then he claimed my mouth in a deep kiss. Holding me tight, he pushed my lips apart and slipped his tongue underneath mine, and I had to lean into him just to keep myself on my feet.

When he broke that kiss, I was out of breath and, Jesus, already trembling.

“I love you too,” I whispered.

“I don’t have much time,” he whispered. “But I…I don’t want to let you go.”

Like nothing else that had been said tonight, those words almost knocked my knees out from under me. As he kissed me again, holding on as tight as I did, it was hard to believe we were here. That we were back in the exact place where things had started between us. Just a few feet from where we were standing now, he’d dropped to his knees and given me a blowjob I’d never forget. A few feet in the other direction, I’d frantically done the same for him.

And now, somehow, we were here again, and he wasn’t leaving.

He guided me back a few steps. My calves hit a booth seat, and he didn’t stop. He leaned into me, and together we sank onto the plush leather cushion.

As he kissed my neck, I bit my lip, struggling not to come unglued. Jesus, I hadn’t touched him since we’d split up, and now it was like the first time all over again—overwhelming, familiar and yet completely new.

I stroked his hair. “You’re gonna…be late for your show.”

“They can wait,” he panted against my neck. “They’ll dance to anything.”

“But you—”

His hand slid over my very hard cock. “They can wait,” he said again. “Right now, I need you.”

“Likewise.” I closed my eyes, groaning softly.

“God, I wish we were at home,” he murmured. “So I could strip you down and fuck you.”

I moaned, holding him tighter.

"Later tonight." He ground his cock against me. "My place."

"Yes, *please*."

He pinned me to the bench and rubbed against me. "Definitely not letting you go without getting you off, though."

I bit back a moan. "Didn't you say one of your coworkers busted a table in here having makeup sex?"

"Mmhmm," he said against my neck. "But unless you've got condoms with you…"

"Damn it."

"S'okay." He nipped just above my collar. "I can…I can work with what we've got."

Before I could ask what he had in mind, his hand was between us, and he was drawing down my zipper. I couldn't speak, so nudged him gently with my shoulder until he lifted his head, and in the same instant, I kissed him, and he wrapped his fingers around my cock.

Holding his shoulder with one hand for balance, I rubbed him through his pants with the other. God knew who moaned—both of us, maybe? I was too turned on to tell Sailo's voice from mine, and way too turned on to care.

"I've got an idea," he said.

"Hmm?"

"Get on top." He gestured at the bench we were sitting on. "I'll lie on my back, and you turn around the other way."

It took a second to make sense of what he'd requested, but as we shifted around, I figured out what he was getting at. Although the space between the table and the back of the bench was narrow, there was just enough room for him to lie on his back and for me to get on top on all fours, and as I took his hard dick between my lips, he did the same with mine.

Good God. What if someone saw this? A quickie blowjob was one thing, but…this?

Sailo didn't seem to worry, though, so I didn't protest. I kept my hips perfectly still so I wouldn't choke him. Besides, he was doing just fine, lifting his head and taking me impossibly far into his mouth, slowly letting me slide out between his lips, and then taking me again. With his talented lips and tongue working at my cock, I could barely concentrate on returning the favor. I tried, though, bobbing my head over his cock and stroking it with my free hand, and judging by the way he moaned and dug his fingers into my thigh, he was enjoying it.

Somehow, we fell into a rhythm together, teasing each other in perfect sync. I stopped caring if anyone might walk through that door and catch us. Let them. Let everyone in the club show up and see me sixty-nining with Sailo like we had all night to turn each other inside out. I didn't care who caught us. All I cared about was making him feel as amazing as he was making me feel.

I want to make you feel like this every night.

I want to feel like this every night.

I want the way you make me feel. Always.

Then something…changed. The rhythm didn't fall apart, but there was a new sense of urgency. A franticness that wasn't there before. We swallowed each other deeper, stroked each other harder. My breath came in rapid, uneven gasps as his rushed across my skin in sharp, hot huffs. The urge to thrust into his mouth was almost irresistible. It must've been mutual, too—he lifted his hips slightly, pushing himself deeper into my throat, and I took him because God, yes, I loved hearing and feeling and tasting him as he came apart. As *I* came apart.

He whimpered softly, his voice reverberating against my cock, and my whole body was trembling, electrified, ready to fall to pieces, and I groaned too. I had no idea whose orgasm started first, only that I couldn't have stopped if I'd wanted to; in the same instant, I shuddered violently and his semen filled my mouth.

And just like that, we were still. Silent. Breathing hard, each with a hand resting on the other's leg as the spinning room slowed around us.

When I was sure I wouldn't black out, I carefully sat up on my knees. We shifted around again, straightening our clothes and hair, and rose, our legs unsteady enough that we both had to lean on the table for a few seconds.

Eyes glazed and tan cheeks flushed, he met my gaze and grinned. He cupped my face with a shaking hand. "I'm so glad you came back."

"Me too." I kissed him softly. "I'm sorry. It—"

Sailo cut me off with a gentle kiss. "Don't. You've already explained yourself." Our lips brushed as he whispered, "I love you." The words may as well have been an incantation that let him relax completely, and he melted against me, holding on as he released a long breath. Barely whispering, he said, "God, I really do love you."

"I love you too."

He touched his forehead to mine. "And I'm so not finished with you tonight."

"Good. Meet me at my apartment when you're off?"

Drawing back, he licked his lips. "My show's over at midnight. I'll be there as soon as I can."

I kissed him softly and whispered, "You might as well plan on staying the night."

"I love the sound of that." He cupped my face in both hands and kissed me softly. "I have to go for now, though."

"I know."

"But I'll see you soon?"

I grinned. "Definitely."

One more kiss, one more long look, and then we left the VIP lounge and walked downstairs together.

Beneath the exit dividing the back hallway from the rest of the club, we stopped.

I put a hand on his waist. "See you after your show."

"I'll be there as soon as I can." He grinned. "And when I get there, I'm planning on fucking you until you can't move, so I want you ready for me."

I shivered so hard, my toes curled inside my shoes. "I will be."

"Promise?"

"Promise."

"Good." He kissed me one last time, letting it linger for a moment.

Then he really had to go, so we separated. He continued toward the door I'd been leaning on the night we'd crashed into each other, and I paused, watching him go.

This time, it didn't hurt to watch him leave.

Because later tonight, he'd be in my bed, in my arms.

And deep down, I knew that was where he'd stay.

Epilogue

Christmas Eve, the following year

My doorbell rang just as I was peeling shrimp. "Shit." I looked down at my hands, then over at Sailo, who was checking on some sauce simmering on the stove. "Could you get that?"

"Of course." He put the lid on the pot and disappeared from the kitchen.

A moment later, Kurt, April, Mark, and their respective partners—not to mention my granddaughter—filed into the kitchen, setting down bags of gifts and unzipping parkas.

"Sorry we're late." Devon groaned. "We had to wait for the damn landlord to come by and fix the water heater."

"What's wrong with it?" I asked.

"Nothing now." He turned to Nathan. "Do you need a hand getting the rest of the presents?"

"I could definitely use some help," my son-in-law said. "There's…a lot."

Sailo looked at me. "Can you hold down the fort for a minute while I help them?"

"Not a problem."

April kept an eye on Kayla and Mika, and everyone else went back down to help unload the car. Alone in the warm, fragrant kitchen, I smiled to myself as I tended to all the dishes.

Everything in my world had changed over the last year, but I was happy now. Happier than I'd been before. I hadn't even realized how much of a rut I'd fallen into, how unhappy my ex-wife and I really were, until that part of our lives was behind us.

But it was behind us now. This was my first Christmas in the new place, and I did the best I could to ignore how alien it felt. No, not alien. Just…new. Different, but good.

Having Sailo here, that felt pretty damned normal these days. In fact, it was starting to feel weird when he wasn't here, even though I was used to him working nights at Wilde's. Whenever he wasn't working, and we weren't out somewhere, we always ended up back here or at his place. It was only a matter of time before we moved in together. As it was, bits and pieces were creeping over to each other's houses. Sailo's grill was still on my back patio after the Fourth of July. We each had clothes hanging in the other's closet.

"I guess I should bring your grill back over one of these days," I'd said to him as summer came to a close.

He'd shrugged. "Might as well keep it there. By the time it's grilling weather again, we'll probably have a place together anyway."

So the grill stayed, and so did he.

He'd waited a few months before introducing me to his son, which I completely understood. After he'd met me a few times, we started taking him along on outings and day trips. I was pretty sure I won the kid over forever at the fair over Labor Day weekend—Sailo couldn't stomach carnival rides, but I went on every last one with Mika.

In the last year, I'd spent more time with my own son than I had in the past several years combined. Mark was finally opening up again, and we'd gone from tensely cordial to the kind of friendly father-son relationship I'd always hoped for.

I'd gone with him when he'd decided to come out to Becky. She'd also taken it well—in fact, if she was uncomfortable with anything about that conversation, it was my presence. But Mark had been too nervous to approach her on his own, and having me there relaxed him. Once that conversation was over, it was smooth sailing. He told me not long after that Becky and Devon absolutely adored each other.

As time went on, I empathized even more with Mark's struggle to come out to us and everyone else in his life. My own coming out had been a slow, challenging process. I'd told my youngest son not long after Sailo and I reconciled, and he'd taken it in stride. If anything, he was relieved that I knew about Mark being gay—now he didn't feel like he was keeping this enormous secret from us anymore.

My kids were at peace with it, so I was happy, but I still had to eventually come clean to the extended family. My mother and stepdad weren't thrilled, but they started lightening up after they met Mika over the Fourth of July. Something about seeing the three of us together—and realizing that Sailo's son was, for all intents and purposes, their new grandson—softened them, and this year's Christmas card had come addressed to both of us. Telling my father, well…the less said about that, the better.

As for Becky and me, we were more or less amicable, but we were still a long way off from being as friendly as Rhett and his ex-wife, and since all of our kids were grown, we didn't have co-parenting as an excuse to force ourselves to interact. We'd sent each other Christmas cards with "hope you're doing well," and signed them individually rather than including our respective boyfriends' names—cordial, civil, but not terribly warm. Maybe we'd never be friendly. I was okay with that, though. We'd had some good years, and we'd raised three great kids together. If moving on meant parting ways, then

I could make peace with that if she could be happy and so could I.

I also didn't see as much of the friends Becky and I had once socialized with. We kept in touch but had sort of drifted apart. Instead, Sailo and I spent a lot of time hanging out with Rhett and Ethan and their friends. Sailo didn't even mind a little playful ribbing about spending all his time with a bunch of old men. And since my kids would be at their mother's on Christmas Day, we were joining the guys tomorrow, along with Sabrina and her family.

Rhett and Ethan were enjoying the hell out of being grandfathers. Sabrina's baby was a few months old now, and that woman never had to worry about finding a babysitter if she and her husband needed some downtime. Ethan especially had taken to his new role like a duck to water. He'd come into Sabrina's life when she was already eight years old, so this was the closest he'd ever had to raising a baby, and he loved it.

So, overall, though, things were settling. My social circle had changed. My love life had changed. My identity had changed. And though it had been a painful process, it was hard to look at the way things were now and believe it hadn't been for the better.

The best part? Even as the need to rebound from my marriage wore off, along with the novelty of being able to live as a gay man, my breath *still* caught whenever Sailo came through the door.

And right at that moment, the apartment door opened, and paper crinkled and feet shuffled as the troops returned with…

"My God," I said as they passed by the kitchen doorway. "How many gifts did you guys bring?"

"Blame your daughter," Nathan called over his shoulder.

"I heard that!" she said from the living room.

Chuckling, I shook my head.

Sailo stepped in, brushing a few raindrops off his sleeves. "How's everything coming along?"

"Nothing's on fire yet, so I'll call it a win." I pulled off my oven mitts and paused for a quick kiss. "Can you keep an eye on it while I get everyone situated?"

"Of course."

We exchanged smiles, and of course another kiss, and I left the kitchen. After I'd taken everyone's coats into the spare bedroom, I came back out to see them unloading a shitload of gifts. April and Nathan really had gone all out—there were mountains of packages under the tree, and Mark and Devon had brought quite a few too. Not that Sailo and I had exactly been stingy either. It was our first Christmas together, so we'd gone…a little crazy.

"Dad, I think we should probably start opening these before dinner," Nathan said. "Or we're going to be here all night."

"No!" Kayla looked up from playing trucks with Mika. "We have to be home for Santa!"

"You'll be home in time for Santa," I said. "I promise." To Nathan, I added, "Yeah, we should get started soon. This is going to take a while."

"That's an understatement." Devon laughed

"Well, let me wrap up a few things in the kitchen, and then we'll get started."

"Do you need a hand?" April started to stand up.

"I think we've got it, but you're welcome to join us."

She glanced at her daughter, who was playing happily with Mika by the Christmas tree. We left them under the watchful eyes of the boys and headed for the kitchen.

April pressed her shoulder against the doorway and chatted with Sailo and me while we finished putting dinner together.

"Are the potatoes done?" I asked.

"Five more minutes." Sailo glanced at me. "Do you want me to put the green bean casserole in when it comes out?"

"Yes, please."

"Will do. Just let me finish…" Sailo took the lid off the chicken curry dish, something from a Samoan recipe his mother had always prepared for special occasions.

Instantly, April clapped her hand over her mouth and turned away, making a gagging sound. "Oh God…"

Sailo and I froze, exchanging glances.

"April?" I asked. "You okay?"

"Yeah," she croaked. "Sorry."

Sailo put the lid back on and glanced at me. "I thought you liked curry?"

"I do. I do. I…" She turned to us, and some color bloomed in her cheeks. "Just wasn't expecting the smell. It's, um, strong."

"It's never bothered you before," I said. "Are—"

Our eyes locked.

I faced her fully, absently drying my hands on a kitchen towel. "You've never been sensitive to strong smells except…"

The corners of her mouth rose slightly.

"April…"

She laughed. "Well, I was *going* to wait until dinner to say anything."

My jaw dropped. "You're serious."

She nodded. "Yep. Twelve weeks last Thursday."

"Oh my God." I crossed the kitchen and hugged her gently but tightly. "Congratulations, kiddo."

"Thanks, Dad." She laughed. "Merry Christmas."

I kissed the top of her head. "Merry Christmas. Does your mom know yet?"

She shook her head, releasing me. "No. I…guess I wanted to tell you guys first. Except I was, um, going to be a little less…nauseated about it?"

I laughed, pulling her into another hug. "Yeah, way to make the announcement—by insulting my boyfriend's cooking."

"Yeah." Sailo huffed sharply. "What the hell?"

"I'm sorry!" She let me go and hugged him. "You know I love your cooking!"

"I know, I know." He embraced her gently and patted her shoulder. "And in all seriousness, congratulations."

"Thanks." As she stepped back, she glanced toward the living room. "I guess I should go make sure the kids aren't diving into their presents early."

Sailo craned his neck, looking past her. "I think Nathan was watching them, wasn't he?"

"Yep." She smirked. "Exactly why I'd better check."

The three of us laughed, and she left the kitchen.

As soon as we were alone, I exhaled and rested my hands on the counter "Wow. That was…unexpected."

Sailo put a hand on the small of my back, and when I turned to him, he smiled. "Going to be a grandfather all over again, aren't you?"

"Yep." I grinned, wrapping my arm around his shoulders. "Don't get too smug. Technically, you're the step-grandparent."

"Technically, not unless we're married." He paused, then winked. "So maybe by next Christmas."

My heart fluttered, and I leaned in to kiss him lightly. "Sounds like next year's going to be a big year."

"Yeah." He grinned, drawing me in closer. "It is." He pressed his lips to mine and whispered, "I love you."

"I love you too."

"Guess we should go join everybody else?" His eyes sparkled mischievously. "I want to open presents too."

"Oh, well, I suppose. Let's grab the munchies." I turned to pick up the bowls of chips and dip, but before I could, he wrapped his arms around me and kissed the side of my neck.

"By the way," he murmured, "I meant to tell you, I looked into renting the VIP lounge. They're willing to give me an employee discount, so it's not as bad as I thought."

"Yeah?" I put my hands over his. "How's their schedule look?"

"Wide open for May." He nuzzled my neck. "Still think you want to do it in May?"

"What do you think?"

He shrugged. "Works for me."

"Do they have a lot of receptions up there?"

"Now and then. Most people don't want to bring their families to Wilde's, so…"

I laughed. "Fair enough."

One more kiss, and we continued into the living room to join the rest of the family. As I sat on the couch, surrounded by the most amazing people on the planet, I couldn't stop smiling.

This time next year, we'd be living somewhere together. Maybe married, or maybe we'd put it off for another year, but both our names would be on a lease. Maybe even a mortgage. These decorations would be in a different place, with a different array of gifts stacked beneath the branches of a different tree, and it would be amazing.

All this change was kind of terrifying, but it was exciting too. The life I'd had before was, to an extent, over, but I was moving on. Moving forward. Moving toward something even better than I'd ever imagined.

I was okay. I was happy.

And I was living again.

About the Author

L.A. Witt is an abnormal M/M romance writer who has finally been released from the purgatorial corn maze of Omaha, Nebraska, and now spends her time on the southwestern coast of Spain. In between wondering how she didn't lose her mind in Omaha, she explores the country with her husband, several clairvoyant hamsters, and an ever-growing herd of rabid plot bunnies. She also has substantially more time on her hands these days, as she has recruited a small army of mercenaries to search South America for her nemesis, romance author Lauren Gallagher, but don't tell Lauren. And definitely don't tell Lori A. Witt or Ann Gallagher. Neither of those twits can keep their mouths shut…

Website: www.gallagherwitt.com
Email: gallagherwitt@gmail.com
Twitter: @GallagherWitt

CPSIA information can be obtained
at www.ICGtesting.com
Printed in the USA
LVOW12s1804260118
564005LV00024B/14/P